LARGE PRINT
EDITION

MURDER

AT THE

GALLIANO CLUB

CARMEN AMATO

Also by Carmen Amato

Available in Large print

GALLIANO CLUB SERIES
ROAD TO THE GALLIANO CLUB: Prequel
MURDER AT THE GALLIANO CLUB: Book 1
BLACKMAIL AT THE GALLIANO CLUB: Book 2
REVENGE AT THE GALLIANO CLUB: Book 3

DEDICATION

The Galliano Club series is dedicated to the memory of

Celine McIndoe

First cousin. First playmate. First and best friend. My maid of honor.

In our hearts forever.

COPYRIGHT

Published 2024 by Laurel & Croton

ISBN Large Print: 979-8-9891403-2-9

Key characters in the Galliano Club series

Luca Lombardo: Orphaned in Italy, Luca doesn't own the Galliano Club, but it's all he has after losing his wife and baby to the Spanish influenza shortly after arriving in America. *His secret:* He killed the man who murdered his parents. *He wants:* To truly be an American.

Karol Dombrowski: From Poland, Karol has one of the most dangerous jobs at the Lido Premium mill and lives in the same boarding house as Luca. *His secret:* Karol is ambitious but sees no opportunity to move ahead. *He wants:* A position of influence to improve the lives of fellow newcomers to America.

Owen Forbes Fisher: A graduate of Syracuse University, Owen is the accountant for the Lido Premium mill. *His secret:* He fears his wife will leave him for a richer and more socially connected man. *He wants:* To be an admired figure in Lido's high society.

Ruth Cross: A former Broadway chorus girl, Ruth rents the apartment over the Galliano Club and runs the Tapping Toes School of Dance. *Her secret:* She was once convicted of public indecency and lewd behavior and spent time in jail. *She wants:* To be more than Luca Lombardo's friend.

Tess Kennedy: A graduate of Vassar College, Class of 1924, Tess works in the prestigious First National Bank of Lido. *Her secret:* She is a brilliant mathematician. *She wants:* To break the bonds of family and societal expectations for women and decide her own future.

Benny Rotolo: Previously a hitman for Chicago's North Side gang, Benny was chased out by Al Capone and came to Lido where his cousin lives. *His secret:* He's wanted for murder in Chicago. *He wants:* To build a bootlegging empire with the Galliano Club as his signature speakeasy.

Hanna Gorski: An artist's model and young widow, Hanna is on the hunt for the person who killed her sister and dumped the body in the Mohawk River near Lido. *Her secret:* She has ties to Al Capone's Chicago Outfit. *She wants:* Revenge for her sister's murder.

Eighteenth Amendment - Prohibition of Intoxicating Liquors, effective 16 January 1920

Section 1. After one year from the ratification of this article the manufacture, sale, or transportation of intoxicating liquors within, the importation thereof into, or the exportation thereof from the United States and all territory subject to the jurisdiction thereof for beverage purposes is hereby prohibited.

Section 2. The Congress and the several States shall have concurrent power to enforce this article by appropriate legislation.

Volstead Prohibition Enforcement Act, 28 October 1919

Sixty-sixth Congress of The United States of America;

To prohibit intoxicating beverages, and to regulate the manufacture, production, use, and sale of high-proof spirits for other than beverage purposes, and to insure an ample supply of alcohol and promote its use in scientific research and in the development of fuel, dye, and other lawful industries.

Be it enacted by the Senate and House of Representatives of the United States of America in Congress assembled, that the short title of this Act shall be the "National Prohibition Act."

... The words "beer, wine, or other intoxicating malt or vinous liquors" . . . shall be hereafter construed to mean any such beverages which contain one-half of 1 per centum or more of alcohol by volume . . .

"Prohibition has made nothing but trouble" – Al Capone

CHAPTER 1

Find a man's weak spot

By the time Benny Rotolo was in Lido, New York, for a week, he had a plan, a partner, and a line on a patsy with access to big money. As he waited in the Model T, twilight bled into evening and Benny thought about what a swell education Chicago's North Side gang had given him.

Dean O'Banion. Hymie Weiss. Bugs Moran. In their own way, each had taught him how to find a man's weak spot.

The Model T was parked in the lot next to the huge Lido Premium Copper and Brass Rolling Mill, which stretched into the night for two city blocks. Five stories of red brick full of giant forges and block-and-tackle machinery that shaped crucibles of molten metal into copper sheeting to build everything from teakettles to telephone switchboards. Its iron-framed windows glinted in the moonlight.

Compared to the mill, the Lido Premium office building on the other side of the lot was no bigger than a shoebox. A light shone in one of the windows.

Another lit the entrance.

Benny squirmed a bit in the passenger seat, trying to find a comfortable position for the Colt Pocket Hammerless concealed in the inner breast pocket of his sixty-dollar suit from Marshall Field's. The wool suit had been right for windy Chicago, but upstate New York's summer humidity turned it into a steam bath. He couldn't afford to buy a new suit until the business got going. The few hundred in his pocket when he left Chicago was running out fast.

The mill faced Hamilton Street in the section of the city known as East Lido. At this time of night, any road in Chicago would be clogged with cars and buses and people heading to the next good time, but not here. From where they were parked, Benny could see a sliver of Hamilton Street. The wide boulevard was empty and quiet.

Perched on the Mohawk River, Lido was right smack in the middle of the state of New York and duller than dishwater. Summer nightlife meant a dance at Saint Rocco's Catholic Church, a lecture at the Women's Institute, or a moving picture at the Strand Theatre. Six years into Prohibition, too, like nobody knew how to take advantage of a good thing.

A smart fella could step into empty shoes, so to speak.

East Lido was home to Italian mill workers like his cousin Nick Procopio who lived crammed into the warren of narrow lanes above Hamilton Street. At this hour of the night, those chumps were playing cards at a neighborhood fixture called the Galliano Club.

Nick used to belong to the Galliano Club, but not anymore. That suited Benny just fine; it meant Nick was available to go into business with him.

Behind the wheel of the Model T, his cousin produced a hunk of cheese and half a loaf of crusty bread from a wrinkled napkin. The smell of ripe provolone thickened the night air.

"You got to eat now?" Benny demanded.

"I worked all day," Nick said and held out a fistful of food. "You want some?"

"Jesus, Nick. No." Benny waved the cheese stink away. "You sure Fisher works late every Friday, all by himself?"

Benny had asked the question a dozen times. The situation was too good, too easy.

"I told you. I seen the night watchman's logs."

"You think Fisher's dipping his hand into the petty cash?"

Nick grunted and chewed. "What else would he be doing?"

Deputy foreman of the Lido Premium mill, Nick

was a bull of a man, with shoulders that jutted like twin cliffs, hands the size of iceboxes, and a pumpkin head that sat directly on his shoulders. A frayed bandana was tied around the spot where his neck should be, distracting from an oil-stained canvas shirt, dirty dungarees, and the steel-toed boots he wore to the mill six days a week.

Benny's cousin might look like a roughneck and be saddled with a horse-faced wife and four snot-nosed kids, but Nick was smart enough. When Benny appeared on his doorstep, having fled Chicago one step ahead of Al Capone's enforcer Frank Nitti and his trigger-happy torpedoes, Nick didn't flinch. Not only that, but he helped Benny make a plan that was going to make both of them richer than the Rockefellers. According to Nick, this Fisher fella was somebody who could be persuaded to help.

Benny had lots of experience in the persuasion business.

It all began in Chicago when Hymie Weiss throttled a fella named Tricker Egan in the back of a car that Benny happened to be driving. That was before Dean O'Banion died and Hymie took over the North Side gang. Benny was sure that when he had enough dough to go back to Chicago, Hymie would help him take down Capone and Nitti and the rest of the Chicago

Outfit.

Slouched against the passenger door, Benny adjusted the Colt again. His thoughts moved on to dames. In Chicago, his dark hair, blue eyes, expensive clothes, and confident swagger attracted them like bees to honey. Made their clothes fall off, too. Too bad the blonde he'd picked up on the way out of Chicago was old news. Too prim. Meanwhile, East Lido was a bastion of Italian women like Nick's wife. One eyebrow and a pack of mewling kids.

"He shut off the light." Nick gulped down his last mouthful. The low brick office building was dark now except for the entrance.

Benny sat up. A slight figure in a suit and fedora came out, pausing under the light to put a key in the lock. Fisher, the accountant. The fella looked to be ten years or so older than Benny, maybe 35 or 36 years old. A plain face but dressed real swell in a seersucker suit and bow tie. White handkerchief in the breast pocket. Polished shoes.

A signet ring glinted as he locked the door. Somebody liked expensive things.

Obviously unaware that he was being watched, Fisher headed toward the only other vehicle parked in the lot, an older Ford. Nick and Benny met him halfway.

"Evening, Mr. Fisher," Nick said.

"Ah, Procopio," Fisher said with a visible start. "The whistle blew hours ago. What are you doing here so late?"

"Need to talk to you," Nick said, looming over the smaller man.

"Can't it wait until Monday?"

"I brung my cousin."

Benny stuck out his hand, real friendly. "I'm Benny Rotolo, Nick's cousin."

"A pleasure to meet you. I'm Owen Forbes Fisher, the accountant for Lido Premium." Fisher shook hands, evidently relieved to see that Benny wasn't another mill worker like Nick. Clearly admired the suit, as well as the black fedora that Benny had hastily lifted from a bespoke men's shop on his way out of Chicago.

"I've got a business idea," Benny said. "Nick here had a notion that you could help us get it off the ground."

"Is this related to Lido Premium?" Fisher asked, looking from Benny to Nick and back again. "Speak to Henry Blick on Monday. He's the operations manager."

"No, this is up your alley." Benny moved closer. "You being a money man and all. I could use your expert investment advice."

"Expert investment advice?" Fisher preened a bit.

"Exactly." Benny rubbed his hands together. "What would you say to becoming a partner in a business with a guaranteed two hundred percent return?"

Fisher's eyes nearly popped out of his head. "Two hundred percent?"

Benny nodded. "I'm from Chicago. Looking to set up a Chicago-style business. A partner with some seed money to invest could recoup their investment in thirty days. Even less. Everything after that is money in your pocket, free and clear."

"There is only one business with a return like that," Fisher said.

"That's right," Benny agreed, still real friendly. "The beer racket."

Fisher took a step back. "I can't help you with anything like that."

"You got a nice position here, I take it." Benny cut his eyes to the office building. "But you're still driving yesterday's Ford. Bet you'd like a La Salle or a Packard."

"It's not worth going to jail over a car," Fisher said.

Benny was still his best friend. "Bet you got a wife."

"Yes." Fisher swallowed hard, making his Adam's apple jump like a champagne cork. "Cynthia."

"She like pretty things?"

"Yes."

"Guaranteed two hundred percent return," Benny emphasized.

Fisher dabbed at his upper lip with the white hanky from his breast pocket. "I don't have any money to invest."

"Nobody's expecting you to invest your own money." Benny pointed a thumb towards the office building. "Not when this place is lousy with it."

Unaware of his own move, Fisher's free hand pressed on his jacket pocket to keep it closed.

Guilty. The best kind of patsy.

"We need cash and equipment," Benny went on. "A thousand dollars more or less, plus the kind of equipment you order for the mill. Nick will tell you what to get. You place the order and square it with the books. Me and Nick handle the rest. See? Nothing too complicated."

"I'd be stealing from my employer. Embezzling."

"Borrowing," Benny countered.

"Stealing," Fisher repeated, trying to sound indignant. "You want me to steal. Fake receipts and cook the books."

"You're doing it now," Benny said coolly. "What's the difference?"

Fisher's face twisted in alarm. "Who told you that?"

Quick as a wink, Nick smacked away Fisher's hand,

allowing Benny to find out what was hidden inside the pocket. He pulled out a couple of folded bills and nearly laughed. "Ten dollars! In Chicago you can't even get laid for ten dollars."

"That's mine," Fisher gasped. "It's none of your business."

"It is now." Benny grinned and cut his eyes to the office building. "You take it out of petty cash? What would Whatsisname, uh, Blick, think about that if Nick here told him?"

Fisher's chin dimpled like he was gonna cry. "Cynthia wants a mink jacket."

"What else does she want?" Benny stuffed the bills back into the other man's pocket. "Take the same risk for our little business proposition and you could buy her the moon."

"You don't understand what you're asking," Fisher gulped. "A brewery needs industrial equipment like chemical tanks. Hoses. Pumps. Heating coils. It's an expensive proposition."

"See," Benny said to Nick. "Man knows what he's talking about. Just the partner we need."

"I'd have to perform miracles of accounting to hide paying for it all."

"But you know how," Benny said leadingly.

"False receipts. Changes to inventory accounting.

And the quarterly report. No, it's impossible."

"Two hundred percent return on investment," Benny reminded him.

Fisher plied the handkerchief against the sweat on his forehead. "Exactly where would this equipment go?"

"The old mill that burned down." Nick crowded into the conversation. "On the river below the Settlers Rest cemetery. The stone pump house is still standing. Big enough but you can't see it from any road."

"The old mill?" Fisher was agog. "That riverfront property still belongs to Lido Premium and the Packham family."

"Nobody goes there," Nick growled.

"But they could."

"Then you'll see that they don't," Benny said.

Fisher's face was shiny with sweat. "An illegal brewery at the old mill built with funds embezzled from Lido Premium. Dear Lord."

Benny grinned; the hook was in the fish's mouth. "Nick and I will handle customers and delivery. We need cash for trucks and payroll until the beer sales start rolling in. Won't take long. Lido is lousy with fellas who want a beer when the whistle blows and even more that don't want to work in a mill no more."

"We'd be partners?" Fisher dabbed again and again.

"The three of us? Splitting profits three ways?"

"Sure." Benny stuck out his hand. The man was hooked. "Shall we shake on it?"

"I need some time to think about it," Fisher said, but he extended a limp paw.

Benny reeled him in the next night when they met up at Perk's Diner, a rough spot on the south side of Lido. Lumped between the freight railyard and a scrap heap, it was the kind of place that served soup and pie to teamsters and stevedores. A blue neon sign advertised Fresh Coffee 24 Hours. A row of seen-better-days Fords nosed against the side of the building.

Fisher was out of place, darting glances at the rough customers and fidgeting with excitement. Benny knew the feeling, knew what was going on in the accountant's head. Fisher was scared at the notion of being in the beer racket, but it put some steel in his spine, too. He was going to be a rich gangster, not just some mealy-mouthed bookkeeper scamming petty cash.

They ordered coffee and pie. Fisher produced a pocket-sized business ledger book covered in gray linen with maroon leather corners. Benny wrote "The Lido Outfit" on the flyleaf and they all signed their names. Then they got down to business and hammered out the details. The equipment and supplies needed to be delivered fast.

Fisher took the ledger book with him when he left Perk's. Maybe the accountant thought it was some kind of insurance policy. Benny didn't care. The only insurance he needed was the Colt Pocket Hammerless and cops on his payroll.

Through the plate glass window, Benny watched Fisher get in his Ford and rattle off across the gravel. "Got us a new pet, Nick. A dog who comes when ya whistle and all it took was writing names in a book."

Nick grunted and shoveled in some apple pie.

As Benny ate, his plans expanded. Once the beer racket was printing money, he'd collar other rackets. Protection, brothels, gambling. Every racket from Buffalo to Albany would be his in a swath of money and power across his newly adopted state.

He'd run it all from the finest speakeasy in New York. Al Capone's Four Deuces on Wabash Street in Chicago was a shack compared to what Benny had in mind.

A floor show with a chorus line, gambling in the back, lottery sales, and girls turning tricks upstairs. Red velvet everywhere. Crystal chandeliers. A bar as long as Hamilton Street. Cocktails the size of punchbowls. Torpedoes with Tommy guns to keep the peace. A road in back and a couple of extra Cadillacs for quick getaways.

Capone had run Benny out of Chicago, but in six months Benny was going to suck enough dough and firepower out of upstate New York to go back. Join forces with Hymie again and bust up Capone's Chicago Outfit. Divvy up whatever was left standing.

Benny was just about to tell Nick about the place he had in mind to transform into his new speakeasy when two blondes walked into the diner. One of them gave Benny an appraising look that melted into a slow smile and he lost his train of thought.

CHAPTER 2

Tonight at the Galliano Club

Luca Lombardo didn't own the Galliano Club, but it was his all the same.

He finished tacking up the big banner, jumped off the ladder and surveyed his handiwork with satisfaction. White letters on red cotton blazed across the wall facing the bar:

B R A V I S S I M O 45 G I O R N I

Tony Bilotti shuffled up and shook a crooked finger at Luca. "It's bad luck to say congratulations already," he rasped. "Too soon and you bring the evil eye. *Malocchio.*"

Luca grinned, ignoring the nervous flutter in his stomach. "You think they'll break their streak on the very last day?"

"You laugh, eh? Just wait." Tony was an old-timer who passed his days playing pinochle in the corner, dealing cards with hands crabbed from years in a wire mill. His glare implied that a young man like Luca had yet to learn the many ways *malocchio* could find those who tempted fate.

"I'll bet you a glass of wine," Luca promised. "I have a good feeling about tonight."

He put the ladder away and went behind the enormous mahogany bar running the length of the saloon, the club's main gathering space. Above the bar, a giant swag created from two draped flags bore witness to the club's dual loyalties: Italy's tricolor on the left and America's stars and stripes on the right. The two flags curtained rows of empty liquor bottles mounted on the mirrored wall, although careful draping left the tapered bottle of Liquore Galliano on full display.

Nearly as tall as Luca, the stunning spear of imported golden liquor from which the club took its name stretched nearly to the pressed tin ceiling. Impossible to overlook, the bottle had never been opened. As long as Prohibition dragged on, it never would.

With the ladder stored in the hallway, Luca double checked that everything was ready, starting with the keg of beer hidden in a well below the bar. There were more kegs in the cellar. Besides the beer, the bar was stocked with a few bottles of real whiskey. Luca expected that sales of shots of whiskey would pay for the food waiting under dishcloths, plus a keg or two.

Beer would be free tonight, but hard liquor was too valuable to give away.

The bar was crowded with platters holding mountains of pickled eggs, onions, and watermelon rinds, as well as cheese, salami, oil-cured olives sprinkled with crushed red pepper, and crusty rolls delivered fresh from the bakery. Even curls of candied lemon and orange peel, plus almond and pistachio-studded *torrone* nougat candy from the Bella Napoli pastry shop a few blocks away.

All that was needed now was the signal from the Lido Premium mill.

Back in August, Nathan Packham, owner of the Lido Premium Copper and Brass Rolling Mill, promised an extra 250 dollars to every worker if the mill filled a Boston shipyard's huge order within 45 days. The amount was more than most earned in two months.

The bonus was contingent on two things. Avoid all accidents for the duration. Fulfill all current and standing orders at the same time.

The audacious challenge was accepted. The mill went from six to seven days a week. The workday stretched to 14 hours. Workers rolled out endless sheets of copper and spun miles of wire and cable. Cured the metal in vats of chemicals. Stacked the metal on rail cars.

The brutal pace continued as summer humidity gave way to the crisp days of a golden New York autumn.

Fulfilling the contract and earning the bonus became a matter of city pride. Newspapers from Buffalo to Boston picked up the story, questioning how workers came together at Lido Premium when there was no union. In Albany, the state Assembly praised Lido Premium as a model of modern industry. At home, the *Lido Daily Clipper* published a daily countdown of days that passed without an accident in the mill. Luca read it religiously. These were his friends, his community, his refuge.

Today, October 2, 1926, was the forty-fifth day.

Luca poured the pinochle players glasses of red wine and mineral water as more club members trooped in to join the two dozen already in the saloon, bringing staccato bursts of nervous conversation in English and Italian. Everyone noticed the swagged flags and congratulatory banner.

Nearly every member of the Galliano Club was Italian, lived in East Lido, and worked at the mill, one of the largest industrial complexes in the northeast United States. Most of the Lido Premium workforce was Italian, with a few exceptions like Luca's friend Karol Dombrowski, who was Polish and belonged to the Warsaw Club on the other side of Lido.

"Fifteen minutes," someone shouted, pointing to the clock on the wall above the card tables. Guido Serra, the club's portly doorman, abandoned his stool in the vestibule enclosed by a pony wall to admit a steady stream of members who worked in nearby shops and businesses. They surged in, buzzing with anticipation.

Luca left the bar and went down the hall. No one was playing pool in the back room or idling in the postage stamp-sized library. Everyone was too agitated to do anything but gather in the saloon and sweat out the last minutes of the last day of the last shift at Lido Premium.

At the end of the hall, the door to the boss's office was partly open. The walls displayed a jumble of framed pictures and last year's Lido Industrial League baseball pennant. Vito Spinelli sat behind the desk with a glass of amber fluid. His eyes were closed. An unlabeled bottle sat within reach.

"Boss." Luca went in without knocking or breaking stride. "It's almost time. We've already got a crowd."

Vito drank the contents of the glass in a swift gulp, not reacting at all as the illegal rotgut hit bottom, then wiped his mouth and generous mustache with the back of his hand. "First one today," he said.

"Sure," Luca said, keeping judgment out of his

voice. It was a lie and they both knew it. The same as yesterday and the day before that. And the day before that.

Luca had walked into the Galliano Club with a hole in his soul and a Help Wanted ad in a language he didn't speak. Not yet 20 years old, he'd been in America less than a year, earning his way as a bare-knuckled fighter in an Irish saloon in the Bowery while his young wife Rafaella waited to give birth. And then she and their newborn son were gone, swept away by the Spanish influenza, like so many others in New York City's crowded Italian immigrant enclaves.

His cousin Enzo Russo had already established himself in Lido, six hours north by train. Luca joined Enzo but Vito Spinelli was the man who saved him.

The unofficial mayor of the close-knit East Lido neighborhood, Vito gave Luca a job at the Galliano Club, arranged for English lessons, and found him a room in a nearby boarding house. The Galliano Club dominated Hamilton Street, which ran from the mill on one end to Saint Rocco's church on the other, and was the social hub for the neighborhood. Vito's patronage gave Luca a position of respect and status that he never had before, neither as an orphan in Calabria nor as a new immigrant in a Mulberry Street tenement.

In return for everything Vito did for him, Luca took

care of things when blue dogs days came around. That's what Vito called the drinking binges when he tried to dull the pain of losing the soldier son who went to France with General Pershing and never came back. At first only a few close friends knew about the blue dog days, but now they were more frequent and harder to conceal.

Luca took the half-empty bottle to the floor safe next to the leather Chesterfield sofa and spun the dial. The door swung open to reveal two more whiskey bottles, a pile of papers, and the big green account books that kept the club solvent. Luca added the bottle. The door shut with a humorless *thunk*.

Vito sat slack in his chair behind the desk, chest rising and falling under his fine plaid wool vest with the silver watch chain strung across it. "First one today," he said again.

Luca helped him out of the chair, relieved to find that Vito was steady on his feet and gave him a stick of Black Jack licorice chewing gum.

The crowd in the saloon was swelling by the minute. Tobacco smoke wafted to the ceiling. Vito passed through, shaking hands and cracking jokes, before going behind the bar and tying on an apron.

Luca went outside to check on Guido. "All good?" he asked the doorman.

"You think they did it?" Guido shifted from foot to foot on the sidewalk under the door's striped awning. On the wrong side of forty, his round, guileless face was creased with worry.

"One hundred percent," Luca replied. Another familiar conversation.

Guido smiled, comforted yet again.

Luca surveyed Hamilton Street, lined on both sides by two- and three-story brick buildings. Signs in Italian and English advertised everything from insurance services to cigars and bicycles. He waved to the knots of people in front of the newsstand, Fiori's fish market and the Bella Napoli pastry shop. Panetta's Hardware next door was already closed. Everyone was waiting, despite the early October breeze and the lengthening shadows.

He could just make out the cross on top of Saint Rocco's as it diffused the last rays of the setting sun into a brilliant halo. Luca took it as a good omen, although he hadn't been inside a church since Rafaella died.

With a last word of reassurance to Guido, Luca went back inside.

"Three minutes," someone sang out. The saloon hushed but the nervous energy remained, sparking like electricity. Someone gave a shaky laugh. Matches flicked flame as nervous hands juggled another cigarette. Vito removed the dishcloths, revealing the heaped platters. Luca filled pitchers with beer from the hidden keg.

The clock on the wall above the card tables chimed seven o'clock. Everyone froze. In the quiet, the gushing beer sounded like Niagara Falls.

Vito pulled out his pocket watch and shook his head. "Two minutes fast," he announced.

The last chime faded away. Feet shuffled, men coughed, tobacco smoke drifted upward.

Luca focused on keeping the pitcher at the right angle so the sudsy bootleg beer wouldn't foam over the top.

The mill whistle shrilled, long and hard. The crowd in the saloon surged toward the big front window as if the view would change fate. Luca twisted the tap to close off the flow of beer and carefully set the full pitcher on the bar.

The blast subsided.

Luca silently counted seconds. *One, two, three, four, five--*

The whistle sounded a second time, a long, strong howl that rattled the empty liquor bottles on the wall behind the flags. Everyone in the saloon cheered, competing with the whistle to deafen every ear in East Lido. Vito threw his arms around Luca and kissed him on both cheeks before charging into the crowd for a wild flurry of handshakes and embraces.

The saloon was still a circus when the tired but elated workers from Lido Premium stampeded in. Raucous congratulations and shouts of *Bravo, bravo!* circled the saloon. Heady scents of soot, honest sweat and damp wool competed with the spiraling miasma of tobacco smoke.

Hands gesticulated as war stories from the past 45 days were shared at freight train volume in both English and Italian, with a little Calabrese or Sicilian thrown in for emphasis. Luca worked his end of the bar like a machine, shaking hands, filling glasses, replenishing snacks, and ringing up whiskey sales. On the other end of the long bar, Vito did the same, beaming with pride and looking ten years younger.

Guido gave a shout from the vestibule. A cheer went up from the crowd. Luca joined in, abandoning his normal reserve. Vito banged a hand on the bar top.

Jimmy Zambrano walked in and made his way through the room, shaking more hands than Governor Al Smith at a re-election rally. The mill foreman was nearly fifty, the same age as Vito, with a wiry build, a Roman nose, and closely cropped hair fading to gray above his ears. Like the other mill workers, he wore a canvas jacket over a flannel shirt and dirty dungarees.

After a circuit of back slapping, Jimmy motioned to Vito. The two were good friends and Luca was not surprised when they cut through the crowd and disappeared into Vito's office. So much for locking Vito's stash of whiskey in the safe.

The saloon was bursting at the seams and Luca's ears were ringing from the din when Jimmy and Vito reappeared. Vito still wore his apron and seemed no more impaired than before as he started refilling glasses.

Jimmy reached across the bar top to shake Luca's hand. "Thanks for the party, Luca."

"Congratulations, Jimmy," Luca raised his voice to be heard as he pumped the man's work-hardened hand with real respect. "What can I get the man of the hour?"

"How about some real beer?" Jimmy shouted back.

Luca filled a glass and used a ruler to slice the foam off the top before sliding the glass to the foreman. "On the house tonight."

Jimmy raised the glass in a salute. "Thanks, Luca. Here's to Sonny's college fund." He drank down a third in a single swallow before wading into the throng again.

The celebration was in full swing when Jimmy climbed onto a table in the middle of the saloon, prompting wild cheering, applause, and foot stamping. Luca got a good view of Jimmy's leather work boots famously splashed with pink stains from a chemical spill.

Jimmy raised both hands for quiet. "We did the impossible," he shouted as the ruckus subsided. "A sharp stick in the eye to everybody who said we couldn't."

More cheering and laughter rang out, forcing Jimmy to gesture again. "Mr. Blick asked me to pass on a message about the bonuses."

Luca opened a bottle of lemon-lime rickey from the West End brewery in nearby Utica and took a big fizzy swallow.

"There's been a hitch," Jimmy continued. A pall fell over the upturned faces surrounding him. "If we all take the bonus on Monday, Vito here will be the richest man in Lido on Tuesday. The mill will be closed because we'll be in the courthouse jail on account of public drunkenness." He gave a bark of rueful laughter. "So, if your name starts with A through G, you'll get your bonus on Monday. H through M on Tuesday. The rest of us get it on Wednesday."

There was a murmur of surprise.

Luca raised his glass in a silent toast to the foreman's craftiness.

Throughout the 45-day period, the assumption had been that once the workers got their hands on the bonus, they'd drink themselves blind and be unable to work the next day. Jimmy had just made sure that the money didn't disappear down thirsty gullets all at once, which would have closed the Lido Premium mill for a day or more. Not only that, but most of the men had too many mouths to feed and winter was coming, meaning that every wife and mother in East Lido had been hoping and praying for that bonus money. Plus, by waiting to reveal the staggered bonus payout, Jimmy kept the issue from dividing the men or eroding morale as they struggled to do the impossible.

"You'll be the last to get paid, Jimmy," a voice called.

"Suits me fine," Jimmy shot back. "Mr. Blick isn't going to welch on the deal."

Someone else spoke up. "What about the Polacks?"

"Same for everybody," Jimmy said. "Dombrowski is spreading the word at the Warsaw Club."

Luca had a pang of concern for his friend. Breaking the news to the Polish workers, most of whom held the least skilled jobs at the mill, would not be easy.

"What about Procopio?" The question came from the card tables, where Tony Bilotti and the old-timers still clustered around their game.

Everybody quieted.

Nick Procopio was Jimmy's deputy. When it came

to running the mill, Jimmy was respected but Nick was feared.

He wasn't a member of the Galliano Club and the entire saloon knew it. A few months ago, Nick was kicked out for cheating and fighting, inciting a melee that ended only when Luca clocked him twice with the Commodore baseball bat kept behind the bar for emergencies. Nick enjoyed a certain status in East Lido because of his key position at Lido Premium, but club rules were ironclad, and few were sad to see him go.

"I've already told him," Jimmy told the crowd. "Plus, Carmella is spreading the word in the neighborhood, so all the wives know when to see the cash."

"Hey!" Vito shoved past Luca and swung around the end of the bar. He made his way through the saloon and glared up at Jimmy standing on the table. "That's no good. You tell Mr. Big Shot at the mill that everybody gets their money on the same day."

"Don't worry, Vito," Jimmy replied. "Everybody will still buy their beer from you."

Uncertain laughter rippled through the crowd. Luca slowly put down his glass of tonic. Clearly Jimmy hadn't discussed this with Vito ahead of time, which was normally the case with anything that impacted so many in East Lido. Everyone came to the Galliano Club to consult with Vito.

This was a slight by one of his best friends, who was also a man of stature in the community.

"It's a cheat," Vito said, his mustache trembling in indignation. "Everybody needs to get their bonus at the same time."

"It's already been decided."

"Tulipano's getting cheated out of two days." Vito jabbed his finger at faces in the crowd. "Same for Rosselli and Staglione. You, too, Zambrano."

"Nobody's getting cheated," Jimmy said forcefully over a fresh murmur of discontent. "Everybody gets paid, and the mill stays open."

"Jimmy?" Luca stayed behind the bar, within reach of the Commodore, but his voice carried. "Did you say that Dombrowski and the Poles agreed?"

"Sure did."

Vito tugged at his mustache, clearly nonplussed by the new direction.

"A through G on Monday," Luca went on. "H through M on Tuesday and the rest on Wednesday. Besides Dombrowski, how many of the Poles will get their bonuses on Monday?"

Jimmy quickly caught on. "He's the only one."

"Everybody gets treated the same. Italian, Polish, Irish. Doesn't matter." Frank Conti, a respected crew chief, came to stand next to Jimmy's table. The solidarity was not lost on the crowd.

"We ain't letting the Polacks get the better of us, are we?" Gio Tulipano spoke up again. He was a crane operator, a skilled position at Lido Premium with a certain status of its own. "If they can wait, so can I. Jimmy's plan is all right."

Murmurs gave way to chest thumping and self-congratulations for putting one over on the Polish contingent. Jimmy jumped off the table and immediately threw an arm around Vito's neck. Luca held his breath for a moment, but the two men had known each other for a long time. After a muted conversation, Vito resumed his spot behind the bar and the celebration was once more in full swing.

The crowd ebbed and flowed for the next few hours as members went home to tell their families then returned for another round in the saloon.

Gio Tulipano reached across the bar to shake Vito's hand before stumbling out. "No hard feelings, eh, Vito?" the younger man slurred. "Gotta keep those Polacks in their place, you know."

Vito wrung the other man's hand with sincerity. "You're a good boy, Gio. Go home."

By the time the club closed at eleven o'clock, Luca's head was pounding from too many shouted conversations and too many lungfuls of someone else's tobacco smoke. Guido gave him an exhausted embrace and went home. Vito left his apron on the bar and disappeared into the office. The distinctive clicking of the spinning safe dial said the boss wouldn't be available to clean up.

Luca left the dirty glasses on the bar, trotted down the hall and let himself out the back door. The narrow porch overlooked the gravel lot where Vito's big black Packard made an opaque rectangle against the starry darkness. The window on the second floor, which belonged to the apartment rented by Vito's tenant Ruth Cross, was dark.

The air was cool and fresh. Luca's second wind was infused with pride. So much for Tony Bilotti's talk of *malocchio*.

The yard behind the club dissolved into an unpaved alley that ran parallel to Hamilton Street. Most main thoroughfares in Lido had a companion alley, designed for servants, trash collection, and access to stables, although few kept horses inside the city limits anymore.

On the far end of the two-story Galliano Club building, the ground sloped away enough to accommodate the small cellar door. Originally conceived to deliver heating oil for the big boiler, Prohibition gave it a new purpose every few weeks when the Antonelli brothers showed up with barrels of bootleg beer.

A crescent moon backlit the sugar maples on the other side of the alley, along with the club's bocce and handball courts. The leaves were scarlet now but would soon wither away. One of the first lessons Luca had learned in upstate New York was that winter always came early.

Another hour to clean up the saloon and Luca would head to his room at Mrs. Esposito's boarding house a few blocks away. Maybe he'd see if Karol, who rented the room next to his, had survived the celebration at the Warsaw Club.

Something on the ground next to the Packard caught Luca's eye. It took him a moment to realize that he was looking at a pair of heavy cordovan leather boots with dirty white laces and whorls of pink chemical stains.

Jimmy Zambrano's legs were stretched out on the gravel, but his head and shoulders were hidden, as if tinkering with the undercarriage of Vito's pride and joy.

"Jimmy?" Luca squatted beside the Packard, careful not to get a handprint on the shiny japanned finish. The foreman had left the club more than two hours ago. Had he gone drinking elsewhere and passed out like a mechanic under the big automobile? "Jimmy? What are you doing under there? It's past closing time."

The man didn't react, not even when Luca shook a boot.

"Jimmy, are you all right?"

Again, there was no reaction, no attempt to come out from under the car.

There was a smell in the air that reminded Luca of the time that his cousin Enzo had slaughtered a pig.

Luca grabbed Jimmy's boots, dragged him clear of the Packard, and stumbled backward in shock.

"Luca!" Vito's rounded silhouette filled the doorway. Light haloed around him, brightening the gravel yard. "What are you playing at?"

"Boss." Luca's voice cracked before he could steady himself. "Boss, we got trouble."

"*Madonna santa*! Did somebody scratch my car?" Vito clomped down the steps, releasing the light.

Luca pointed at the ground.

Vito recoiled and made the Sign of the Cross.

A copper wire was buried in Jimmy Zambrano's throat. Like a gruesome handlebar mustache, coils of wire protruded from either side.

The smell of blood, cloying and vile, rose from the foreman's deeply stained shirt and canvas jacket. Jimmy's hands rested lightly on the gravel. His eyes were unnaturally wide, staring in sightless surprise at the stars above.

CHAPTER 3

Perhaps she imagined the whole thing

Curled in her parlor armchair with the lights off, too agitated to get back in bed, Ruth Cross swallowed a scream when she heard a knock on the door below her second-floor apartment. Heart thumping, she twitched aside the edge of the curtain to peek at Hamilton Street.

Luca waited on the sidewalk below; her own personal savior in corduroy trousers, suspenders, and a band-collar shirt with the sleeves rolled to reveal muscular forearms. Apart from him, Hamilton Street was deserted. No shadows lurked beyond the streetlight's glow or beckoned from Fiori's fish market across the street.

Ruth didn't know if she should be relieved or terrified that Luca was knocking on her door in the middle of the night.

Her bedroom overlooked the alley behind the Galliano Club where a stray tabby often prowled for mice at night. Ruth had been woken by a scrabbling noise.

Instead of a cat, Ruth witnessed a strange struggle

between two faceless shadows. Her landlord's Packard touring car was parked on the gravel directly below her window. The struggle moved in and out of the car's blocky silhouette. A soft night breeze carried away sounds of grunting and urgent footfalls.

One moment the shadows were there, and the violence was real. The next they were gone, leaving Ruth wondering if she'd imagined the whole thing. Only the Packard remained below her bedroom window, mute and immense and inscrutable in the darkness.

Luca knocked again. Still in her flannel dressing gown, Ruth left the apartment and ran down the stairs. Her front door and the entrance to the Galliano Club were identical, topped with striped awnings and inset with a rectangle of wavy glass. They were separated by the big plate glass window with *GALLIANO CLUB EST. 1912* lettered in gold across it. Ruth's address was 601½ Hamilton Street, while the club was located at 601 Hamilton Street.

Her door opened directly to stairs leading to the second floor. Ruth rented the entire floor from Mr. Spinelli, which was divided into the furnished apartment and the Tapping Toes School of Dance, of which she was the sole proprietor and instructor.

Ruth cracked open the street door. "Luca, what's

going on?"

"I need a sheet," Luca said. "Quickly. Please."

"Oh, God." She was risking an impropriety, but Ruth opened the door all the way and beckoned for Luca to come in. He locked the deadbolt behind him.

"I saw people in the alley," Ruth said, a hand at her throat to keep the dressing gown closed. "Fighting. Was it you?

"No, not me." Luca was close enough for Ruth to see the tension in his eyes and smell the smoke clinging to his clothes.

"They were only there for a moment. Fighting next to Vito's car."

"One of them was Jimmy Zambrano," Luca said. "Strangled and left under the car."

Ruth swayed. "Murdered? The foreman at Lido Premium?"

"I need a bedsheet or a blankct."

"A sheet?"

"To cover him."

"Of course." Rubbery legs carried Ruth back up the stairs. Luca waited in the parlor as she whipped the quilt off the bed to expose her second-best sheet with the seam down the middle. As Ruth untucked the heavy linen, she was acutely aware that she was in her nightclothes and that Luca had never been in her apartment before.

Of course, he was far too young and had never given her even a sliver of hope. Nor would she expect him to forgive her past if he ever found out about it.

They'd met the day that Vito offered cheap rent in exchange for giving English lessons to his bartender. Expecting a thankless chore, Ruth discovered that Luca already had a solid self-taught foundation and absorbed information like a sponge. At this point, there was little more that she could teach him, but they still met once a week to challenge each other with esoteric vocabulary words. Sometimes they read one of her precious National Geographic magazines.

"Lock both doors behind me," Luca said when Ruth returned to the parlor with the sheet.

"Am I in danger?" Ruth quavered. She wanted to fling herself at Luca, feel him stroke her hair and tell her it was all a bad dream.

"I don't know," he said simply.

They were halfway down the dark stairway, Luca ahead with the wadded linen sheet under one arm, when the knob on the street door rattled. Luca froze. Ruth grabbed his shoulder to keep from falling against him.

The knob rattled harder. Someone was testing the door's strength.

"Anybody home? Miss Cross?" The Irish rasp

belonged to Officer Sean O'Malley, the strapping policeman who kept the peace on Hamilton Street.

Ruth stopped breathing. If he peered through the window in the street door at just the right angle, O'Malley would see them poised halfway down the stairs.

An unmarried woman in her nightclothes and an Italian immigrant carrying a bedsheet. O'Malley would arrest them both for indecency. The scandal would be tomorrow's headline in the *Lido Daily Clipper*, eclipsed only by the discovery of the poor man strangled behind the club. Panic surged into Ruth's throat at the thought of being arrested for murder, too.

"Go back," Luca murmured.

Without turning around, Ruth eased up a step. Luca did the same. She kept her hand on his shoulder.

The club door squealed open as Vito nearly shouted the police officer's name. "Officer O'Malley."

"Your tenant always lock her door?" O'Malley asked.

"Sure, sure."

"Smart, being a single lady and all."

"Sure," Vito said again.

Ruth willed herself up another two steps. Luca moved with her.

"Past closing time," O'Malley said. "How come

you're still around?"

"Big night, big clean up."

"Where's Serra?"

"He went home," Vito said.

"Lombardo, too?"

"Sure."

"You got a lady friend hiding back there?" O'Malley asked.

"No, no." Vito gave a falsely hearty chuckle. "No ladies allowed at the Galliano Club."

"Can't take Communion from the priest tomorrow if you lie today."

"The priest don't need to know everything, eh?"

Ruth wasn't religious but nearly everyone she knew in Lido was Catholic. The Italians went to St. Rocco's, the Irish went to St. Brigid's, and the Polish went to Holy Angels.

Doctors, lawyers, mill owners and the mayor went to Trinity Episcopal, the church with the bell tower instead of a steeple. Those were the people who sent their children to the Tapping Toes School of Dance. Rich people. Respectable people.

Outside, a faint rustling sound ensued, followed by a satisfied click of the tongue.

"Nice doing business with you, Spinelli," O'Malley said. "I'm going to close you down someday, but seeing as today is payday, you just bought yourself a little more time."

"What's folding money between friends?" Vito gave another strained chuckle.

"Now that's a dangerous word." O'Malley's tone changed from jocular to insolent. "Wops and Irishmen aren't friends. We just help each other out from time to time. You wops need to keep with wops. Mix it up with your betters and we'll have no end of trouble. Am I right about that, Spinelli?"

There was a dull thumping noise. Ruth imagined O'Malley slapping his nightstick into his palm the way she'd seen him do on his evening rounds. Vito said something indistinct. O'Malley barked a laugh. The door to the club slammed shut.

Luca leaped up the remaining stairs, Ruth on his heels, and they rushed to the parlor window in time to see O'Malley stride down Hamilton Street twirling his nightstick. He passed under the streetlight, an impressive figure in domed helmet and ironclad wool uniform pinched at the waist by a leather belt.

A panel truck passed O'Malley going in the opposite direction, decorated with a smiling penguin wearing a top hat. *Penguin Ice. Delivery Day or Night.*

"*Oddio*," Luca muttered.

Ruth had never heard him swear in Italian before.

O'Malley rattled the doorknob at Panetta's Hardware, peered in the window of D'Agostino's bicycle store, and read the specials tacked up in the window of Red's Meat Market. Ham was 19 cents a pound, Ruth recalled as if the price of meat was suddenly the most important thing in the world. She'd bought some that morning.

Luca tucked the wadded sheet under his arm again. "Lock all the doors behind me. You were asleep all night. No shadows, no fighting, nothing."

"What about Vito?" Ruth pressed. "He knows about . . . about the dead man, too?"

"Even if Vito asks, you saw nothing." Luca held her gaze until Ruth nodded her understanding. Vito Spinelli was a prince among men, but she knew about his blue dog days. Alcohol made her landlord thoughtless.

When Luca left, Ruth bolted the street door behind him. A moment later, she heard the club door open and close.

Back upstairs, with the lights off, the apartment door locked, and a chair braced under the knob, Ruth curled up again in the armchair, next to the table with her cherished photograph of George M. Cohan and the 1904 Broadway cast of *Little Johnny Jones*. She was the tall girl in the middle of the chorus line.

A murder had happened just below her. The killer

could be anyone, even an East Lido neighbor. What if the killer recognized her face in the window? Everyone knew that she lived above the Galliano Club and ran a business there, too.

Before she knew it, Ruth was weeping uncontrollably.

Four years ago, she was Ruthie June Crosswater, a Broadway chorus girl too old for the big shows, reduced to playing the bottom-tier vaudeville circuit in an all-girl song-and-dance act. She loved her friends and life on the road, but when a fellow hoofer named William Wilson offered love and big-time success, she grabbed the chance with both hands.

William was a talented acrobat as well as a dancer. He dazzled Ruth with his seeming devotion and show business contacts. Envisioning the ballroom fame enjoyed by Vernon and Irene Castle a decade before, Ruth agreed to everything William suggested, from calling herself "June Wilson" to delaying the wedding until they got their big break and could do it up right.

The new act never had a chance. William ran out on Ruth one freezing day, leaving her destitute and pregnant. Hunting for work, Ruth miscarried on a park bench in Poughkeepsie. The police charged her with public indecency, lewd behavior, and more. The local newspapers never printed her name, but she was excoriated as *Park Mother,* a modern model of abject immorality.

Ruth spent six months in prison.

No one in Lido knew about her scandalous past. To the parents who paid her to teach their children to twirl and waltz, Ruth Cross was a respectable spinster who had known famous Broadway impresario George M. Cohan.

To Vito and Luca, she was tenant and teacher. Not even a friend.

Alone in the dark parlor, Ruth couldn't stop sobbing. She didn't know if it was because she was frightened by the murder or terrified of the scandal so narrowly averted as O'Malley passed by.

Or perhaps the hopeless burden of her own yearnings was simply too heavy to bear.

CHAPTER 4

This death was different

Luca skidded into the vestibule with the sheet and locked the club door behind him.

"Which way did O'Malley go?" Vito's eyes were red, but he was cold sober.

"Toward Saint Rocco's," Luca said, skirting the pony wall. "The Antonelli's truck passed him coming this way."

"The Antonelli's? You sure?"

"Penguin Ice," Luca confirmed. "Did you know they were coming tonight?"

Vito passed a shaky hand over his face. "*Madonna santa*, but I forgot."

Every few weeks Sal and Milo Antonelli left their farm near Gananoque on the Canadian side of the border with a load of rye whiskey and home-brewed beer, took the ferry across the neck of Lake Ontario to Clayton, and drove south through upstate New York. They supplied Italian-owned establishments from Watertown to Lido. To avoid coming to the attention of Prohibition Bureau agents, they delivered late at night and kept their circle of customers small.

Luca met the brothers soon after coming to work at the Galliano Club when he pointed out that their kegs weren't full. Amid forced laughter and muttered excuses about mistakes, Luca made sure the brothers understood their cheating days were over. Since then, the relationship had evolved into a grudging friendship based on bootlegging profits and mutual distrust.

Jimmy's body had released its bowels. The stink was undeniable as Luca knelt on the gravel and shook out the linen sheet. Jimmy's head lolled to one side. Bone, blood, and copper wire shone in the gloom.

"What did Ruth say?" Vito asked. "What did you tell her about needing a sheet?"

"I said you were asleep in your office," Luca lied. There was a humming in his head that said this wasn't real, that Jimmy Zambrano was home with his wife Carmella and their children.

Vito helped Luca enshroud Jimmy in the sheet, tying it at both ends to keep his head or boots from flopping out. A brief discussion ensued about how to hide the body from Sal and Milo, who always expected to use the club's toilets and down a sandwich or two.

Just in time, they wrestled Jimmy into the Packard and laid him on the floor in the rear. A minute later they heard the Penguin Ice truck coming down the alley, although no headlights announced its arrival.

The truck came to a stop on the verge just above the cellar door. As always, the truck dripped water from a leaky box inside; a clever ruse to make believe the vehicle was full of melting ice.

Sal Antonelli spilled out of the passenger side. "We saw a cop not a block from here." His brother Milo eased himself out from behind the wheel.

"O'Malley was making the rounds," Vito said. "Just a little later than usual."

Luca unlocked the cellar door, hoping to get this over as fast as possible.

"Our last stop was at Pino Barone's in Boonville." Sal was taller and the brother in charge but otherwise the Antonellis were identical. Walrus mustaches, tweed caps, baggy trousers, and the kind of woolen pea coats that sailors wore. "Said you was selling the club."

"Selling?" Vito blinked in surprise. "Pino said I was selling?"

"Said he heard it from a real slick type."

Luca climbed up the slope in two big steps. "A slick type? Who?"

Sal shrugged. "Barone didn't have a name."

"Well, that's Barone's problem," Vito said as if that was the end of the conversation. "Nobody is selling the Galliano Club."

"Wait a minute, boss." Luca kept his attention on Sal. "Why wouldn't Barone say who told him?"

Milo shoved his way into the discussion. "You've been a good customer, Spinelli. But if this is some kind of trick to beat us down on prices, there's going to be trouble."

"It's a mix-up." Luca clapped Milo on the shoulder. "Nobody's trying to cut you down. Same price as before, right? Let's get the beer moved before O'Malley decides to come back."

"Eh, sure," Milo said, mollified.

Luca opened the cellar door and heaved out the empty kegs while the brothers unloaded the truck. With Jimmy's body stiffening in the Packard and Vito looking like he was going to fall over dead of a heart attack, time was in short supply.

Ten minutes later, the cellar was stocked with enough beer for more than a month. The truck was loaded with empties and straw to keep them from rolling. Luca locked the cellar door, and they went into the club.

Vito extracted payment from the office safe, and Sal counted it carefully as Luca split crusty bread lengthwise, spread both sides with pesto, and added slices of provolone and salami from the remains of the celebration. The meat and cheese were topped with roasted red peppers oozing with olive oil.

"Here you go." He handed across the giant sandwiches. The brothers helped themselves to olives and candy. Two glasses of beer followed.

It was long past midnight when the Antonellis pulled out of the gravel yard. As the sound of the truck faded and East Lido grew silent, Luca sank onto the cold cement porch steps.

"What do you think?" he asked.

The boss looked bad, like the blue dog was nipping at his heels. "I never said I wanted to sell."

"I know." Luca hesitated. "But somebody might think they could buy the club cheap if you were in trouble. Real big trouble."

"What kind of trouble?"

Luca waited for the boss to figure it out, too. O'Malley's presence at the club took on a new importance. Did the cop come by because he expected to see a murder victim and make an arrest? Or did the killer know the policeman's routine?

"*Madonna santa*," Vito swore softly as he made the connection. "He was supposed to find Jimmy and arrest me for murder. But everyone knows I got no reason to kill Jimmy."

"You argued with him about the bonus," Luca said miserably. "Everyone heard."

"It's wrong, the way they want to do it."

"The bonus isn't important." Luca thought about the heavy copper wire and the strength it must have taken to kill the tough foreman. "Even if O'Malley arrested you, boss, he'd know that you couldn't have killed Jimmy. Whoever did it was taller and strong, real strong."

Vito swabbed his forehead with his handkerchief and lowered his bulk to the steps next to Luca. "Like you," he said slowly. "You're strong enough. O'Malley could blame you."

A fresh wave of cold sweat washed over Luca. Vito was right. Luca had inherited height and hazel eyes from his father, a military officer from Italy's northern Lombardy province, along with the muscular frame and iron constitution of his Calabrian mother.

Luca shoved himself upright. A man was dead in Vito's car, and they were blubbering on the back porch instead of figuring out what to do. "Right now," he said, "the only people who know for sure that Jimmy is dead are you, me, and whoever killed him."

"You think if he's not found here, nobody can connect the club to his murder?"

"What if Jimmy was found at Saint Rocco's?" Luca suggested. "We could leave him in back of the church. The priest will take care of him."

"That's good," Vito said mournfully. "The priest can tell Carmella."

Luca was reminded again of Vito Spinelli's innate decency. Amid all the fear and uncertainty, the boss was thinking of Jimmy's family.

They locked the club, climbed into the Packard with Jimmy's body, and set out for the corner of Hamilton and Union Ave where Saint Rocco's served the faithful. The massive church, made of rough-hewn ruddy stone, resembled a modest cathedral, with wide steps, arched doorways, and a giant rose window. The steeple soared into the sky from an offset squared tower. The gold cross on top winked against the stars, a symbol of absolution to a sinner's eye.

It was past midnight but just a few blocks away, the downtown district beckoned with neon lights and a parade of cars. The second showing at the Strand Theatre was just ending. A dozen restaurants were still open.

Before they reached the main intersection, Vito veered down a narrow lane. Saint Rocco's stone walls loomed on the right, stained glass windows glinting blood-red in the beam of the Packard's headlights. The Catholic elementary school, where every parent in East Lido sent their children if they could afford it, squatted dark and low on the left. Next door to the school, the nuns who taught there lived in a convent with the same soulless architecture, as if all the glory belonged to Saint Rocco's and none to its acolytes.

Vito was just about to swing into the drive behind the church when Luca gripped his arm. "Don't stop. Keep going."

Light glowed from the convent's windows on the first floor. Candles flickered in the prayer garden next to it and female voices were lifted in song.

"The nuns are outside for midnight vespers."

Vito swore and drove on.

"What if we take Jimmy to the mill?" Luca suggested when the church grounds were well behind them.

Vito glanced at him with the eyes of a frightened child. "Yes, the mill. They'll find him."

The stench in the Packard was becoming unbearable. Luca cranked down his window as they passed through the warehouse area. The giant lumberyard went by, as did the Teaberry Knitting Mill, the club's baseball arch-rival.

It was fitting to leave Jimmy at the mill. He'd spent most of his life there, smelting, rolling, and dipping copper sheeting. During the Great War, Jimmy stamped copper into shell casings. But the Great War was the war to end all wars. Nobody except gangsters needed ammunition anymore.

To Luca's frayed nerves, it felt as if they would never get there. Eventually the mill came into view. Two big smokestacks stabbed into the sky; black fingers silhouetted against a milky light emanating from behind the massive building. That's where a rail spur carried ore in and shining metal out.

Luca's heart sank. He'd expected Lido Premium to be deserted after the exhausting 45-day marathon, but several night watchmen guarded the front, light from their lanterns dancing across the bottom tier of windows. More lingered in front of the small office building. More than a dozen cars waited in the lot.

"They haven't shipped out the order yet," Luca guessed. "They must still be loading."

Vito didn't slow. Luca glimpsed a row of freight cars standing on the track and the hook of an unseen crane dangling above.

"This is no good," Vito said. He pulled out his handkerchief and mopped his eyes as he drove. "Maybe the devil took Jimmy and doesn't want him to be found."

They rattled over the Bell Street bridge. Luca saw the dark outlines of farmhouses and barns. He knew the area well; his cousin Enzo's farm was on Bell Road, where the Mohawk River curved to create a basin of rich soil. Like Enzo, most of the farmers had a few cows and aspired to an entire dairy. In between milkings, they grew vegetables and garlic from the peppery black earth and supplied grocery stores from Plattsburgh to Manhattan.

Vito muttered something about *malocchio* as Bell Road dwindled into a gravel track running parallel to the river. He cut the headlights. The Packard rolled through an endless black tunnel.

The river was on the left. Air freshened by running water and autumn leaves soon diluted the smell of Jimmy's body. Dense foliage scraped at the sides of the big boxy vehicle. The Packard slewed from side to side as it passed through unseen openings, coming ever closer to the water's edge.

Vito stopped on a little swell above the river and set the brake. Luca opened the passenger door and heard rushing water. The current flowed past the riverbank in a series of white-tipped ripples. Vines and wild scrub surrounded birch, maple and pine trees, creating an enclosure that reminded Luca of a chapel.

"What is this place, boss?"

"Jimmy's secret fishing spot," Vito said. "It'll be iced over in a few weeks. Jimmy can rest in peace where the devil won't find him."

"You want to leave him here?"

"Not where the animals will get him," Vito said sharply. "We put him in the water, like a sailor."

Luca looked around. Moonlight gilded the foliage. The river would wash away the violence of Jimmy's last moments.

And no one would ever be able to connect his murder to the Galliano Club.

Getting the stiffened body out of the Packard was a wretched task. Tears ran down Vito's cheeks as they set Jimmy on the ground, untied the sheet, and carefully emptied his pockets, finding 40 cents, two keys, a pipe, some tobacco in a pouch, and a book of matches. No watch, wedding band, or cross around his neck.

Vito refused to take any of it. Luca stuffed everything in his own pockets. Somehow, he'd make sure that Carmella Zambrano got her husband's effects.

A few heavy rocks to weight the body and the heavy linen sheet became a true death shroud. Luca wondered if the linen would be imprinted with Jimmy's face, the way the Shroud of Turin bore the likeness of Jesus Christ.

"Do you want to say something?" he asked Vito. "A prayer?"

Vito made the Sign of the Cross, his voice barely audible. *"In nomine Patris, et Filii, et Spiritus Sancti."*

Luca bowed his head and waited for Vito to go on.

The river gurgled below them. An owl hooted in the distance. Leaves rustled.

When Vito didn't speak, Luca found himself reciting the Hail Mary as it had been taught to him so many years ago, in the language of the Catholic Church. He had not said the prayer in nearly a decade, but the Latin came back to him without effort.

Ave Maria, gratia plena, Dominus tecum. Benedicta tu in mulieribus, et benedictus fructus ventris tui, Iesus. Sancta Maria, Mater Dei, ora pro nobis peccatoribus, nunc, et in hora mortis nostrae. Amen.

"Amen," Vito choked out.

It took both of them to heave the weighted body over the lip of the riverbank. The ungainly bundle sent up a plume of freezing water, forcing Luca to jerk back to avoid getting soaked. When he peered over the edge, Jimmy had disappeared into the depths. The river rippled downstream as calmly as before.

Mopping his eyes yet again, the white handkerchief a flag of surrender in the darkness, Vito plodded to the Packard.

As he made to follow, an icy hand squeezed Luca's heart. Dizziness engulfed him. Blindly reaching out for the nearest tree to steady himself, Luca threw up everything he'd ever put in his stomach.

Somehow, the return trip through the woods was

even more harrowing than the odyssey to get there. Luca hung on grimly as the Packard lurched through the woods. The rutted track leading back to Bell Road felt as smooth as glass compared to jouncing through a tunnel made of thickets and sorrow and silent night. When they finally saw city streetlights ahead, the release of tension was so sudden Luca was nearly overcome with dizziness again. They were back to Hamilton Street before they saw another car.

Vito cleared his throat as they neared Mrs. Esposito's boarding house. "I'm not going to drink anymore," he said. "I swear on Jimmy's soul, no more drinking."

Luca got out of the Packard without saying a word.

Before collapsing into bed, he tucked the handful of items from Jimmy's pockets into the tin box where he kept his personal treasures. His American citizenship papers were there, along with his dead wife's Italian passport and a leather portfolio decorated with a military crest that contained his father's military records.

Despite being desperately tired, Luca lay awake, staring at Mrs. Esposito's cabbage rose wallpaper. The memory of Jimmy's body hitting the water would be a stone in his heart forever, just like the night in Calabria when he took the life of a military officer named

Humberto Orsini.

As a child, Luca saw Orsini execute his father Matteo for desertion from King Victor Emmanuel's army, then shoot his mother Viola when she protested.

A dozen years later, Luca was reluctantly studying for the priesthood when he learned that Orsini was now head of the local army garrison. Luca confronted the officer, determined to make him beg for forgiveness. Wily as ever, Orsini stabbed the teenager before Luca pulled the trigger of his father's gun.

No one ever found out. Orsini's death was ruled a suicide by the local authorities.

Luca sold the gun to a smuggler, married Rafaella, and bought passage to America. When she and the baby died in that horrible New York City tenement, Luca knew it was his punishment for the sin of taking another man's life.

He was a sinner, yet he could not confess to a priest and ask for absolution. Luca felt no remorse for killing the man who murdered his parents.

Leaving Jimmy in the river was different. Someone else had taken that life.

Someone Luca intended to find.

CHAPTER 5

A successful man

"Owen Forbes Fisher, you are a successful man." Owen whispered the words to his reflection in the bathroom mirror. It was the morning mantra, said only when Cynthia was downstairs making breakfast. "You are clever. You are capable. You are in the inner circle."

He murmured the mantra three more times, then opened a tin of pomade, smoothed it over his cowlick, and slicked his light brown hair into place. Washed the comb before putting it back in the cup Cynthia kept for just that purpose.

"Owen!" Cynthia's voice floated up the stairs. "Your egg is ready."

"Coming." Owen winked at himself in the mirror before buttoning his vest. The new windowpane suit was a little loud for the Sunday service at Trinity Episcopal, but Cynthia insisted that it was the latest fashion. It was from Van Dyke's, Lido's finest clothing store.

She had a vinegary poached egg on store-bought bread waiting for him in the dining room. Their shiny new electric percolator stood ready on the buffet with fresh coffee. He gave Cynthia an air kiss because she didn't like to be mussed and took his seat at the head of the table.

"Don't you think we should get a maid now?" Cynthia asked.

"A maid?" Owen hesitated, fork in the air.

"You said with this new raise that the sky's the limit." Cynthia smiled at him over the rim of her coffee cup.

"I'll think about it," Owen promised.

Cynthia believed his story about getting a raise, but the truth was that the new partnership with Benny Rotolo and Nick Procopio was a roaring success. The brewery inside the stone pumphouse near the charred ruins of the original Lido Premium mill made money faster than Owen could count it.

Benny signed up customers.

Nick ran the crew.

Owen kept the books.

It would take a squadron of auditors to unravel how Owen used Lido Premium funds to pay for the brewery equipment. Not only was the accounting a thing of beauty but he discovered a flair for forging signatures, too. All the receipts and invoices looked completely genuine.

Of course, the timing was perfect. Everyone at Lido Premium, from the frighteningly efficient operations manager Henry Blick to the lowliest stoker sweating to keep the boilers hot, had been too consumed with the 45-day challenge to focus on the minutiae of Owen's bookkeeping. The staggered bonus payout plan created more useful complexity.

Cynthia adored her mink jacket, also from Van Dyke's, and the new Gorham sterling silver flatware.

The pattern was called Etruscan and featured a Greek key design. Not content with just forks and knives, Cynthia had bought every piece imaginable, from a jelly spoon with a curl in the bowl to a shovel-sized sardine server that Owen doubted they'd ever use. Next on Cynthia's list was a set of Limoges china with hand painted roses.

Hopefully, she was happy enough to stop listening to her mother complain that Owen wasn't climbing the ladder of success fast enough for her only child. A pillar of Syracuse society, Owen's mother-in-law had wanted Cynthia to marry someone richer and more socially connected. Any of Owen's Delta Kappa Epsilon fraternity brothers at Syracuse University, for example.

Owen always wondered if Cynthia chose him just to spite her mother. His wife was blonde and beautiful and moved through Lido society like a swan. He was desperate to keep her.

Cynthia poured his coffee, her silky hair shining in the sunlight streaming through the lace curtains. A new rope of pearls, also from Van Dyke's, swung across her cream-colored dress as she bent over the table. Owen thanked her and told her she looked lovely and finished his egg. The coffee was rich and strong.

Things were going so well that losing his pocket ledger was simply not an option. He'd kept it with him at the mill where ledger books were a dime a dozen, cleverly hiding it in plain sight. A big mistake. Sadder but wiser and all that, of course, but it was a matter of some urgency to find it.

The ledger was his private accounting, not the one he showed to his partners in the Lido Outfit. Who knows what would happen if it fell into the wrong hands.

Cynthia topped her mink jacket with a new cloche hat with a curling peacock feather and they drove to Sunday service. Trinity Episcopal was the usual dull mix of pious and pretentious but all the best people attended. Owen and Cynthia made sure to see and be seen after the service. He couldn't help preening a bit as the mink jacket earned a few envious looks.

"Let's take a walk," Owen suggested as the crowd thinned. He steered Cynthia to the sidewalk running in front of the church. "Show off your new mink jacket."

"Did you see Osa Rutherford?" Cynthia whispered with a giggle. "She's so jealous."

Owen was sure that the scion of Lido Lumber could afford to buy his wife ten mink jackets but he smiled and tucked Cynthia's hand through the crook of his elbow. "Of course, she is."

Every Sunday, weather permitting, everyone who was anyone visited Lido's expansive city green. Anchored by a granite obelisk chiseled in Vermont to commemorate the Revolutionary War, the park spanned two city blocks and was bordered on all sides by the best shops and restaurants, as well as the Strand Theatre.

Clusters of businessmen lit post-church cigars and cigarettes as they discussed the news coming out of Albany and Washington. Housebound during the week, wives window-shopped and gossiped while children ran around on the grass. After an appearance in the park, most families migrated to the Varsity Restaurant for lunch, with the Bloomfield Hotel and the Canal House vying for second choice. Men spent the rest of the day at the Bison Club if they were in the inner circle; the Shanks or the Willett clubs if they weren't.

Today Owen walked east toward Hamilton Street, bypassing the park entirely.

"Where are we going?" Cynthia asked, frowning. The curling peacock feather jiggled with every step.

"It's a surprise," Owen said vaguely.

"But we're going toward East Lido. What kind of surprise could be there?"

Owen belatedly thought of taking her to the pastry shop he passed every day coming and going from the mill. "Just wait, dear."

They strolled through the intersection of Hamilton and Union as the congregation spilled out of Saint Rocco's church. Little traffic blocked their view. Most people walked in this neighborhood where everything was jammed together, from the tall clapboard houses where multiple families lived on top of each other, to the rows of brick buildings full of shops and services and fronted with signs in Italian.

The Papists liked living on top of each other, Owen supposed. They were all swarthy people in rough clothes with packs of children like wolves with runny noses. When they knew a bit of English, the Italians made good workers, and they took it in stride if they lost a finger or got burned by molten metal. Some of them could even be downright clever, like Benny Rotolo, when they could read and dressed properly. Of course, those types were few and far between. Right-thinking people knew that God had not blessed either

Italians or mules with much more than the capacity for manual labor.

Nick Procopio came out of the church with a shabbily dressed woman and the requisite swarm of grubby children. A big barrel-chested man, the deputy foreman was easy to pick out of the crowd. Ignoring his wife and children, Nick looked up and down Hamilton Street.

"Why are we stopping?" Cynthia asked.

"I think I have a stone in my shoe."

Owen made a show of bending down to fiddle with his shoe, staring across the street the entire time. He caught Nick's eye and got a nod that spoke volumes. Owen was so giddy with relief he could barely stand upright again.

The nod meant that Nick had taken care of the little matter of the lost ledger.

Fixed and forgotten and Benny none the wiser. Owen would pay Nick on Monday for handling the problem.

Owen began walking again, his mood almost exuberant. Cynthia made a little huffy noise of distress. "You're going too fast," she complained.

Owen stopped. "Would you rather go to Buckner's for lunch?"

"Buckner's?" Cynthia exclaimed. "Oh, Owen."

Tucked into the exclusive West Circle neighborhood, Buckner's was widely acknowledged to be the most elegant restaurant in Lido. In all the time they'd been married, Owen and Cynthia had only been twice.

Now Owen could take his wife to Buckner's every week. Every day, if he wanted.

As long as Benny never saw the pocket ledger. Not that he'd understand. But better to be safe than sorry.

CHAPTER 6

As if nothing happened

Luca woke up on Sunday struggling to call out, to warn Jimmy just before the river swallowed him up.

The water gurgled away and was replaced with Mrs. Esposito's cabbage roses. Tangled in sheets and blankets, for a long moment Luca was unable to do much more than lie in the narrow bed, suck in air and will the nightmare away.

There was no way to turn back time, no choice to make. The only option was to do what he normally did on Sunday, then Monday, and every day after that.

And lie.

Luca always spent Sunday at his cousin Enzo's farm, helping with chores that required four hands and two strong backs. The club was closed on Sunday, which Vito insisted was still the Lord's day despite the money the club could make. In the evening, back at the boarding house, he and Karol caught up over a game of chess.

When the other lodgers went to Mass, Luca took a piping hot bath, a luxury when the bathroom was shared with seven other lodgers and Mrs. Esposito monitored every drop of water they used. Shaved and dressed, he paced the frowzy little parlor with its uncomfortable sofa, crocheted antimacassars, and glowering photograph of the late Mr. Esposito, until he saw Enzo's truck pull to the curb in front of the house.

Enzo honked and waved as Luca trotted down the steps. In the front seat next to her husband, Rosaria held the baby swaddled in a quilt on her lap. Luca leaned through the window to give her a kiss before vaulting into the bed of the truck to join 8-year-old Rocco and his sister Matilda, who was two years younger.

"*Zio!*" Matilda squealed as Luca presented both children with a peppermint. Both children always addressed him as *Uncle,* and it always felt right.

Sundays at the farm were a substitute for having a family of his own.

"*Zio,* are you listening?" Rocco waved a hand in front of Luca's face as the truck rattled along Bell Road.

"Yes," Luca lied. It was just cold enough riding in the back of the open truck to finally clear his head. "Tell me, what's the solution? Remember you add each individual number as you go. Twenty-five. Sixty-two. Seventeen."

"That's a hard one," Matilda said doubtfully and huddled into her coat.

"Wait." Rocco's face screwed up in concentration, then opened in a broad smile. "I know. Five!"

"Very good." Luca gave him an approving grin.

"Give me another one, *Zio*!"

They played the counting game that Luca had played with his father, adding digits in a linear quest to find a final single-digit solution, until Matilda wanted to tell him about her teacher. Luca listened as the scenery went by, the same view he'd passed in the darkness less than ten hours ago.

The trip ended in front of the Russo family's clapboard farmhouse with its steeply pitched roof. Luca helped the kids clamber over the tailgate.

Twenty minutes later, after a cup of coffee and two homemade doughnuts, Luca and Enzo were nailing wall boards to the half-finished structure that would become the new barn. Each board was 12 feet long and took two men to hold against the uprights and nail into place. With a sturdy stone foundation they'd laid during the summer, once the walls were done and the metal roof in place, the barn would be strong enough to withstand the harshest winter winds.

The cousins built up a sweat despite the cool day. They made a good team and their work fell into an easy rhythm of sawing, lifting, fitting, and nailing. The pine boards were rough and aromatic, and it was satisfying to watch the wall grow.

"You doing all right?" Enzo asked when they took a break.

"Sure." Luca downed a dipperful of water from the drinking bucket.

"You've barely said two words."

Luca sluiced a dipperful over his head, both to buy time and dilute his salty sweat. "Long day yesterday," he said at length.

Enzo was a dark-haired and dark-eyed Calabrian, with none of Luca's northern Italian looks. He rolled his shoulders to ease his muscles. "Everyone at Mass was talking about the big celebration at the club last night. I should have come into town for it."

For a moment, Luca couldn't catch his breath. Enzo was a member of the Galliano Club but like so many who lived outside East Lido, he didn't come very often. Now and then he enjoyed a Saturday night at the club, bringing Luca to the farm afterward.

"Did I say something wrong?" Enzo wiped sweat off his forehead with the back of a hand.

Luca couldn't look his cousin in the eye and covered by dousing himself with another dipperful of water. "No, sorry. Just a long night."

"How was Vito?" Enzo knew about blue dog days.

"He held up." Luca passed the dipper to his cousin.

What were the chances Enzo knew something about a rumor passed from Pino Barone in Boonville to the bootlegging Antonelli brothers? "Some people think he should sell the club."

Enzo sucked down the cool water, but his eyes were wide. "Is his drinking getting so bad?"

"No, Vito's doing all right. Just something I overheard."

"Vito can't sell," Enzo said stoutly. "East Lido would never be the same."

"If you ever hear anybody talk about it, tell me, okay?"

"Sure." Enzo was completely without suspicion or guile.

Dusk was lengthening the shadows when Rosaria shouted from the house that it was time to eat. Luca pounded in the last nail before washing up for dinner.

The dining room was the hub of the farmhouse, with dark wood furniture, striped wallpaper, and a brass ceiling fixture with three electric light bulbs.

Enzo poured homemade dandelion wine into stubby glasses for everyone, they said grace, and Rosaria brought out the *prima piatti*, a huge bowl of homemade linguini swimming in silky tomato sauce. Matilda trailed her mother, assigned to carry in the cheese and grater.

Luca wolfed the linguini, expertly twirling every forkful against the bowl of his spoon. Rosaria was an excellent cook who knew how to feed a ravenous working man. The sauce was rich with garlic and basil, the pasta cooked to *al dente* perfection.

The *secondi piatti* was a mountain of pork cutlets pounded flat, coated in breadcrumbs and fried golden brown, along with a bucket-sized bowl of boiled potatoes and another of just-wilted spinach glistening with olive oil and speckled with garlic and coarse salt. Enzo filled the plates, which were passed down the table. For a few minutes, the room was silent except for the chime of fork against plate, satisfied chewing, and slurps of wine.

"So, did you tell him?" Rosaria posed the question to her husband, but her eyes strayed to Luca.

Enzo kept his attention on his plate. "Not yet," he mumbled around a mouthful.

"What are you waiting for?" Rosaria demanded. "You were outside together all afternoon."

Luca paused with a bite of cutlet speared on his fork. "What's going on? What's the matter?"

"Ma says you need to get married, *Zio*," Rocco announced.

Matilda jabbed her brother with an elbow. "*Cafone.* You weren't supposed to tell him."

Enzo reached out and clouted Rocco on the side of the head. "Eat your food, both of you."

Luca winked at Rocco. The kid winked back and stuffed half a potato into his mouth.

Matilda giggled, holding her cutlet like a cookie.

Rosaria pointed her fork at both children, who obediently bent over their plates. "I told Enzo to tell you the good news."

Shaking his head, Enzo tore a chunk off the big loaf of crusty bread sitting in the middle of the table.

"What sort of good news?" Luca asked warily.

"Do you know Al Genovese?" Rosaria asked. "The dairy farm across the road. Big yellow house. His wife is Claudia."

"Sure, he comes to the club every now and then." Luca recalled the Genovese farm. It was the closest property to the river.

"They have fifteen cows," Matilda said and made a mooing noise, which her brother immediately copied.

"That's right," Enzo said, loud enough to be heard over the silliness. "Fifteen cows. Al sells the milk to Gulla's Dairy."

Still wary, Luca merely nodded.

"His sister arrives this week from Italy," Rosaria said. "Claudia tells me Annunziata kept house for her sainted mother until the woman passed away. She's a nice unspoiled girl who knows how to cook. A regular churchgoer, too. And lovely, so I hear."

This was nothing about last night, merely an attempt by Rosaria to play matchmaker. "No," Luca said.

"I told you," Enzo murmured, loud enough to be heard by his wife at the other end of the table.

"No means nothing." Rosaria bristled. "He can say no after he meets her. But he won't. From what Claudia says, the girl is perfect for him."

Luca helped himself to a hunk of bread. "No."

"I told you," Enzo said again.

Rosaria was hardly the first person to play matchmaker for Luca. When Luca went to work at the Galliano Club, news of an eligible bachelor with a good job and all his teeth spread like wildfire through East Lido. Every member's wife aimed to introduce him to a sister or a cousin or a daughter. Even Mrs. Esposito trotted out a cousin for him to admire. The worst was when they ambushed him at Lido Industrial League baseball games when he was playing first base.

Luca tried hard not to insult East Lido's would-be matchmakers, but he'd already been married to a girl who only knew how to cook and clean and pray. Rafaella had been frightened of this new, unfamiliar place called America and had clung to her fears until the day she died in their tiny room in a Mulberry Street tenement. Luca wanted to explore America, grasp it in both hands, shake a new life out of it.

Neither could he marry in the Church again after taking Orsini's life, nor explain his reasons why. This alone put every Italian woman out of reach.

"You're almost 30 years old," Rosaria said. "You need a wife."

"Twenty-seven," Luca countered. "Not so old."

"You can't keep living like a priest," she declared. "Alone. No children. No family."

Luca grinned tiredly at her. "You're not my family anymore?"

"You know what I mean." Rosaria shook her fork as if Luca was another troublesome child. "You should have a wife to cook and look after you."

"I know how to cook."

"You make sandwiches at the club," Rosaria argued. "That's not cooking. Besides, it's not right to live in a boarding house with strangers. A man needs his own house."

"A house costs money."

Rosaria threw up her hands. "Stop sending all your money away. Have they ever once thanked you? Said that it was enough? No, they just take and take. You need to live your own life now." She lifted her chin at her husband. "Tell him, Enzo."

"It's been a long time," Enzo mumbled.

Luca sighed and wiped his mouth with his napkin. "Have you met her? This Annunziata?"

"No," Enzo replied before Rosaria could reply.

"Claudia told me all about her and Annunziata sounds perfect." Rosaria grimaced at her husband, evidently irritated at his less-than persuasive attitude. "What's the harm in meeting her? You can see if having a wife isn't better than living with strangers."

"What if this girl likes baseball, *Zio*?" Rocco asked.

"She won't."

"You shouldn't live with strangers, *Zio*," Matilda said seriously.

"They aren't strangers," Luca told the little girl. "They're my friends."

"Still," Matilda said, sounding far too much like her mother.

Rosaria topped up Luca's wineglass. "See?"

Luca mopped his empty plate with a bite of bread. He had no energy left to counter Rosaria's determination. "All right," he said resignedly. "What does she look like?"

"You'll meet her next Sunday," Rosaria said. "They're coming for supper."

Luca stopped with the bread halfway to his mouth. Enzo doggedly kept his eyes on his plate.

Rosaria smiled, sensing victory. "Wear your suit."

The dandelion wine's alcohol content was low and last month's vintage tasted like dirt, but it softened defeat.

"So next Sunday, we'll have a nice meal." Rosaria stood up and began collecting empty plates. "I'll make lasagna and veal. You'll meet Annunziata. Maybe take her for a walk down to the riverbank, then talk to Al. Nobody says you have to decide right away."

"That's good, eh?" Enzo topped up his own glass.

"Your ma's real clever," Luca said to Rocco and Matilda.

Rosaria banged Luca on the side of the head with her elbow as she carried away the plates, but he could tell that she was pleased.

Enzo drove him back into Lido just as twilight blanketed the fields along Bell Road with a purple haze.

The truck rattled over the new bridge. Above the latticework of iron trusses, the electric sign proclaimed Lido as America's Copper City. One-tenth of all copper used in American manufacturing came from Lido.

It was the same bridge he'd crossed in Vito's Packard the night before, but Luca had no memory of seeing the sign then.

"So, you'll meet the Genovese girl next week," Enzo said as the truck idled in front of Mrs. Esposito's boarding house. "She could be the one."

"Or a disaster." Luca climbed out of the passenger seat with the tin pail Rosaria had pressed on him, convinced as always that he would starve until the next time he came to the farm.

Grinning, Enzo gave a wave, then put the truck in gear and drove off.

Luca hustled upstairs before Mrs. Esposito could see the pail and rapped on Karol Dombrowski's door. It opened at once.

"Hey, Luca." Karol stepped to the side to let Luca enter the tidy room.

Karol was a gentle giant from Poland, with bright blonde hair, pale blue eyes, and a jaw like granite. A competitive swimmer in his youth, he had broad shoulders and the wingspan of an eagle.

They'd met five years ago in the boarding house and discovered a mutual love of chess. About the same age, the two immigrants were both single men trying to build a new life in a new country. An initial language barrier disappeared as Luca's English improved. The Sunday night chess game was now a ritual, alternating between Karol's desk and the small table in Luca's room.

The desk wasn't quite big enough for the chess board, Rosaria's roast chicken, plus a pile of books. A small brown volume fell to the floor. Luca picked it up. The title was written in slanting cursive. *The Civil Government of the United States.*

"What's this?"

"Let's eat, then I'll tell you." Karol moved the book to the bedside table.

Rosaria's food disappeared quickly as Karol talked about the previous night's revelries at the Warsaw Club and how he handled telling the Polish workers about the bonus scheme. "I'll get mine first, so I offered to divide it into equal parts and share," Karol said. "Everyone could pay me back when they get theirs.'

"That was a very Solomon-like offer." Luca was amazed at Karol's generosity, but then he was always looking out for everybody else. It's why he was a crew chief at Lido Premium, the only chief who wasn't Italian.

"They voted me down. They said they would wait."

"Still, they'll remember that you offered."

"It was the fair thing to do," Karol said.

Luca kept yawning. The chess pieces swam in and out of focus. After less than 30 minutes, Karol called checkmate. Luca stared at the board, chagrined but not surprised that he'd been defeated so easily.

"You played badly," Karol said frankly, stretching out long legs.

"I know." Luca gave his friend a baleful look. "Rematch?"

"Look at this first." Karol held out a newspaper advertisement.

It was a notice from the *Lido Daily Clipper*. The City of Lido invited men of good character to apply for positions within the Police Department to "safeguard citizens and valuables of our growing metropolis."

"I'm going to become a policeman," Karol announced. "That's why I'm studying the government book."

"You want to be a policeman?" Surely, Karol wouldn't quit a secure job at Lido Premium to become another O'Malley, taking money with one hand and twirling a nightstick in the other? He was too honest.

"What's the matter?" Karol frowned. "Don't you think I can be a policeman?"

"What about your job at the mill?" Luca parried. "You're a crew chief. You get the bonus tomorrow."

Karol shook his head. "Italians run the mill and I'm Polish. I have ideas to make things better, but they only want me to do the dangerous jobs and manage the Polish workers."

"You think things will be better if you're a policeman?"

"Maybe."

Italians run the mill. Luca's thoughts slid back to last night. Did Jimmy Zambrano have a rival who saw an opportunity when Jimmy was drunk? "Anybody have a hard time with Jimmy Zambrano lately?"

"A hard time with Zambrano? What do you mean?"

"I don't know." Luca shrugged and began putting the chess pieces away in their box, hating that he had to hide the truth from his friend. "Was anybody mad at him when the pressure was on?"

"No, Jimmy knows everybody," Karol said with grudging respect. "He knows what's going on in every corner of the place."

"A good leader?"

"Especially if you're Italian," Karol said dryly.

Luca closed the box with the chess pieces lined up neatly in their satin-lined beds. Had he expected Karol to say that one of the workers had announced to the entire rolling mill that Jimmy was to be killed? Brandished a spool of copper wire to demonstrate the murder weapon?

Of course not.

Luca slept fitfully that night, dreaming of Jimmy Zambrano rising from the depths of the river, Ruth's linen sheet a slimy cape across his shoulders. The dead foreman yoked Luca to a plow in front of a yellow house. As Luca dragged the blade through rocky ground, the sun beat down and Rafaella watched from the far end of the field, standing next to an Italian army officer. Dressed all in black, she held a glass of lemonade that Luca desperately needed but never reached.

CHAPTER 7

Time to buy insurance

Benny had been in and around lots of public buildings in Chicago, but only as a driver, slugger, and torpedo for the North Side gang. Somebody else worked the inside, shelling out dough and making deals with political hacks and union leaders. Now, as Benny walked up to the Lido courthouse on this bright and shiny Monday morning, it was his turn to work the inside.

Things had come together, just like he'd planned. Fisher was a real nervous type, but he'd come through with cash and equipment purchases. Nick found a couple of fellas who needed work and weren't too particular about what. The beer racket was making money, although not quite as much as Benny expected.

It was time to buy insurance.

The courthouse was a hefty pile of gray painted brick, with a round cupola perched on the roof like an oversized pillbox hat. The entrance boasted half a dozen columns stretching up three stories from granite steps that spanned the entire front facade. The immense double doors were dark wood. The brass handles were as big as Benny's head.

Once inside, he was stopped by a dog-faced police officer in blue wool and shiny buttons glowering behind a rounded desk. Next to the desk, a low wooden rail blocked the riffraff from going any further.

The view over the cop's shoulder was of an open vault that reminded Benny of Chicago's Union Station, minus the buzz of excitement and chug of trains. White fluted panels covered the walls between long mullioned windows. The black and white checkered marble floor reflected long oblongs of light coming from far above. Benny had to crane his neck to see how the light streamed in from glass panels below the cupola's dome, while the ceiling surrounding it was a circle of blue decorated with hundreds of plaster stars like a damned church.

Fellas in dark suits passed by, carrying briefcases and papers, and engrossed in conversation. Benny figured they'd seen the swell ceiling before. They disappeared through a set of doors marked *Courtroom 1*.

"Can I help you, mister?" The uniformed cop evidently didn't care for sightseers.

Benny swaggered closer to the desk. "I'm here to see Chief Doyle."

"Chief Doyle?" the officer repeated. A brass nametag proclaimed his name as Finnegan. The Irish in his voice confirmed it.

"The chief of police, right?" Benny pressed. Doyle was always in the newspaper, usually because he'd made a windy speech to schoolkids or a ladies' luncheon. Two weeks of the *Lido Daily Clipper* was enough to take the measure of the man.

"Do you have an appointment?"

"He wants to see me," Benny bluffed. "Told me to come today."

"Oh." The officer pushed a visitor book toward Benny. "Sign your name here. Chief's office is on the top floor."

Benito Rotolo. Benny signed his name with a flourish and was allowed to pass through the wooden gate into the courthouse proper. Officer Finnegan didn't frisk him or nothing, proving that the police in Lido were a bunch of mugs, just like Benny expected. He could have kept his Colt Pocket Hammerless with him instead of leaving it at Nick's house.

Opposite the entrance, the big curving staircase was another reminder of Union Station, although there was no Harvey House restaurant serving up roast beef sandwiches to hungry travelers.

At the top of the stairs, little brass signs directed him

to hot spots like the chief's office, the usher's cloakroom, and the law library. Benny tipped his fedora to a brunette carrying an armload of books and considered following her into the law library but he was there for business, not pleasure, and went the other way. Besides, she wasn't blonde.

A secretary with gray hair and thick tortoise shell spectacles guarded Chief Doyle's office. "Who are you, young man?" she snapped.

A nameplate on her desk proclaimed her to be Mrs. Theodora Clancy. Benny instantly felt real sorry for Mr. Clancy. Not only was she a wizened old apple, but the missus also had a voice that could crack marble.

"I'm Benny Rotolo," Benny announced. He took off the fedora, real respectful-like and flashed his best smile. "Here to see Chief Doyle. I know he wants to see me."

"Mister Rotolo." Mrs. Clancy didn't melt like a normal woman. Her eyes were suspicious pin dots behind the spectacles. "What is your business with Chief Doyle?"

"I'm a new businessman in Lido and wanted to pay my respects to the chief." Benny had to hand it to Fisher for coming up with that gag. The line sounded real professional.

"How nice." Mrs. Clancy softened. "You say you're

new to Lido?"

"Sure am," Benny said. "Lido's real nice, real nice."

"Where are you from?"

"Illinois, ma'am. But it ain't half as swell as Lido." Benny gave her another dose of pearly charm and this time it worked.

Mrs. Clancy left the safety of her desk and knocked on an inner door decorated with a giant brass plaque. There was no mistaking that this was the chief of police's personal entry. Benny decided to have a similar inner and outer office setup when he built his speakeasy. Plus, a blonde secretary who took dictation every day.

Benny grinned at his own cleverness.

Mrs. Clancy escorted him into the inner sanctum.

His first impression was that the chief sure knew how to decorate because the place was nicer than a North Side brothel, even the places that catered to Chicago aldermen. Dark blue velvet curtains, polished wood paneling, a wagon load of leather armchairs and a desk that somebody could mistake for a grand piano. Every corner was filled with flagpoles waiting for the next parade. Old Glory, New York's Empire State banner, a green silk with an Irish harp, and a few others Benny didn't recognize, all topped with brass eagles.

The real centerpiece of the office was smack in the

middle of a wall where nobody could miss it. Watermarked with the etching of an overweight cow with a neck hump, a framed scroll the size of a Pullman sleeper proclaimed in gold letters that Gerald Francis Doyle was a member of the Loyal Order of the Bison. Half a dozen signatures attested to that fact.

Benny didn't know nothing about the Bisons, but they sure put out an impressive diploma.

"Welcome to Lido, Mr. Rotolo." Doyle stood up and came around the side of the desk. His considerable belly strained the buttons of his blue police uniform and the collar pinched ample jowls. A thicket of silver hair offset a nose bulging with red veins, but nothing distracted from the foghorn voice and an Irish accent thicker than a porterhouse steak.

Benny shook Chief Doyle's hand. "Thank you."

"Sit down," the chief boomed and settled back in his desk chair. "Tell me, where are you from?"

"Just arrived from out of state," Benny said, not wanting to play his cards too soon. He sat in a leather armchair fronting the desk, pinching his trouser legs so the chief would notice the swell suit. "I have family in Lido. My cousin says he's going to find me a good Catholic girl."

"Family first, I always say." Chief Doyle pulled a glass ashtray closer to himself. Half a thick stogie waited on the wide groove in the rim. "So, what can the Lido police department do for you?"

"Well, I'm starting a business and wanted to make sure the department extends protection, so to speak." Benny tried not to rush his words. Chief Doyle was a big, intimidating man and knew it.

"What's your business, Mr. Rotolo?"

"The beverage trade." Another one of Fisher's gags. Benny waited to see how it would go over.

"The beverage trade," Chief Doyle repeated. He stuck the stogie in his mouth.

"Yessir. Serving the public. By that I mean the good people of Lido and the surrounding towns. Lido's a nice quiet place and that's the way I hope it stays." Benny heard himself babbling and shut up.

At length, Chief Doyle took the cigar out of his mouth and examined it. The tobacco at one end was darkened by his saliva. "Where are you from again?"

Benny decided not to waste any more time. "Chicago."

"Chicago." Chief Doyle tapped the business end of the cigar against the glass ashtray, but it was cold, and no ash fell off. "In the beverage business. You must take me for a fool, Mr. Rotolo."

Benny spread his hands in feigned surprise. "No sir, not at all. Takes a very intelligent man to run a department like yours."

"You know Al Capone? He's in the beverage business, too."

"No friend of mine," Benny said, which wasn't no lie. "Capone's a crook."

Chief Doyle grunted in a way that could mean anything.

"My cousin and me, we're planning a small business, serving local clubs and restaurants," Benny said stoutly. "Running everything on the up and up."

"On the up and up," Chief Doyle repeated, the Irish lilt taking on the tone of a threat. "You'll have trucks? Making deliveries and so forth?"

"Sure."

"Workers who need to go about their jobs, ah, unimpeded, shall we say?"

"You understand business, sir." The flattery didn't have any effect. Benny hurriedly remembered another of the accountant's gags. "We're aiming to be a real credit to Lido."

Chief Doyle shifted in his chair and brass buttons clacked against the edge of the desk. "Have you joined the Chamber of Commerce yet?"

"My next stop," Benny lied.

"Well, I wouldn't be in a rush now." Chief Doyle struck a match and applied the flame to the end of his cigar. He puffed a few times before dropping the match into the ashtray.

"No?" Benny watched the sliver of wood curl into black carbon and fizzle out.

"The chamber is run by a fellow named Jack Rutherford. A real straight arrow." Chief Doyle puffed out a hazy blue smoke ring.

"Rutherford. Sure, I've seen his name in the papers."

"Lido's got two kinds of businesses, Mr. Rotolo." Chief Doyle gestured with the cigar. "The first kind join the Chamber so Rutherford can cut a ribbon in front of their store on opening day. They go to Chamber meetings and pester the mayor about new sidewalks."

"And the second kind?"

"Those are the businesses that I personally look out for."

"I see." Benny nodded. Now they were getting somewhere.

Chief Doyle puffed on the stogie and blew another smoke ring.

"Is there a Police Benevolent Association in Lido?" Benny asked into the silence. In Chicago, the North Side gang funneled graft through the Association and received favors in return, although nobody talked about the exchange that way. But if a gang member got collared, the Association made sure that evidence was lost, witnesses recanted, and charges were dropped.

A reciprocal relationship, as Dean O'Banion used to say before Capone's goons made him into Swiss cheese.

"Aye, sure." Chief Doyle sent another smoke ring to the ceiling. "It's affiliated with the Women's Temperance Society."

"Ah."

"Aye, 'tis a shame." Chief Doyle lowered the cigar. "Of course, laddie, we do have a Police Widows and Orphans Fund."

"Have many police officers in Lido died in the line of duty?" Benny asked.

"No, not a one." Chief Doyle's jowls wobbled as the corner of his mouth quirked up in a knowing smile.

Benny took an envelope out of the inner pocket of his suit jacket. It contained three hundred smackeroos, which was pretty generous for a small burg like Lido.

He put the envelope on Chief Doyle's desk. "It's important to me that your people are taken care of, sir. Consider that my donation."

"That's very generous of you." Chief Doyle placed a beefy hand over the envelope and made it disappear with the skill of a magician. "I'm sure you want to make it a regular thing."

"Monthly," Benny said.

"Weekly," Chief Doyle growled. "Wouldn't want those starving orphans on your bad side, would you, laddie? Those kids have a direct line to the Prohibition Bureau. That's who they call when they get hungry."

Benny's smile was weak. "Weekly."

"That's settled then." Chief Doyle puffed another smoke ring into the air. "Welcome to Lido, Mr. Rotolo."

CHAPTER 8

The last link is broken

The newsstand was a short walk away from the boarding house, under a grayish sky with scudding clouds that foretold a rainy afternoon. The headline of the morning edition of the *Lido Daily Clipper* was an ironic alert about hurricanes hitting Florida. So far more than 100 were dead as the storms continued.

There was no mention of a missing mill foreman, or a body fished out of the Mohawk River.

Luca tucked the newspaper under his arm and set out briskly for the First National Bank of Lido, located on the prime piece of downtown real estate known as the American Corner. It was the first Monday of the month and that meant a trip to the bank. What happened on Saturday was not enough to change the routine, especially when so many depended on it.

He was dressed for the monthly ceremony, both a point of pride and a reminder of tragedy, in his good suit, camelhair overcoat, and the dark green fedora that matched his tie. The clothing was secondhand, but the hat was brand new from Nelson's Department Store.

When he first established the account at the First National Bank of Lido, Enzo and Rosaria were puzzled. Italians kept their money under the mattress or in an account at the post office. They didn't have mortgages and loans from banks but used Italian community societies. If they sent money back to the old country, the post office did it for them with a money order and didn't require the transaction to be conducted in English, like the banks did.

But Americans put their money in banks.

The sky was grim, but the sidewalks were dry. Luca walked west on Hamilton Street, passed Saint Rocco's, and left East Lido behind. The buildings rose from two to four and even five stories. Canvas awnings brightened the murky reds and browns of brick and stone. The streets grew wider. Signs were only in English.

United Cigar. Jackson Dry Goods. The Stanley Hotel. Seegar's Fitness Academy.

Luca could have taken the trolley, but he liked to walk downtown, striding along the wide sidewalks like he belonged there. The buildings were tall and impressive, showing the world that Lido was prosperous. Crenelated rooflines on one block, dentil molding on the next. Windows were arched or topped with a keystone. He passed dozens of stores and offices offering insurance, picture framing services, legal advice, harness and leather goods, books, toys, clothing. There was a barber shop on every block, of course.

Towering wooden electrical poles were topped with cross bars studded with blue glass insulators. Electrical wires swagged from block to block and across the main streets to connect every structure and every business. A bell rang as the trolley passed him, gliding along tracks fused into the pavement and powered by a metal arm hooked to wires far overhead.

The First National Bank of Lido was an elegant place of polished mahogany and darkly veined marble. Luca thought it resembled pictures of Italian palaces. Crystal and brass chandeliers hung overhead. Half a dozen tellers presided over a long counter, while an ornate wooden rail created a line of demarcation between the lobby for customers and the vast space where bankers presided over accounting ledgers and speckled file boxes. Black paneled doors proclaimed *President* and *Vice President* in big brass letters.

The bank was always quiet. Everyone spoke in hushed tones.

A tall table offered customers a selection of forms and pens attached by long chains. Luca filled out the form to deposit his salary from the Galliano Club and another slip to send an international money order to the bank in Reggio di Calabria. Half of his earnings every month, without fail.

"Good morning, Mr. Lombardo." Ralph, the young teller in the stiff collar, was a familiar face in his green eyeshade and black sleeve protectors.

"Good morning," Luca said. "This is for my deposit." He handed Ralph his passbook, the deposit slip, and the cash.

"Of course." The transaction was accomplished with a flurry of activity, ending with a brisk stamp in Luca's passbook.

"Next, I wish to make a wire transfer." Luca passed the request form across the counter.

Instead of processing the transaction right away, Ralph pursed his lips and rifled through a tray of index cards. "Mr. Lombardo, did you receive a letter from the bank?"

"No," Luca said.

"Excuse me one moment." Ralph hopped off the stool clutching both Luca's passbook and an index card. He disappeared through a door behind the counter.

Luca looked around, his pulse quickening. Was he about to be arrested for Jimmy's murder after all? Did the bank have orders to delay him and call the police? He thought wildly about rushing out, running all the way to Canada, but the teller still had his passbook and all the savings it represented.

The low murmur of banking conversations continued. It began to rain. The glass door opened and closed as customers came and went. Several had wet umbrellas. Damp footprints marred the plush carpet.

Ralph reappeared on the other side of the wooden gate, speaking to a woman at one of the desks. She had short red hair and wore round wire spectacles. Definitely not a policeman.

As Ralph murmured in her ear, the woman glanced up. Luca saw that she was surprisingly young. After another moment of discreet discussion, she passed through the gate while Ralph returned to his post.

The woman held out her hand to Luca. "Hello, Mr. Lombardo. I'm Tess Kennedy, one of the bank's account managers."

Coppery hair swept across a high forehead and settled into soft waves that hid her ears but left her jawline exposed. She wore a dark blue plaid dress. The pointed ends of a white sailor collar were chased by a red satin ribbon and her white cuffs closed with pearl buttons.

"A pleasure to meet you." Thoroughly uncomfortable, Luca snatched his hat off his head with his left hand and slid his right into her grasp for a brief, uncertain shake. "Is there a problem?"

She gave him his passbook. "If you would follow me, Mr. Lombardo, I'd be happy to explain the situation and help you decide what to do." Tess Kennedy gestured for him to follow her through the wooden gate. It latched behind him with a distinct click, like the bars of a jail cell.

Surely, this was a trap, but he couldn't think of what else to do but follow her like a lamb to slaughter.

The knife pleats of Tess Kennedy's dress swirled around her calves as she led him to her desk and indicated that he should sit in the chair next to it. She took the chair behind the desk, adjusted her spectacles, and opened a file folder.

"First, let me apologize," Miss Kennedy said. "The bank should have sent you a letter concerning wire transfers to Italy."

"My money is honest," Luca said. "My account is good."

"Your account status is not in question, Mr. Lombardo," Miss Kennedy reassured him. She leafed through a few papers in the file folder and drew out a yellow Western Union telegram slip. "The issue is with the receiving bank. The Banco di Napoli in Reggio di Calabria." She correctly pronounced all the foreign words without hesitation.

"I send money every month," Luca explained.

"I can see that. But unfortunately, the transfer was refused last month. We should have informed you right away. I apologize."

Luca shook his head, not sure if he was understanding her correctly. "The bank refused my money? Why?"

"The account in Italy is closed."

"No, that's impossible. I would know if they closed the account." But even as he spoke, Luca knew that wasn't true. Not once did his dead wife's parents write or send a telegram, not even to thank him.

"Maybe this will explain." Miss Kennedy held out the flimsy telegram. "It's in Italian, but I believe it says that the account is closed due to the death of the account holder."

Luca read the missive twice before reality sank in. Pietro and Renata Benedetto, account holders, were deceased. The account was closed by the next of kin. No further transfers would be accepted.

"It's bad news, isn't it?" Miss Kennedy asked quietly. "Family?"

Luca handed back the telegram, trying to process his shock. "You're right. They're dead. The account is closed."

Rafaella's parents were gone, breaking the last link

to her. If the floor had suddenly disappeared, Luca would have been equally unprepared.

"I'm so sorry." Miss Kennedy clasped her hands together.

Luca took refuge in the practical. "If the bank refused the wire transfer last month, what happened to the money?"

"We can credit it back to your account or give you the cash right now."

"Cash, please," Luca said. Money in his hand would be tangible proof.

Miss Kennedy ushered him back to Ralph's window. The teller bobbed his head at her explanation, took the form she'd filled out, and asked for Luca's passbook. It was stamped and returned to him with five crisp ten-dollar bills.

When the transaction was over, Miss Kennedy steered Luca away from the row of tellers. "You deserve an official notification. Perhaps you should send a telegram. Ask the bank in Italy to provide information about the next of kin. Then you could contact them and ask for details."

"Yes, I'll do that," Luca said.

"Let's go to the Western Union office," Miss Kennedy said. "I'll just get my coat."

Luca watched Miss Kennedy go back to her desk,

wondering why he hadn't simply said he could handle it. He'd sent dozens of telegrams. There was even a stack of Western Union forms in the club's tiny library.

A moment later, she came through the wooden gate wearing a fingertip-length navy coat and matching cloche hat. A smart little red leather purse dangled from one gloved hand.

Rain was drumming on the bank's awnings when they walked outside. Rivulets of water gurgled along the edge of the sidewalk and gutters streamed with the sudden overflow. People scurried by, dipping their umbrellas to avoid hitting awnings and each other. Cars churned through puddles, spraying water onto the curb. From a block away, the lights on the Strand Theatre's marquee shimmered through the watery curtain.

"Shall we run?" Miss Kennedy asked. "Dodge the raindrops?"

Luca offered her the crook of his elbow, she threaded her arm through his, and they ran across the street, heels kicking up the rain. It wasn't far but Luca was almost breathless as they skidded into the lobby of the Western Union office. Miss Kennedy let go of him immediately.

He composed a brief request for information from the Banco di Napoli and translated it for her.

Provide details earliest convenience deaths of Pietro and Renata Benedetto of Serra San Bruno and next of kin Stop Reply to Gianluca Lombardo c/o Galliano Club Lido NY.

"I think that's fine," Miss Kennedy said. "Clear and to the point."

Luca paid for the telegram, and they walked out. The weather had worsened in the brief time they'd been inside. They waited in the shelter of the entrance. Dark clouds spit out stinging needles of rain. Miss Kennedy shivered.

"Could I buy you lunch?" Luca asked. "As a thank-you. You've been very kind."

Miss Kennedy glanced across the street to the bank then back to Luca. "I'd like that very much. Do you think we'll drown between here and McSweeney's?"

The diner was further along Liberty Street, its sign nearly obscured by the relentless weather. "How fast can you run?" he asked.

"Fast enough," she replied and took his arm again.

They pelted down the sidewalk, dodging umbrellas and other pedestrians, their strides in sync. Luca yanked open the door and the wind blew them inside. Miss Kennedy shook water off her coat. Rain trickled off the brim of his fedora as Luca looked around.

McSweeney's was a Lido institution, but he had never been inside. The name was painted in flowing script across the top of one white wall, but otherwise the place had no need of decoration. Booths upholstered in red leather filled both sides of the long, narrow space, while a row of tables paraded through the middle. Waiters in long white aprons hurried up and down the checkerboard linoleum in between, juggling platters of food and metal pitchers steaming with coffee.

They sat in a booth facing each other, coats hung on the racks that bookended each bench seat. Miss Kennedy ordered coffee and a ham sandwich. Luca did the same. Wet wool competed with the tastier aromas of coffee and fried potatoes. Chatter from the lunchtime crowd rose above the rain drumming on the roof.

All the women in McSweeney's wore nice day dresses like Miss Kennedy and the men were in suits, the normal attire for downtown businessmen. For the moment, Luca wasn't an outsider from East Lido.

Their coffee arrived first. Miss Kennedy busied herself adding sugar. Luca made halting small talk about the weather and wondered if she regretted accepting his invitation.

Their food arrived before the conversation completely evaporated. The sandwiches were towers of toasted bread piled high with slices of honey ham and beefsteak tomato, accompanied by a giant pickle.

"Don't I know you?" the waiter asked Luca after setting down the plates. "Lombardo, right? Galliano Club team. I tagged you out at second, but you hit a triple in the bottom of the seventh."

Luca recognized the waiter. "Sheehan. Shortstop for the server's union."

"That's it." Sheehan grinned broadly. "Too bad about Teaberry taking the pennant. You Italians put up a hell of a fight."

"Next year," Luca said.

Sheehan winked. "I'll bring you some cheesecake. On the house."

"That was about baseball," Luca said when the waiter left, wondering if he should have introduced Miss Kennedy.

"Of course, it was," she said. "I adore baseball, especially the statistics. Calculating batting averages and such. Didn't you have the same batting average as Lou Gehrig this season?"

"Yes, I did." Luca nearly spilled coffee into his lap. "How did you know?"

"Everyone at the bank follows the Lido Industrial League. My girlfriends and I go when we can. We went to the last game of the season. I'm sorry that your team lost to the Teaberry Knitting Mill."

"Did you cheer for Teaberry?"

"No, absolutely not." Miss Kennedy opened her sandwich and spread mustard on the ham. "I've seen you on Hamilton Street, too. I take dance classes on Tuesdays and Thursdays at the Tapping Toes School of Dance. With Ruth Cross. After class, most of the girls look for you in the window of the club."

"Why would they do that?" Luca studied her prowess with the little wooden mustard spoon. In his experience, cold ham required roasted peppers and layers of spicy pepperoni. Mustard was for hot dogs at the ballpark.

Miss Kennedy's cheeks turned pink. "You do look like Rudolph Valentino, you know."

"It's just a rumor," Luca said.

She laughed out loud and pushed the little pot of mustard to him. Despite the pummeling rain and the crowded diner, Luca felt sunshine on his face.

"I hope you get a reply to your telegram soon," Miss Kennedy said after a bite of her sandwich. "It's a terrible thing not to know about family so far away."

Luca swabbed mustard on his bread. "Not really my family," he said. "My wife's parents."

"Your wife's parents? They died and she doesn't know?" Miss Kennedy hastily wiped her hands on her napkin. "Please don't think you have to thank me with lunch. You should go home and tell--"

"My wife is dead," Luca interrupted.

Miss Kennedy froze, the napkin still clutched in one hand. "Oh, oh, I see. How terribly sad. I'm so sorry."

"It was a long time ago," Luca said. It was how he always dismissed any effort to draw him out on the subject.

"How did it happen?" The green eyes behind the spectacles were bright with a disconcerting mix of sympathy and intensity.

"The Spanish influenza," Luca said.

"My father died of the influenza, too," Miss Kennedy said.

"I'm very sorry."

"I live with my aunt now."

They ate their sandwiches, neither looking across the table at the other. Luca wondered what to talk about besides loss.

Beyond their booth, McSweeney's was a beehive of activity as the lunchtime crowd came and went, water sluicing over the checkerboard floor from dripping umbrellas and wet coats. The buzz of conversations reverberated off the diner's painted brick walls as the rain slashed at the windows and beat a tattoo against the roof.

Miss Kennedy broke their silence. "Did your wife

pass away in Lido?"

"No, in New York City."

"What were you doing there?"

"Fighting." Hoping to lighten the conversation, Luca put up his fists like Jack Dempsey about to punch Luis Firpo out of the ring.

"You were a boxer?"

"Bare knuckle fighting. A man named Finn Conover owned a saloon and was always looking for fighters. Twenty dollars to go five minutes. Seventy-five for a knockout, the only way to win."

"You were a boxer in a saloon?" Miss Kennedy was more amused than scandalized.

"Behind the saloon," Luca corrected her. "There wasn't a ring. Or gloves. Just a crowd making bets."

"Did you win many fights?"

"All of them." Luca gave a rueful smile. "Even the last one, with a giant called Plugger Horan."

"He sounds terrible." Miss Kennedy met his smile with a small one of her own. "But then you came to Lido and now you work at the Galliano Club and play baseball. No fighting there, hopefully."

White apron still immaculate, Sheehan set down two forks and a single slice of cheesecake.

"I think he means for us to share," Luca said awkwardly when the waiter left.

Miss Kennedy nudged the cheesecake toward him. "You have it. I couldn't manage another bite."

She'd saved him embarrassment, but Luca didn't know how to acknowledge her thoughtfulness, so he simply forked up a chunk of cheesecake. "Is that your job at the bank?" he asked. "Helping people with wire transfers?"

"I'm what Mr. Howland calls a Customer Account Manager." Miss Kennedy sipped her coffee. "Basically, I handle the odd tasks no one else can be bothered with."

"But everything at a bank is important."

"I was led to believe that I'd be assigned the same work as the other account managers. I have a degree in economics from Vassar. I should be helping businesses with loans and mortgages. Buying property. Mergers and acquisitions."

"But you're not?" Luca pronged more cheesecake.

"Mr. Howland won't assign any commercial accounts to a woman. He's so old-fashioned that until last week I had to sit in the inner office with his secretary."

"Is Mr. Howland your boss?"

"Yes, James Howland, vice president of the bank. He says women shouldn't be involved in business affairs. I'm not even sure why he hired me." Miss

Kennedy rolled her eyes. "His father is president of the bank and someday Mr. Howland will run it in exactly the same old stodgy way. He even tries to look like his father. Undertaker suits and a baseball mustache."

Luca laughed. "Nine hairs on a side?"

"Exactly!" Miss Kennedy blushed. "Oh, dear. I should not have said that."

"Is it true?" Luca smoothed a fingertip over his upper lip and raised his eyebrows in a question.

She turned even pinker. "Yes. But please don't ever tell anyone I said that. I actually quite like working at the bank. I can do number puzzles all day long."

"What kind of number puzzles?"

"All kinds."

"Give me an example. I like number puzzles, too."

The paper menu was in a metal stand, and she pulled it to the center of the table. "See the dinner special for two? It's three dollars and seventy-five cents. Three and seven is ten. Add one and zero to make one. Add five. The solution is six."

"My father and I used to play counting games like that when I was little," Luca said. "We counted everything. Stones in the *piazza*. Olives in the bucket--" The memory of harvesting olives with his father made him stop talking. Orsini had dragged Matteo Lombardo out of the olive grove to his place of execution.

"In Italy?" Miss Kennedy prompted.

"Yes," Luca said shortly, burying the memory deep inside. "Now I play it with my cousin's children."

"You're the first person I've ever met who knew what I'm talking about." Miss Kennedy slid the menu back to its spot by the sugar bowl. "Usually when I try to explain how to add digits like that, people think I'm talking nonsense. But I do it all the time. I don't even think about it."

"It's a good habit to have." Luca tapped the side of his head. "Keeps your brain working."

He paid the bill and helped Miss Kennedy on with her coat. Outside, the sky was still the color of a battleship, but the rain had dwindled to a spiteful drizzle. There was no need for another exhilarating run, her arm locked in his.

They walked back to the bank and paused under the awning in front.

"Thank you again for your help, Miss Kennedy," Luca said.

"Tess," she said unexpectedly. "Please call me Tess."

"Tessa." Luca's accent added a vowel.

She smiled, seemingly delighted with his mispronunciation. "Is that Italian for Tess?"

"Maybe." Luca placed a hand on his heart and gave

a small bow. "Please call me Luca."

"Not Gianluca?"

"No, just Luca."

"You'll let me know if you get a reply to your telegram, won't you?"

"Yes, of course."

"Thank you for lunch."

She extended a gloved hand and Luca pressed it. He opened the door and watched as she went through the lobby and out of sight.

Luca walked to Hamilton Street lost in thought. Rafaella's parents were gone. He'd just eaten a meal with a woman who was the opposite of any woman he'd ever met before. Saturday night might never have happened. He barely felt his feet on the pavement or heard the trolley bell clang.

By the time he reached the Galliano Club, it was long past opening time. Behind the gold lettering, the front window was dark. The morning deliveries from the deli and bakery were stacked by the still-locked front door.

A phalanx of regulars, led by Tony Bilotti, waited on the corner. Guido was there, too, shifting from foot to foot, the doorman's round face puckered with concern.

Luca unlocked the door with an excuse about going

to the bank. The saloon was just as sloppy as he and Vito had left it Saturday night. He cleaned up, put away the deliveries, and made sandwiches and small talk as if nothing was wrong.

Vito never showed up.

As the afternoon wore on, Luca used the office telephone to call the boss's house. He listened to the other end ring, hoping that Vito would answer rather than wife Louise. Remote and flinty, still grieving for the loss of their son Ciro in the Great War, Louise Spinelli rarely visited the club and was not inclined to be friendly to the hired help.

There was no answer and the operator disconnected. Luca tried again half an hour later, with the same result.

He opened the safe. The bottles of rye whiskey were gone.

Yesterday, when the club was closed and Luca was with Enzo, Vito had come back to retrieve his precious whiskey. Today he was too drunk to answer the telephone. A blue dog day.

"Luca!" Guido came puffing down the hallway to the office.

"What's the matter?" Luca shut the safe door and spun the dial to lock it.

"The whistle blew, and the day shift is coming in." Guido vibrated with excitement. "They say Jimmy

Zambrano never showed up."

Luca followed the doorman back to the saloon, which was soon full of sweaty workers, clouds of tobacco smoke, and agitated voices. Jimmy was the main topic, eclipsing even the excitement of those who had a bonus in their pocket. Working both ends of the bar, Luca filled glasses, made change, and listened.

The hot rumor was that Jimmy went to Boston to personally deliver the shipbuilder's order, although that didn't explain why Mr. Blick, the operations manager, was looking for him. It was universally accepted that while Blick might wear an eye patch, he had two eyes in the back of his head and a finger on every worker's pulse.

Others suggested that Jimmy was holding out until he got his bonus on Wednesday to teach Blick and the owners of Lido Premium a lesson. Still others claimed to have seen Jimmy in the whorehouse down by the freight yards, although he was widely known to be a family man.

As twilight faded into evening, the early crowd went home to have supper and was replaced by those who ate first and came to the club afterward. Jimmy's disappearance might be good for business, but Luca would have given anything for a slow Monday night.

"What do you think, Luca?" Gio Tulipano leaned on

the bar. "You think Jimmy went fishing and forgot to come back?"

"I don't know anything about Jimmy." Luca slid a fresh glass of beer to the other man and collected twenty-five cents.

"Luca?" Guido rushed in, practically falling over himself in his haste. "Carmella Zambrano is outside, asking for Vito."

A hush fell over the saloon.

"I'll talk to her," Luca heard himself say.

CHAPTER 9

Creative accounting

Owen watched through the reeded glass of his office door as Miss Camden picked up the telephone that connected directly to the mill floor and said something indistinct. Next to the secretary's desk, Henry Blick repeated the message that the foreman still hadn't reported for work and abruptly walked out of the building.

No one could accuse Owen of eavesdropping. He was merely concerned with the smooth operation of the mill. Just like Henry Blick, that humorless bastard.

Out of everyone who might be interested in Owen's creative accounting, Blick was the person who concerned him the most. To begin with, Blick was the oldest nephew of Nathan Packham, owner of Lido Premium Copper and Brass. As if that wasn't intimidating enough, Blick was a West Point graduate, an Army veteran of the Great War, and wore an eye patch.

Tall and lean, with a skullcap of prematurely white hair, Blick's single ice-blue eye could stop a Rolex watch from twenty paces.

Owen and Blick were both members of the Bison Club, the most prestigious men's club in Lido, but that didn't mean they were equals.

The Blick family was even older than the Packhams, with generations of empire builders buried in the old Dutch cemetery by the river. They were old Lido. They weren't just in the inner circle, they owned it.

The bottom line was that Blick was the heir apparent to the Lido Premium fortune. On the board of directors, his role as the mill's operations manager gave him wide-ranging authority for virtually everything that happened at Lido Premium. When Nathan Packham made a rare appearance at a board meeting, Blick always sat at his right hand and knew the business down to the last detail.

The morning stretched out; the minutes mired in molasses. Yet if anyone bothered to look at what Owen was doing, they would have witnessed intense industry. He consulted charts and ledgers spread out on the desk and wrote reams of figures, his pen scratching industriously. With every pull of the lever, his adding machine produced a veritable fusillade of gear-grinding sound that announced that he was too busy to be interrupted. Miss Camden left him alone.

In the afternoon, Blick rapped on Owen's open

door. "Are you ready for the bonus payments?"

"Yes, of course. Of course, of course," Owen heard himself gabble to the unnerving single eye. "We'll distribute to the men right after the whistle blows."

Owen had bundles of cash ready. The pay window that disbursed workers' weekly salaries was just inside the rear entrance of the mill, not far from the lockers. Each man who received a bonus had to sign for it, the same as when it was payday.

"Good." Blick's ramrod posture added to his ever-present aura of command. "Just for your information, Zambrano never reported for work this morning. I sent a man around to his house. No one knows where he is."

"That's odd," Owen said.

"Procopio is managing the shift," Henry said. "He keeps production high, but he's a brute. I'll be watching him."

Owen delivered the bonus cash to the paymaster and loitered afterward. A through G got their money with no fisticuffs. Nick was there but looked past Owen as if they'd never met, which was fine.

Lido Premium was a different place when it shut down for the day. The boilers went to half power, simmering until fired up the next morning. Machinery was switched off, chains and hoists lowered to rest positions. Chemical tanks were closed, pressure gauges checked, valves adjusted to keep pipes and fittings from bursting. A thin thread of vapor trailed out of the big smokestacks, wisps of white against the setting sun. The only things that moved were the freight cars on the tracks running behind the mill.

Quiet settled over the immense pile of brick. Twilight stretched over the pavement between the mill and the office building. Owen huddled inside his overcoat and walked as fast as he could without running. The night watchmen were used to seeing Owen on a Friday evening, not Monday.

It took him fifteen minutes to reach the small shed used by the rail yard gangs, whose shift started in half an hour. It was a sooty box cluttered with a pot-bellied stove, table and chairs, and other things that could ruin Owen's overcoat with just a touch.

He barked his shin on a crate and swore under his breath.

Nick showed up five minutes later, a plaid mackinaw thrown over dirty canvas dungarees. His face glistened with oily sweat and his body odor was rank.

"Let's be quick," Owen said. "Give me the ledger."

"Zambrano didn't have your book."

"What are you talking about? Of course, he had the book. I saw him pick it up."

"Maybe you was wrong." Nick gave a shrug. "You

still owe me two hundred."

"Don't play games with me." Owen backed up a step and nearly stumbled over the same crate as before. "Give me the ledger."

"He didn't have it."

"Then where is it?"

Nick shrugged. "I don't know. He didn't have it."

Owen glared. Zambrano had to have the ledger. Nick was being a stupid lummox trying to squeeze more money out of him. "Why didn't Zambrano come to work today?"

"Why do you think he didn't show up?"

"Because he's drunk in a gutter, of course." All Italians succumbed to drink sooner or later, Prohibition or no Prohibition. "He obviously dropped it. Did you look around afterward?"

"I was in a hurry."

"Then go back and look."

"When?"

"Now!"

"You think I should go back for your ledger?"

"Yes, for my ledger," Owen said impatiently. "For two hundred dollars, you were supposed to get it."

"I told you; he didn't have it."

"What about his house? Look there."

"How am I supposed to search his house?"

"Doesn't he live in East Lido, too?"

Nick swiped the back of his hand across his nose. "Maybe it's in his locker."

"Yes, excellent idea," Owen said. Finally, the lummox was showing a spark of inspiration. "Look in his locker."

"I don't got the key."

"Pick the lock."

"Yeah, I could do that." Nick looked curiously at a smear of snot on the back of his hand.

Owen grimaced. "Be alert. Blick told me he's watching you. Doesn't like the way you handle the men."

Nick jabbed a finger in the general direction of the office building. "Blick can either make me foreman or go to hell."

"Make you foreman?"

"It's my turn." Nick narrowed his eyes. "Settle up. You owe me two hundred."

"Two hundred for the ledger," Owen said stiffly.

"You want me to keep looking for the ledger it's going to cost you double." Nick held out a grimy hand the size of a Thanksgiving turkey.

Snot smeared the length of the sausage-sized thumb. Owen stared at the glistening slick, revolted and mesmerized at the same time.

"Two hundred now and two hundred so's I keep looking," Nick said. "Unless you want Benny to look instead of me."

"Yes, well. All right." Owen handed over the money.

Nick counted the money, snorted in satisfaction, and gave a friendly shove that sent Owen staggering into the crate yet again. "Same time tomorrow, eh?"

Owen stayed in the shed until he heard Nick's footsteps fade away. He hoped that he hadn't just made a dreadful mistake, but if four hundred bought him the ledger and Nick's silence, then so be it.

CHAPTER 10

An honest man would have told

Luca walked outside. Carmella Zambrano waited on the sidewalk.

"Hello, Carmella." Luca hoped his voice sounded natural.

"I come to ask if you've seen my Jimmy." Carmella Zambrano was a handsome woman, but her eyes were red and swollen under a brown cloche hat. A sack coat ended at her knees, showing the hem of a much longer dress. "He never came home Saturday night."

Luca avoided looking directly at her. "The boys say he didn't make his shift at the mill today."

"I thought maybe he got drunk and went fishing with Vito."

The streetlights glowed brightly. Traffic was heavy up and down Hamilton Street. A police car rumbled past; the yellow shield of the Lido police department emblazoned on the side.

"Vito's home sick," Luca said.

"Do you know if Jimmy is with him?"

Luca shook his head. "I don't think so."

Carmella's mouth twitched but she didn't break down. "He's never missed a day. They sent the Ferlo boy to the house to fetch him and all I could say was that he never came home. Jimmy hasn't been home since Saturday morning."

"He was definitely here Saturday night," Luca said. It was such a pitiful poor bit of truth. "Everybody saw him."

"Was he drunk?"

"No," Luca said. Again, that was the truth.

"Did anything happen Saturday night?" Carmella pressed. "Was there trouble?"

"He made a speech," Luca said. "Told everyone about the bonus schedule. Not everyone was happy but enough of the men stuck up for Jimmy that it was all right in the end."

"Who didn't like the plan?" Carmella asked sharply. "Do you remember?"

"Vito, for one." Luca jammed his hands in his pockets, encountering the refund from the bank. "But he and Jimmy settled it. You know what good friends they are. No hard feelings."

Carmella's eyes brimmed over as cars cruised by heading in the direction of Saint Rocco's. "Jimmy would never leave me and the kids like this. Sonny was up and down the neighborhood yesterday, asking everybody if they've seen him. I made him go to school this morning, telling him Jimmy would show up at the mill. But he didn't. I don't know who else to ask."

Luca nearly choked on the confession knocking against the back of his throat. "Is there anything I can do?"

"Ask Vito to come to the house. They're good friends. He'll know something."

"Carmella, wait." Luca stepped closer, remembering those murderous coils of copper wire. A dozen mills in Lido made wire, including Lido Premium. "Did Jimmy argue with anyone at the mill lately? Maybe over the contract?"

She shrugged. "It was a hard time for everybody."

"What about Nick Procopio?" Luca recalled the day Vito kicked the deputy foreman out of the club for cheating. Procopio had a temper and was a big man, too. "Did they have a problem?"

"Jimmy and Nick make a good team. Everybody knows that."

Luca floundered on. "What about . . . what about promises Jimmy made? Promises to the men that he couldn't keep?"

"What sort of promises?"

"I don't know." Luca was groping in the dark. "Maybe somebody was in trouble and Jimmy went to help?"

"What are you getting at, Luca? You think somebody took out their problems on my Jimmy?"

"No, no," Luca said hastily. "I'm just wondering where he is, too."

Carmella patted him on the cheek. "You're a good boy, Luca. I know what you do for Vito. How you keep the club going. Jimmy always says that it was a lucky day for Vito when you walked into the club."

Luca wanted to fall to his knees, admit the whole truth and beg Carmella's forgiveness. Instead, he held out the money from the bank. "Here, take this. Jimmy has a credit on his club account."

Carmella shook her head. "No, Luca, this is your own money."

"Where would I get fifty dollars?" He closed her fist around the bills. "Go on. Take it. I checked the account book. He's due a refund."

She walked away. Luca stayed where he was, knowing that an honest man would have told Carmella that Jimmy was in the river and that she was a widow.

When he went inside, Luca pulled down the swagged flags and the congratulatory banner. He'd been too quick to scoff at *malocchio*.

CHAPTER 11

You're a role model, Ruthie June

Tuesday morning, Ruth bundled up in a red wool coat, pinned her best beaded broach on her shoulder, and settled a cunning plaid cloche over her russet curls. The vision in the parlor mirror was cheerful, even if the weather was as sullen as yesterday. She grabbed her shopping basket and headed for the stores along Hamilton Street.

She didn't have to teach until the evening, when her class of chorus girls met. Most of the girls dreamed of going to Broadway and dancing in a Rodgers and Hart musical. They drank up Ruth's stories of dancing in *Little Johnny Jones* with George M. Cohan. She always made vaudeville so exciting. Traveling on the circuit, living out of a suitcase and coming alive every night on the stage.

Good times, until William Wilson came along.

Ruth chose a fresh trout at Fiori's market. At the fruit stand, Mrs. Medina pressed a cup of coffee on her, and the two women chatted for half an hour, before Ruth selected a bouquet of carrots and beets and a bag of apples to share with her class.

The basket was heavy after the stop at Medina's, but Ruth pressed on to the Bella Napoli in search of *pasticciotti* tarts filled with chocolate cream. She bought two. She'd treat herself to one tonight after the class and save the other for breakfast. The girl behind the counter double-wrapped them in waxed paper to stay fresh.

Ruth was halfway home, hurrying to beat the rain, when Officer O'Malley emerged from a doorway and fell into step beside her as smoothly as a blue steamship with brass buttons. "Good afternoon to you, Miss Cross," he said and touched the rim of his helmet.

"And to you, Officer." He was a tall and vigorous man. Ruth had to look up to see his face.

"I stopped by to see you Saturday night," O'Malley said.

"Me?" The word tumbled out of Ruth's mouth in surprise.

O'Malley nodded to two men who scurried past, overcoats flapping around their legs. "Sure, and your door was locked."

"Yes, it was," Ruth said. She walked a little faster.

"Oh, aye." O'Malley kept pace, the nightstick bumping against his right side with every step. "Would you be keeping Saturday nights warm for your landlord,

Vito Spinelli?"

"Your implication is vulgar." Ruth felt a cold shiver which had nothing to do with October weather. "If you need to talk to Mr. Spinelli, find him at his place of business."

"He was still at the Galliano Club when I came by Saturday night." O'Malley seemed to be enjoying the conversation. "Past closing time, but he was still there."

"Mr. Spinelli's business hours are no concern of mine." Ruth transferred her shopping basket to her left arm to make a barrier between them. Half a block away, the red and white sign for Ventimiglia's Deli beckoned like a life raft.

"We need to make an arrangement, Miss Cross." O'Malley smiled at her, but his eyes were as hard as nails. "You're a fine woman and I'd be pleased to court you. In other words, I won't say anything about your arrangement with your landlord as long as you extend the same arrangement to me."

"I'm not making any arrangement with you, Officer O'Malley," Ruth gasped. She backed away from him. "You are coarse and low to even make such a suggestion."

"Don't run away from me, Miss High and Mighty." O'Malley caught her by the elbow. "I know all about you and I mean to use it against you, if you make me."

"I have no idea what you're talking about." Ruth tried to shake him off, but his grasp was tight. His fingers pressed through the thick fabric of her coat hard enough to loosen her grip on the heavy basket. Her groceries nearly spilled into the street before Ruth grabbed the handle with her other hand.

"I did a little investigating about Miss Ruth Cross," O'Malley said. "Guess what I found?"

"I have no interest in what you do in your spare time, Officer O'Malley," Ruth said. She spoke tartly but inside she was terrified.

"Miss Ruthie June Crosswater was found bleeding and unconscious on a park bench in Poughkeepsie two years ago." O'Malley let go of her arm to hold his gloved hand sideways, like he was reading from a book. "Taken to the hospital where it was discovered she'd delivered half a deformed child. Miss Crosswater is not married, nor is she a resident of Poughkeepsie. She gave no fixed address when she went before the judge on charges of public indecency, vagrancy and a few other things too nasty to speak about. Six months in jail."

Ruth was speechless, the air knocked clean out of her. Deep down, she'd always expected this day to come, but that didn't lessen the blow.

"A friend of mine is a cop down there," O'Malley

said. He kept his voice low as his eyes bored into hers. "I heard about the police report. How would all those mamas like it if they knew little Suzy's dance teacher was a knocked up, vagrant whore?"

Ruth reeled but he caught her by the arm again.

"You're a role model, Ruthie June," O'Malley said. "You think the upstanding citizens of Lido would let you stay if they knew how soiled you are? Teach their children to dance so they can grow up to be whores, too?"

O'Malley looked away from her to take in the storefronts and the cars cruising up and down Hamilton Street. Ruth knew what his gaze meant. Her business, her new-found place in the community, the friendships she'd made. It was all hers to lose.

Ruth bit her lip to keep the tears from falling. "Get to the point, Officer O'Malley."

"I can forget I ever heard of a place called Poughkeepsie if you want me to," O'Malley said slowly, as if savoring the suspense.

"You mean to blackmail me," Ruth whispered.

O'Malley gave a soundless laugh. "The club is closed on Sunday nights," he said. "Spinelli and Lombardo aren't around. You leave your door unlocked so I can come courting."

"Come courting?" Ruth echoed.

"You and me, Ruthie June," O'Malley said with a mean smile. "We got some real good times ahead of us. You just leave that door unlocked Sunday night and everything will be just fine."

He gave her a wink and strode off whistling, right hand on the handle of the nightstick hanging from the loop on his belt.

CHAPTER 12

He heard wrong

"I drove up to Boonville yesterday," Vito said after a slurp of coffee. "Pino Barone said that Sal heard wrong. Pino talked to a fella that wants to sell liquor. Sell *to* the club. Sell *to* me."

"*Oddio*," Luca swore.

They were in the office with the morning's first batch of coffee from the electric percolator. The boss looked tired, but not as if he'd wrestled the blue dog all day yesterday.

Vito drank more coffee. "So, I says to Pino, who is this fella, and he says a rumrunner. An Irishman willing to bring a boatload of whiskey upstate if he can get enough buyers."

"Then it had nothing to do with Jimmy?"

"Nothing."

Luca leaned forward from his perch on the Chesterfield. "Carmella Zambrano was here last night, asking if we knew anything about where Jimmy could be. She asked if you would go over."

"What did you tell her?"

"I told her that he left after the announcement about the bonus payout." Luca paused. "Nobody talked about anything else last night. Everybody was asking where's Jimmy. How come he didn't show up for his shift. First time he wasn't in church on Sunday, too."

The day wore on. As Luca expected, Jimmy Zambrano's absence from the mill for the second day in a row was the major topic of conversation in the saloon. The theories grew wilder by the hour, inflated by beer and tobacco smoke. A woman. A bigger mill. A union organizer. None of it made sense to anyone who knew Jimmy.

Luca listened with one eye on the clock and the other on the crowd. Who looked strong enough to strangle Jimmy? Who fretted about the bonus schedule? Who didn't talk about Jimmy at all?

No one looked guilty.

Vito went home at nine o'clock. Luca installed Guido behind the bar, grabbed the doorman's broom and went outside. He got a few jibes from members coming and going.

At last Ruth's door opened and her students began coming out. Luca swept as if they gave out medals for tidy sidewalks. Icy wind swirled off the striped awning and found its way down the back of his neck.

A gaggle of girls pranced out, laughing and talking.

"Good evening, ladies," he said as they passed him on the sidewalk.

They responded with giggles, although a bold one with a fur hat blew him a kiss. Luca kept sweeping.

More girls trooped out, including Tess Kennedy wearing wide-legged trousers, a brown mouton jacket, and a matching cap that hid her curls.

He didn't try to catch her eye but industriously applied the broom to the frosty pavement. The night air whistled through his cotton shirt and woolen undershirt as though he was wearing cheesecloth.

"Good evening, Luca." Tess stopped next to him. Her friends clustered nearby.

"Hello, Tess. It's nice to see you again."

"Did you get things sorted with your family?" she asked. "With that telegram and all?"

"Not yet." Luca stopped sweeping; glad he had the broom to hold. "How was your class?"

"Very nice. I know all the steps now." Tess frowned. "Aren't you cold? It's freezing and you're out without a coat."

"It's not so cold," Luca lied.

Tess made a little gesture toward the girls waiting near a green Model T Ford coupe parked against the curb. "I have to drive my friends home."

The coupe was the very latest model. "Is that

yours?"

"Yes." Tess hesitated and wrapped a hand around the broom handle so that the heel of her hand rested on his thumb. "Did you ever play this game, Mr. Lombardo?"

He didn't know what she was talking about, but as long as she didn't rush off, it didn't matter. "I grew up in Italy," Luca said. "We were too poor for games."

"You stack hands like this." She made him grasp the handle above her hand and followed his hand with her other. Four hands climbed the broom handle until they ran out of wood.

Luca's hand ended up at the top. "I win," he said. "What is my prize?"

"A wish."

The heel of her hand against his felt like electricity. "Have you ever eaten cannoli?" Luca asked.

"What's that?"

"It's pastry with cream in it. They make them at the Bella Napoli. It's just down the street."

He lifted his chin to indicate the green and red sign in the next block of Hamilton Street. Tess looked over his shoulder to see.

"My wish is to buy you coffee and cannoli after your class on Thursday," Luca said.

Tess placed the flat of her hand over his fist on top

of the handle. "We didn't finish the game. I won."

"Then you get the wish," Luca said, feeling like a fool.

Tess put her hands in her coat pockets again, leaving him hanging onto the broom handle alone. "I wish to be Tessa when we have coffee on Thursday."

Luca was no longer cold.

It was only when he went inside and heard the agitated talk in the saloon that Luca remembered that Jimmy Zambrano was dead.

CHAPTER 13

Your number one beer supplier

The Galliano Club topped Benny's list of would-be customers. First, he'd sell beer to the club and force the owner into debt. Then he'd buy the club out from under him. The whole process would take two months. Three at the most.

In Chicago, Capone would just smash up a place and take it, but Benny didn't want the Galliano Club wrecked before it was his.

He'd been there before, when he was in Lido to cool his heels after witnessing Frankie Yale and friends shoot up Dean O'Banion in Scofield's Flowers. His cousin Nick was still a member back then and brought Benny as a guest.

The grub was good, Benny recalled. Fresh coffee and sandwiches loaded with salami, provolone and roasted red peppers lousy with fresh garlic, all heaped on crusty bread.

Besides the food, Benny's lasting memory of the Galliano Club was one of size and space. A long bar, tall ceilings, space for two pool tables, and a room they called the library for tracking the lottery. Not much in the way of glitz and glam, but Benny would fix that.

He'd driven past a few times, with a girl in the car because Hymie Weiss had taught him that dames make good cover, not that anybody noticed another car on Hamilton Street. Drove the alley in back of the place once, too, to see handball and bocce courts tucked between a row of trees and an old shed. Everything would have to come down to make space for cars.

The place was deader than a doornail during the day. A couple of old coots came to the club around noon and spent the rest of the day taking up space and swapping lies. Things picked up in the afternoon and the big surge happened when the mills closed.

To Benny's surprise, the club was not open on Sunday, which was a big mistake. Whoever owned the place was too good a Catholic. Thirsty men were still thirsty on Sunday. They still wanted a girl, too.

The doorman was outside, a fatso acting like standing on the sidewalk in a cold drizzle was the highlight of his life. When Benny tried to go in, the fella said the club was just for members.

"I got an appointment with Vito Spinelli," Benny bluffed.

Fatso's face wreathed into a smile. "With Vito? Okay, go on, tell Luca. He'll help you."

"Who's Luca?"

"Luca Lombardo. Behind the bar."

"He run things around here?"

"Sure. Luca's real smart." Benny guessed that the doorman had a bad case of hero worship.

The place was just how Benny remembered it. A giant mahogany bar with a brass footrail that took up the entire side of the room, all carved curlicues and reeded panels that glowed with polish. Mirrors above reflected rows of empty bottles, their labels still intact. The big daddy of a bottle in the middle was still full of Liquore Galliano. Benny decided that he'd keep the mirrors and bottles when the place became his, but he'd replace the green wall paneling with velvet flocked wallpaper. Add brass sconces dripping with crystals so customers would know they were in a swank place and wouldn't chafe at paying swank prices for booze and girls.

"Can I help you?" The fella behind the bar was tall for an Italian and corded with muscle. Light brown hair and smoldering eyes that reminded Benny of Valentino, the actor who played a sheik from Araby and caused a ruckus among the dames when he died last August.

"You must be Lombardo."

"That's right."

"I'm looking for Vito Spinelli." Benny rested a foot

on the brass rail.

"I'm Spinelli." A barrel-shaped man in a tweed vest rose from a table of card players on the far side of the room.

Benny could barely suppress a laugh. The name Spinelli was etched into the stone pediment topping the front façade of the building, like the owner was a somebody. But this mug was a nobody with a soup-strainer mustache, bloodshot eyes, and a gut like Santy Claus.

"Welcome to the Galliano Club," Spinelli said. "What can I do for you?"

"The name's Rotolo. Benny Rotolo. I'd like to talk a little business."

"What kind of business?"

"I'm in the beverage trade."

"Beer?" Lombardo asked softly from behind the bar.

"That's right." Benny lowered his voice, pulling the same respectful act as in Chief Doyle's office. "The best beer in Lido."

"We can talk in my office." Spinelli led the way down a hallway. Lombardo brought up the rear. Bartender and bodyguard, too.

Benny checked out every open door along the way. Pool tables, sliver of a kitchen, library.

Spinelli's office was at the end of the hall. It couldn't compare to Chief Doyle's palace, but it boasted a big desk, leather Chesterfield sofa, even an icebox-sized safe.

The one thing Benny didn't see along the way to the office was a staircase. How were the working girls supposed to make a big entrance?

"How do you get upstairs? he asked.

"Upstairs is private," Spinelli said.

"What's up there?"

"A dance school," Lombardo said before Spinelli could reply. "Not part of the club."

Benny mentally added a few more dollars to his investment for busting up the ceiling and adding stairs. Curving stairs, with a crystal chandelier above.

Spinelli sat behind the desk and motioned to Benny to take the Chesterfield. Lombardo lounged against the wall with his arms folded.

"The Galliano Club's the biggest spot in Lido, isn't it?" Benny asked to get the ball rolling.

"Sure is," Spinelli said proudly.

"Three hundred members?" Benny pressed. "Four?"

"Almost five hundred." Spinelli thumped a big green ledger on the desk. "We take care of East Lido."

"I want to be your number one beer supplier. How does ten barrels a week at sixty dollars a barrel sound?"

"Sounds expensive," Lombardo said. "Where are you coming from?"

"Right here," Benny replied and trotted out the same gag that had worked with Chief Doyle. "Bringing the beverage trade to Lido. Just made a run to Camden. But my heart's in East Lido, you know? My people are here."

"Is sixty a barrel your best price?" Spinelli asked.

"Name one outfit that can beat it."

"The Antonelli brothers," Lombardo said.

"Never heard of them." Whoever the Antonelli brothers were, they were hauling beer from outside the county, maybe even outside the state.

"How do we know you're not a Prohibition Bureau agent trying to get us in trouble?" Lombardo asked.

Benny decided there and then that when the Galliano Club belonged to him, he'd dump Lombardo and dump him hard. If nothing else, the North Side gang had taught him not to keep a mug around who thought he knew stuff. Bugs Moran was a walking, talking lesson on that very subject.

"Tell you what, fellas." Benny lolled against the back of the Chesterfield and brought out the really juicy bait, the one he really wanted them to take. "I'll let you have the beer on credit. Fifty-seven a barrel on credit. The Prohibition Bureau never offers credit, and we all know it. Nobody's going to beat that offer."

Credit was a tactic used by all the big wheels in Chicago to snatch real estate when saloons ran up a tab with suppliers and couldn't pay.

"We'll buy at fifty a barrel," Spinelli said.

"Fifty-seven on credit." Benny strolled over to the desk and planted both hands in front of Spinelli. "Credit is the best deal of the day, eh?"

Lombardo peeled himself off the wall and jerked Benny around by the shoulder. "I remember you," he said. "You were in once with Nick Procopio. His cousin, right?"

"That's right. Nick's my cousin."

"He's not a member here anymore."

"So?" Benny shrugged. "Do we have a deal?"

Spinelli glanced at Lombardo.

"No deal," Lombardo said.

"I'm offering a fair price and credit besides. Nobody's going to beat that."

"We'll keep the supplier we've got."

Benny elbowed Lombardo aside and addressed Spinelli. "Hey, I didn't come here to waste my time. Let's close this deal, old man."

"Not today," Spinelli said. "You heard Luca."

Lombardo opened the office door. "Thanks for coming."

The fella actually marched Benny all the way down the hall and through the saloon. By the time they got to the vestibule, Benny was ready to whip out the Colt Pocket Hammerless and plug Lombardo just for the hell of it.

"Look, buddy," Benny said. Through the glass in the street door, he could see the moon-faced doorman on the sidewalk outside. "Before the year ends, I'm going to squeeze out every other beer racket in New York. The Galliano Club is either going to do business with me or go bankrupt."

Lombardo didn't respond, just bored into Benny with those Valentino eyes. For sure Benny would have to dump him when the place became his.

Benny adjusted his jacket so the Colt Pocket Hammerless was on display, tucked into its special inside pocket. "Think I'll call you Sheik from now on because you're a dead ringer for Valentino. Dead ringer. That's funny, ain't it? Seeing how he's dead."

The doorman pulled the door open.

"See you around, Sheik."

Hymie Weiss had taught him well. Benny tipped the fedora over his eye and walked away like he owned the world.

He'd be back.

CHAPTER 14

No one can save her

Ruth wasn't sure how she stayed sane since the conversation with O'Malley, much less attend to the demanding schedule of classes offered at the Tapping Toes School of Dance. As time passed in an unhappy blur, she taught tap steps to wiggly toddlers and jazz routines to Broadway hopefuls. After the last student left and Ruth was in her apartment across the hall, she let herself sob in hopeless desperation until she was too weak to lift her head from the pillow.

On Wednesday morning, she splashed cold water on her red eyes, sat at the little dining table, and wrote out five random vocabulary words for Luca's weekly English lesson.

She could have sent word and canceled but he would have asked why, and she had no acceptable excuse. Besides, she hadn't seen him since Saturday night. What happened after he left her apartment?

The rich aroma of coffee hit her as soon as she pushed open the door to the club two hours before it opened. Luca always had the coffee going and a plate of pastries from the Bella Napoli shop to share. Ruth appreciated anew the little ritual that she usually took for granted. Luca set down plates and mugs and napkins. She got herself under control and took her seat.

His notebook and well-thumbed dictionary were already on the table. Ruth watched the sinews of his hand ripple under the skin as he wrote the date at the top of a clean page. Someone had taught him how to be a disciplined student with a vast hunger for information. As a result, Luca mastered English quickly. Ruth had almost finished high school, not that a diploma would have changed anything, but she was finding it harder and harder to teach him something he didn't already know.

She passed him the list of vocabulary words. *Despair. Frivolous. Voluble. Arrogant. Surgeon.*

As Luca copied down the list in his notebook, Ruth clasped the coffee mug in both hands.

"Despair is a very great sadness, no?" Luca had yet to open the dictionary. "Or does it mean feeling the sadness?"

"It's both a noun and a verb," Ruth said shakily. "Sadness and hopeless at the same time."

"Ah." Luca opened the dictionary, flipped a few pages, and found the correct entry. After a moment he began to write in his notebook, head bent in concentration. She always made him copy the definition, then use the word in a sentence.

Ruth fought a whirlwind of temptations. She wanted to brush aside the lock of wavy hair that fell across his forehead. Blurt out everything O'Malley was holding over her. Fling herself against Luca and feel safe inside the circle of his arms.

"Luca," she murmured.

He raised his eyes to hers.

Ruth swallowed hard. "Saturday night," she started. "I gave you my second-best sheet--"

"No," Luca interrupted her. "We don't ever talk about it. Nothing happened."

"At least tell me why O'Malley knocked on my door." It was hard to keep her voice from trembling.

"He wanted his money from Vito."

"Are you sure?"

Someone rapped on the window. Ruth smothered a gasp with her hand.

It was only a Western Union messenger waiting outside on the sidewalk. Luca went to the door and returned with a yellow telegram. His shoulders slumped as he read it.

"Is everything all right?" Ruth asked.

Luca tucked the telegram under his dictionary and picked up his pencil again. "It was from Italy, from

Serra San Bruno. I used to send money but the bank in Italy sent a telegram to the bank here. Miss Kennedy helped me ask for more information and now they sent it."

"Miss Kennedy?"

"You must know her. She works at the bank and takes lessons from you."

Ruth thought of the lovely girl who came to the chorus line class on Tuesdays and Thursdays. A halo of red hair, spectacles, and a captivating personality heralded by a ready smile. "Tess Kennedy. Yes, I know her."

"Tessa," Luca said dreamily. "In Italian her name is Tessa."

When he finished writing his sentences, which needed no corrections, Ruth told Luca that this would be his last English lesson with her. She simply would not be able to face him after what was going to happen on Sunday.

CHAPTER 15

Corridor talk

Procopio was in charge yet again. It was amazing to Karol how quickly the mill's well-ordered routine unraveled. The deputy foreman was either bullying the men or as elusive as a ghost.

Tension thrummed through the mill, a vibration that made everyone uneasy and careless. Karol kept a sharp eye on the crews nearest the chemical tanks. More than once he shouted a warning to prevent an accident. Each time, the worker on the brink of disaster was Italian and rewarded Karol with a look of hostile insolence.

To make matters worse, something was troubling Broz Siwak, Karol's right-hand man on the dipping crew. It was Broz's day to get the bonus, but he barely said two words all morning, wouldn't look Karol in the eye, and disappeared during the midday break.

A whisper passed from man to man in the afternoon. Procopio wanted the machines shut down ten minutes before the last whistle blew. Everyone was to assemble by the lockers for an announcement.

Every worker at Lido Premium was assigned a

doorless locker to store coat, hat, lunch pail, and other personal items. Lining two sides of a long corridor directly off the main shop floor, the lockers were little more than open-fronted metal mesh rectangles. The payroll window was in the same corridor, in a niche that interrupted the row of lockers on one side.

Only the foreman had a locker with a door. The coveted bit of privacy was undisputed evidence of his status in the mill.

The corridor was the first and last stop for workers entering and leaving. It was bookended by the workers' entrance at one end, and the private door used by those from the adjacent office building on the other, including Mr. Blick, the operations manager.

Karol got a locker in the middle of the long row when he first started at the mill, and he'd never sought a more desirable spot. Generally, everyone wanted the lockers farthest from the entrance and closest to the shop floor. Those lockers had the dual benefit of missing an Arctic blast while fumbling for winter galoshes and a shorter walk to grab lunch pails and Thermos bottles during the breaks.

The tension needled everyone as the last hours of the workday dragged on. Broz kept glancing at the clock and nearly lost a glove in a vat. Procopio was noticeably absent.

Exactly ten minutes before the evening whistle blew, the machines cut off. Karol and Broz manhandled the covers onto the chemical tanks. As they joined the crowd in the corridor, Broz was still uncharacteristically silent.

Procopio was already there, the usual red kerchief knotted around his neck. As a jostling and expectant crowd gathered around the deputy foreman, he climbed on a packing crate. It bowed under his weight.

Broz waded in but Karol hung back. He wondered if Mr. Blick knew about the unorthodox assembly.

Using a length of pipe, Procopio banged on the door of the foreman's locker.

The crowd quieted.

"Zambrano took off." Procopio exuded sweat and self-importance. "He ain't coming back."

"Who says Jimmy's not coming back?" someone shouted.

"The police," Procopio shot back. "It'll be in the newspaper tomorrow."

The crowd erupted into agitated protests that Jimmy Zambrano had run away from job and family, with an undercurrent of fear that Procopio would permanently usurp the foreman's job.

Procopio smacked the length of pipe into his open palm. Once. Twice. The crowd quieted. "I'm the foreman now and that means I get the foreman's locker. I'm offering a fifty-dollar reward for anybody who brings me the key."

The steam whistle blew to announce the official end of the workday. Procopio stepped off the crate and bulled his way through the throng.

As the workers who were due to collect their bonuses lined up in front of the payroll window, Karol got his coat. The Warsaw Club was the place to be tonight, to hash over Procopio's announcement and gripe about who favored Italians and rode the Polish workers harder than the rest. Karol thought about the police test and wondered if his compatriots at the mill would think he was deserting them just when things got hot.

Broz was at the head of the line at the payroll window when Mr. Blick walked into the corridor escorting a woman in a black hat and shapeless coat. A woman in the mill was such a rare occurrence that everyone stared.

Tall and commanding with his eye patch and finely tailored suit, Blick tilted his head to speak to Broz. Karol didn't hear what was said, but everyone including Broz shuffled back a step or two. The woman took Broz's place at the window.

Karol didn't need to be told that she was Jimmy

Zambrano's wife. Silence descended over the corridor. Everyone heard her thank the paymaster. Blick walked her out.

Karol caught up with Broz as his friend shoved a bonus envelope into the pocket of his woolen jacket. A damp chill hit them as they walked outside.

Karol adjusted his long stride to that of the shorter man, something he had to do with almost everyone. "Was that Zambrano's wife with Mr. Blick?"

"Sure. She collected his bonus." Broz was lean but strong, with a thatch of brown hair and a nose like a knife blade.

"What's the matter with you?" Karol asked. There was something in the hunched shoulders and hard set of his jaw that said Broz had something to say, but it didn't spill out until they were clear across the parking lot by Broz's old Ford.

"I'm leaving," Broz said. "Gave my paper to Blick this morning. Got another job."

Only one thing jumped into Karol's mind as a possibility. "Are you taking the test to be a policeman?"

"A policeman? Who wants to be a policeman?" Broz was scornful. "No, I'm going to make some real money."

"Where?" Lido Premium paid the best of any mill in Lido.

"The beverage trade."

"The beverage trade?" Karol echoed.

Broz was uncharacteristically defensive. "You heard me."

"You mean bootleggers."

"You said it, not me."

"Don't get yourself involved in anything illegal, Broz," Karol cautioned. "You got a wife and kids."

"Why do you think I'm doing this?" Broz still wouldn't look him in the eye. "I'm going to make twice as much every week."

"The money isn't worth the risk." The thought of someday arresting Broz made Karol's stomach clench. "Don't give up a good job here for something illegal."

"That's your problem, Karol." A spasm of jealousy twisted Broz's face into an ugly mask as he wrenched open the door to the Ford. "You think too small. You took one risk your entire life. Came to America. You've had nothing but good luck ever since. Everybody looks up to you. You never do anything wrong. Such a good man, Father Nowicki always says. An honest man. Why can't you be like Karol? Well, fuck you."

Karol was too stunned to reply. He and Broz had worked together for years. They built the dipping crew into the most reliable and efficient team at Lido Premium and toasted each other at the Warsaw Club afterward. Went to Holy Angels together, celebrated All Saints Day and Saint Sylwester's Day together, ate meat dumplings and cabbage *golumkies* at every church gathering together.

Broz launched himself into the car, making it rock on the narrow tires. "Next time you see me, Karol," he said. "I'll be the one on top."

CHAPTER 16

Bad news and Bella Napoli

Enzo had given Luca a bushel of green tomatoes at the end of the summer to be wrapped in newspaper and allowed to slowly ripen. Now that winter was approaching, fresh tomatoes were a real treat. For Thursday's special Luca heaped steak-sized slices on crusty bread with spicy *soppressata* salami, provolone cheese, onions pickled in red wine vinegar and a drizzle of olive oil. The sandwiches disappeared as fast as they were made.

Yet lunch curdled in his stomach when Luca saw the evening edition of the *Lido Daily Clipper*. Jimmy Zambrano's disappearance was splashed across the front page. Caving to general clamor, Luca read the article out loud.

LIDO PREMIUM FOREMAN GOES MISSING

The Lido police are investigating the disappearance of Giacomo "Jimmy" Zambrano, of 218 Fourth Street, foreman of the Lido Premium Copper and Brass

Rolling Mill. According to Lido Premium Operations Manager, Mr. Henry Blick, Zambrano was last seen at the mill immediately after last Saturday's shift, which Zambrano supervised as normal. The shift finalized the important rush shipment for Boston-based Beacon Maritime Company.

Inquiries by this reporter reveal that Zambrano did not return to his home Saturday evening as expected following a celebration at the Galliano Club, 603 Hamilton Street. Nicola Procopio has been installed as temporary foreman pending approval by the Board of Directors.

Zambrano is not known to be connected to criminal activity. The police are tracing Zambrano's last known movements. Beacon Maritime Company has released a statement disavowing any connection to Zambrano's disappearance.

Anyone with information about the missing man is instructed to contact the Lido Police Department.

The article was worrisome and useless at the same time. It gave no clue as to Jimmy's enemies but tracing his last known movements would inevitably lead to the Galliano Club. Luca sensed the jaws of a slowly closing trap.

"That's all?" Gio Tulipano demanded. "What about

Procopio offering a reward for Jimmy's locker key?"

"See for yourself." Luca rotated the newspaper so the men on the other side of the bar could read the article. He left them to it, grabbed an empty beer pitcher and began refilling it.

The saloon was nearly empty, and Vito was still in his office when the clock chimed nine o'clock. Luca grabbed his jacket and cap, installed Guido behind the bar, and waited outside.

Ruth's door opened, spilling out light and chattering young women. Luca met Tess halfway, extremely conscious of the stares of her friends.

"Did you remember my wish?" Tess asked. Once again, she wore trousers.

"Tessa," Luca said.

"You remembered." She took his arm.

As they turned to go, Luca saw Ruth standing on the sidewalk by the open door leading upstairs. He waved but Ruth went inside and shut the door without acknowledging him.

With Tess's hand through his arm, the walk was short but thrilling. Luca knew everyone in Bella Napoli, which meant introducing Tess before they could take a table for two near the back. Bruno, the waiter who was old enough to be Vito's grandfather and only spoke Italian, went into a spasm of rapture when Tess told him

"*Grazie mille*," for taking their order.

"You never said you knew Italian," Luca said, recalling her reluctance to read the telegram from the Banco di Napoli.

"After I graduated from Vassar, Aunt Evelyn and I did the grand tour," Tess said. "I learned a few words. It's not so different from French."

"What is a grand tour?"

"London, Paris, Geneva, Venice and Rome. And Florence, of course. I loved Italy. Everywhere we went, there was something beautiful."

"You only saw the good parts."

"We were on a train once and these families got on and they had a picnic, right on the floor of the carriage. Roast chicken, oranges, and that wonderful crusty bread. And wine! Even the children drank it."

"Were you scandalized?"

"No, although Aunt Evelyn was."

"So, you like to go places," Luca said. "Is that what you want? To travel?"

"Not really, I like Lido. I think what I want most of all is to make my own decisions."

"What do you mean?" Her words surprised Luca. She seemed so independent, so sure of herself.

"When I was at Vassar, they told us that we could do anything, make our own decisions, decide what's best for ourselves. But in the real world, someone else makes the decisions for women. They say it's for my own good."

"Who says that?"

"Aunt Evelyn. Mr. Howland." Tess cocked her head to examine Luca. "I'll bet no one says that to you. They never do to men."

"Perhaps no one cares so much what happens to me."

"I doubt that." Tess touched his sleeve.

Luca wanted to press her hand against his heart and let the electricity jolt his very core.

"So, you are free to make your own decisions," Tess said. Her hand withdrew into her lap. "What do you want to do?"

Freed of her touch, Luca's brain re-engaged. "Win back the pennant from the Teaberry Knitting Mill."

Tess smiled. "That's a given. What else?"

Luca considered. "I want to see America. It's so big. So different from east to west and north to south. I want to be part of it."

Bruno came with their coffee and cannoli.

"This is beautiful," Tess exclaimed, admiring the golden tubes of pastry filled with cream and dusted with sugar. The ends were studded with chocolate chips.

"Go ahead."

Tess bit into a crisp shell and closed her eyes in rapture. "This is delicious."

Luca was almost dizzy as he watched her lick ricotta filling off her thumb. He ate his slowly, wanting to stretch out the evening.

Conversation came easily after that, jumping from topic to topic. She was curious about places and people, with an array of facts at her disposal. Laughter came easily as they talked about recent films and discovered that Buster Keaton was a mutual favorite. Luca couldn't remember the last time he'd had such an interesting evening.

Tess asked if he liked working at the Galliano Club. Luca said it was the best job in Lido and she asked what his favorite part was.

"Keeping the accounts," Luca admitted. "I do all the orders. Like complicated number puzzles."

"Except the numbers have no personality when you're doing the club accounts or I'm at the bank."

"But they do in the counting game?"

"Of course. We're talking about the scale of single digit numbers. Odd is always better than even and five is the perfect number."

"Isn't seven or nine better than five?"

"Seven is good, too, but tips the scale." Tess steepled her hands, making her fingertips dance together. "This is five, the perfect center. Everything perfectly balanced. That's why it's the best number."

"Tell me about six or eight."

"Too easily divided and conquered." Tess grinned and picked up her coffee cup.

"The same for four and two, then?"

Tess put down the cup without taking a sip. "Sometimes two wishes it was one," she said. Color rose in her cheeks.

Luca knew they were talking about a different kind of number game now.

"A two that becomes one is even better than five," he replied.

"Of course, two can't become one right away," she said softly. "They have to get to know each other first."

They left long after closing time, Bruno waiting patiently. Luca got a wink from the old man as the bell over the door jangled.

A misty fog blotted out the stars as Luca walked Tess back to the Galliano Club. Her green Ford coupe was parked against the curb. The lights were on inside the club, but Guido was not in front. Instead, a man in a newsboy cap lounged against the wall near the door.

Tess noticed the man, too. She said good night and drove off, without so much as a suggestion of another electric moment of intimacy.

Luca watched until the coupe reached the end of Hamilton Street and made the turn.

"That your girl?" the man asked.

Not a club member, even if the Irish accent hadn't betrayed him. "Who's asking?"

"Gleason, Toby Gleason." The Irishman shrugged one shoulder to indicate the club door. He was a sturdy man with a wide mouth primed to smile. "You must be Lombardo. I just made a deal with your boss."

"What kind of deal?" Luca figured that Gleason was the man who'd spoken to Pino Barone about selling to the club, the message that Sal Antonelli had gotten so wrong.

"He's going to buy my whiskey."

"How much is it going to cost him?"

"Two hundred fifty for a case of genuine Irish whiskey." Gleason grinned. "Your boss wasn't interested in the rum."

"Same deal to Pino Barone in Boonville?"

Gleason shrugged. "Barone's place is just a wee thing. The Galliano Club is twenty times the size of any other place around, with the exception of places where the toffs go."

"Toffs?"

"Swank people. The kind who go to country clubs and the racetrack in Saratoga."

"Do you sell to them, too?"

"Be a fool not to," Gleason said cheerfully. "I'm in business to make money."

"You cheat Vito, and you'll have to deal with me," Luca warned.

To Luca's surprise, Gleason grabbed his hand and shook it hard. "Your boss said you were an honest man. Jesus wept, just what I've been looking for."

"We run a decent place here." Luca extricated his hand.

"I've been asking around." Gleason lit a cigarette, cupping his hand around the match so it wouldn't blow out before the tobacco caught. "You've got a good reputation as someone who can hold his own. You're strong, too. I could use a man like yourself. My crew is, ah, a bit short."

"I've already got a job."

"This isn't steady work." Gleason flicked the match into the street. "I bring in rum from the Bahamas. Whiskey from Ireland. Wine from France, too. How about making a run with me? We drive down to Long Island, crew the boat to the rendezvous, take on a load, and drive the goods back upstate. I'll pay you a thousand for the trip and a bounty for every case we bring back to Lido."

"A thousand dollars?" It was a staggering amount.

"What if we get caught?"

"We dump it overboard and say we were fishing. No crime in fishing."

Luca shook his head. "I don't think so. I've never been on a boat."

Gleason was undaunted. "Did you swim here from Italy?"

"I mean a small boat."

"What makes you think it's a small boat?"

Luca found himself liking the irrepressible rumrunner.

"Think about it," Gleason said. "Leave word with the priest at Saint Brigid's."

"The priest?"

"Where do you think sacramental wine comes from?" Gleason tugged on the brim of the newsboy cap and strode off.

CHAPTER 17

Moving, stopping, coming, going

The hash needed salt, not that it mattered. Seated at her tiny dining table, Ruth forced down a few mouthfuls and nearly gagged. Her stomach was too tight to eat.

She pushed the plate aside. As if the week wasn't horrible enough, Luca was smitten with Tess Kennedy. And why not? The girl had everything Ruth never would. A college degree. A secure job at a prestigious bank. A new Ford coupe in the latest color and lovely clothes and dozens of friends.

Until tonight, Ruth had liked the red-haired young woman. Tess wasn't the most promising student of dance, but she was bright and thoughtful, with a way of making everyone in her orbit feel important. Always ready to smile, with a bubbly laugh.

More importantly, Tess was twenty years younger.

The leftover hash went into the icebox. Ruth took a bath and crawled into bed.

She woke with a start, yanked out of a deep sleep by noise below her bedroom window. Intruding on the silent night, footsteps disturbed the gravel behind the

Galliano Club building.

Ruth huddled under the blanket, choking on her fears as she waited for the murderer. It had taken him a week, but he knew she'd been watching from the window Saturday night. He knew who she was.

Slow steps paced the gravel then receded as the unknown visitor moved away. Before Ruth could breathe again, the footsteps came back to the building. The pattern repeated several times as if someone was crisscrossing the gravel lot under cover of darkness. Moving, stopping, coming, going.

Searching.

Ruth expected to hear the back door forced open. A jiggle of the knob as an unseen hand twisted and pulled. Scratching against the lock. Just as a scream rose in her throat to release the pressure of her fears, the steps completely faded away.

The next morning, Ruth wondered if she'd dreamed the whole thing. Did she have a nightmare, or did the murderer really come back to the scene of the crime?

Or was O'Malley lurking behind the building, searching for a less public way to access her second-floor apartment?

Her bones refused to carry her through another day. Ruth lay in bed, eyes shut against the sunlight streaming through the window.

Her career as a Broadway chorus girl in every Cohan and Harris musical was in the distant past. Everything she had, all her money and energy and skill, was invested in the Tapping Toes School of Dance. It all hinged on maintaining the fiction of Ruth Cross: spinster and woman of good breeding.

Ruth Cross belonged to the Chamber of Commerce and directed children's recitals. Ruth Cross was from Philadelphia, where she went to finishing school before appearing on Broadway with George M. Cohan. Speaking roles. Such golden memories, too.

Ruth Cross was nothing like that coal town tramp Ruthie June Crosswater.

Ruthie June Crosswater had run away from a bleak future in Pennsylvania. Was in the chorus of Cohan musicals but never uttered a word on stage. Drifted down the hoofer ranks all the way to the bottom of the vaudeville circuit.

Ruthie June Crosswater met a handsome rogue named William Wilson who left her destitute and pregnant. Ruthie June Crosswater miscarried on a park bench in Poughkeepsie, New York, and wound up in jail.

None of that happened to Ruth Cross.

Sunday was coming. There was no way to avoid the inevitable. O'Malley would show up and Ruth would do what had to be done to buy his silence.

No one, least of all Luca Lombardo, was going to save her.

CHAPTER 18

Blue dog day

Vito had been on a fairly even keel all week but when he stumbled into the club at noon on Friday, Luca knew that it was going to be a blue dog day.

"Wass going on?" Vito slurred.

"Nothing new, boss," Luca said. "You want a sandwich in your office?"

"Sure, sure."

By the time Luca brought him a roll piled high with ham, pepperoni and mozzarella, Vito was sound asleep on the Chesterfield. The office smelled like a distillery but there weren't any bottles on display. Luca put the plate on the desk, made sure the safe was locked, and closed the office door behind him.

The afternoon passed quietly, giving Luca plenty of time to think about the conversation last night with Tess Kennedy. She was lovely, educated, refined, and quick-witted. His reverie evaporated when Guido rushed in, closely followed by two men in dark fedoras and overcoats.

"Luca." The doorman's eyes were wide with fright.

"These men are from the police."

"It's okay, Guido, I'll handle it." Luca nodded at the door. Guido scurried outside.

"Mr. Spinelli?" the taller man rasped at Luca. He pushed aside his coat to show a police badge on his belt.

"I'm Lombardo. I work for Mr. Spinelli."

"Detectives Schultz and Dooley, Lido Police Department." The tall detective pointed at himself, then jerked a thumb at his partner. The shorter Dooley likewise revealed a badge affixed to his belt.

"Lombardo." Dooley took off his hat. He had a broad face spattered with freckles and hair the color of a ripe peach. "I've heard that name before. Ball player? Pitcher?"

"First base."

"Galliano Club had a good team this year," the detective said. "Until Teaberry walked all over you for the pennant."

"Wasn't our best game," Luca admitted. "How can I help you?"

Schultz slapped a hand on the bar. He had blunt features, big ears, and too much pomade slicked through his hair. "We heard that a missing man, Jimmy Zambrano, was a member here."

"That's right," Luca said.

"Were you here Saturday night?"

Luca nodded. "Sure. It was the night that Lido Premium finished the contract."

"Did you see Zambrano?"

"Me and a couple hundred others. Jimmy got right up on a table, and everybody cheered."

"What about lately? Have you seen Zambrano since then?"

"No." Luca wondered what he could say that would make them leave.

"Okay, go back to Saturday night. What happened?"

"We had a big celebration."

"Did you talk to Zambrano?"

"Sure, told him congratulations. We talked about the bonus. He was going to send his son to college with it."

"Did you see Zambrano leave?"

"I don't remember. There were a lot of people here. Lots of smoke, lots of noise."

"And beer?"

Luca didn't answer.

Dooley snorted. "Who else did Zambrano talk to?"

"Jimmy talked to everybody. He's an important person around here."

"Anybody here particularly close to Zambrano?"

Luca thought about the other members who held key positions at the mill. "Frank Conti. He's a crew chief at Lido Premium. Maybe Gio Tulipano."

"What about Vito Spinelli, the owner here? Folks say they're friends."

"Yes. Vito and Jimmy are friends."

"Where's Spinelli now?"

"Taking a nap."

"Let's wake him up," Schultz said.

Luca knocked hard on the door. He waited a beat, then pushed it open. Vito sat up on the Chesterfield, blinking and yawning. The sandwich was still on the desk, exuding a perfume of cured meats and warm cheese.

"Boss," Luca said. "Police to see you."

He got Vito behind the desk as the detectives bustled into the office. "So, tell us about the missing man, Jimmy Zambrano," Schultz began. He licked the end of the pencil and scribbled on a little pad of paper. "A member in good standing?"

"Sure," Vito said.

"Pays his dues on time?"

Vito looked around for his cigar box. Luca pushed it across the desk to him.

"Mr. Spinelli?"

"Sure, Jimmy's all paid up, right, Luca?" Vito fumbled to open the box and select a cigar.

"All paid up," Luca said.

"When did you last see him, Mr. Spinelli?"

"Saturday night," Vito said. He laboriously took the paper wrapping off the cigar. "Big celebration here. Everyone was going to get a big bonus."

"A couple of people we talked to said you argued with Zambrano over the bonus, right in front of everybody. Tell us about that."

Vito gaped at the detective.

Luca jumped in to save the boss. "It wasn't an argument. Jimmy said that they were paying the bonus over three days. Vito thought it should be paid all at once. The men sided with Jimmy. Vito and Jimmy had a laugh later. That's all."

Schultz leaned forward and snapped his fingers to get Vito's attention. "That jive with your memory, Mr. Spinelli?"

Vito gave a start and blinked nervously, the unlit cigar in his hand. "Sure. What Luca said."

"What about strangers?" Dooley asked. "Any strangers talking with funny accents been coming around? Loitering on Hamilton Street?"

"Strangers?"

"Saboteurs!" Dooley exclaimed. "Spies! Anarchists! Bolsheviks!"

"In Lido?" Luca knew about anarchist bombings, but Lido was hardly New York City.

"Lido Premium's an important industry," Schultz

barked. "Zambrano's the foreman of the biggest copper mill in the northeast. Cripple Lido Premium's copper output and what happens to telephone wires and shipping? Sabotage American economic power and the Bolsheviks take over."

"Bolsheviks?"

"This club is ripe for infiltration," the detective went on forcefully. "Lots of Lido Premium workers come here. You hear of anybody with a funny accent asking questions, you need to tell us."

"My boy died," Vito said.

Both detectives swiveled toward Vito like marionettes controlled by the same string. "Say that again, Mr. Spinelli," Dooley said.

"My boy died," Vito repeated. "Nobody investigated what happened to him."

"You mean Zambrano?"

"No," Luca cut in. "His son was a soldier with General Pershing. He died in the war."

"That's too bad, Mr. Spinelli," Schultz said without sympathy.

Vito took out a handkerchief as tears spilled over.

The two detectives grimaced and hastily left the office.

Luca followed them down the hall, hoping they'd leave without poking their noses behind the bar.

"What kind of liquor do you serve here, Lombardo?" Dooley's smirk said that he knew what was going on.

"No liquor," Luca said. "Mostly tonics from the West End brewery in Utica."

"Men come here after a 12-hour shift at Lido Premium and drink ginger beer?" Dooley appeared amused rather than angling for a bribe. He reminded Luca of Toby Gleason. Same swagger, same Irish in the voice.

"The lemon-lime rickey is popular."

Schultz snorted and motioned to the other detective. "Let's go talk to the tenant upstairs. Runs a dance school."

"Miss Cross," Luca said. "Her name is Miss Cross."

Dooley produced a business card and left it on the edge of the bar. "If you remember anything else about Zambrano being here Saturday night, you're obligated to make a statement."

Luca walked out with the two detectives and watched from under the awning as they rapped on Ruth's door. She duly answered and conducted the conversation through the half-open door.

Whatever she said was evidently satisfactory. Both men tipped his hat to her, got in a car parked on the other side of Hamilton Street and drove off in the direction of the mill.

"Ruth?" Luca got to her before she fully closed her door. "Any trouble?"

For a moment Luca was terrified that she was going to cry because the two detectives had wrung the truth out of her. Then Ruth seemed to collect herself.

"I said that I was asleep Saturday night. I didn't see anything. All I know is what's in the newspaper."

Luca took a deep, reassuring breath. "Good, good."

"Do you think this mess will ever be over?" Ruth asked quietly.

"When they catch who did it."

"Luca," Ruth started.

He waited but she shook her head and didn't say anything more.

"Is something the matter?" Luca asked.

"I hope you're happy with Tess Kennedy," Ruth said abruptly and shut the door. Through the glass, Luca caught a glimpse of her running up the stairs.

Gennaro Panetta came out of the adjacent hardware store with a load of tin pails and dishpans. He dropped everything with a clatter on the sidewalk and rubbed palms on his long apron. "Hey, Luca," he called.

"Hey, Gennaro. How's business?" Luca ambled over to the shopkeeper.

"Not so good with police detectives coming

around."

"They ask you questions?"

"What do you think?" Short and stocky, Gennaro stacked the pails in front of his shop to entice passing shoppers. "They asked about Jimmy Zambrano."

"What did you tell them?"

"I said I saw him on Saturday night at the club."

Luca looked around. "Did they talk to anyone else?"

"They were up and down the street." Gennaro created a shaky pyramid of dishpans. "Neither one of those *buffoni* speaks Italian. Like that Officer O'Malley. Nobody cares about Italians."

Still in his white apron, Carlo Fiori came out of the fish market on the opposite side of Hamilton Street and darted across. "Did those detectives talk to you, too?" he asked breathlessly.

As the two shopkeepers compared notes, Luca's gaze was drawn to the display in Panetta Hardware's window. Chunky wooden spools of chain, rope, wire, and cotton lampwick were threaded on dowels, allowing a length to be pulled out and sold by the yard. Luca counted three different thicknesses of copper wire. The medium gauge was the same size as the wire that killed Jimmy.

"You need something, Luca?"

Luca glanced at Gennaro. "You sell a lot of wire?"

"Sure. Wire. Rope. I got it all."

"Anyone bought some lately?"

"Why, you worried that Lido's going to run out?" Gennaro chuckled as Carlo Fiori said his goodbyes and went back to the fish market. "Come inside, tell me what you need."

Inside the cluttered store, Luca was sure about the wire's thickness. He studied the spools and asked questions about customers for wire until Gennaro looked at him sideways. "You thinking about opening a store, too?"

Luca forced a laugh and bought a yard of cotton lampwick, essential for households without electricity that depended on oil lamps. Gennaro drew out the flat woven cord, measured it with a yardstick and snipped off the length.

As Gennaro added ten cents to the club's account, it was clear to Luca that trying to track down Jimmy's killer by asking about wire sales was a dead end. In addition to Lido Premium, half a dozen mills in Lido produced wire. Jimmy's killer could have taken wire from a workplace or purchased it from any number of hardware shops like Panetta's.

Not only that, but Luca could hardly go to every store in Lido and ask about recent wire purchases without calling attention to both himself and the

Galliano Club. Detective Schultz might not catch on, but Detective Dooley had struck Luca as both sharp and dogged.

When he got back to the club, Luca tossed his purchase into the kitchen and Dooley's business card into the cash register. He mopped the bar, lost in grim thoughts of Bolsheviks garroting Jimmy in a plot to destroy the Lido Premium mill, and gave a start when Tony Bilotti reached for a pickled egg.

"What did I tell you?" the old man rasped. "Zambrano's missing. The police are everywhere. *Malocchio*."

CHAPTER 19

Best moxie in the whole wide world

"You're a handful." Trixie rolled onto her side and pulled up the quilt, as if Benny hadn't already seen her best features.

"Wanted to give my best girl a good time." Benny pulled on his trousers and tucked in his shirt.

"I like you, Benny," Trixie said. "You're different. You've got moxie."

"I'm from Chicago, dollface. Best moxie in the whole wide world."

Trixie squirmed into a sitting position against the pillows, letting the quilt slip down enough to reveal her cleavage. "We kick out the last customer at eleven. Why don't you come back then?"

"Have a late supper with you?"

"Sure. You could spend the night. Keep a girl warm."

Benny draped his tie around his collar but instead of tying the knot he put a knee on the bed, caught Trixie by the chin and planted a kiss on her lips. "That's a mighty tempting invitation," he said. "What if I spent every night here?"

"You mean move in?"

"Sure. You and the girls need somebody to keep things from getting out of hand. I'll make sure my fellas come here, too. They're big tippers."

"I'd feel safer if you were around," Trixie admitted.

They sealed the deal with a kiss and a cuddle. Benny left before the mills let out and Trixie's customers showed up.

He'd met Trixie at Perk's Diner the same day that he and Nick and Owen Fisher inked their partnership in Fisher's little ledger. Liked her platinum blonde hair, rouged lips, and slow sultry smile, not to mention the hourglass figure.

Trixie was a few years older than Benny although he knew better than to ask her age. Nor had he asked how she came to be running the only brothel in Lido or how she found the dozen or so girls who worked there. Her establishment wasn't the high-class kind of place the high rollers in Chicago frequented, but it was better than a flophouse where a fella risked getting a dose of the clap.

It was no surprise that she agreed so quickly. Benny had paid some of his new Polish workers to visit her place and cause a little trouble. Throw things around, scare the girls. Then just when Trixie wanted a man around the place, there was Benny. Perfect timing, too. Nick's place was getting on his nerves. The wife had more fight in her than Jack Dempsey, always arguing and yelling. The kids were a pack of savages.

Strategy and nerve were all it took for a fella to get what he wanted. Benny thought about Dean O'Banion swiping half a million from Johnny Torrio over the Sieben Brewery deal a couple of years ago. O'Banion delivered a lesson in cool ruthlessness that day, a ruthlessness that Benny admired to no end. O'Banion got shot up in retaliation, but that was beside the point.

Benny winked at a couple of girls lounging in the parlor on his way out the front door. He was going to be the proverbial fox in a henhouse.

Once he had his own speakeasy, Trixie and the girls would do business there, just like at the Four Deuces in Chicago. Drinks, gambling, and girls all under one roof.

Benny turned onto Railroad Street in his new Cadillac V8 Brougham and bounced over the railroad tracks. As the sun set behind him, Benny slowed, looking for the hidden turn. It was little more than a break in the trees, but he nosed the Cadillac through. The unpaved road carved a line through a wooded glen until the trees petered out and the road became an undulating line curving through the graveyard known as Settlers Rest. Crooked headstones peppered a succession of hilly rises, guarded by castle-like dark stone and stained-glass mausoleums.

It was the final resting place of the Dutch who settled this part of upstate New York. Weathered by a century of wind and rain and snow, the Dutch legacy was visible in the names carved into the headstones. *Brevoort. Van Slyke. Leidecker. Osterhout.* Once a year there was a Founder's Day ceremony. The place was forgotten the rest of the year.

Until Benny started the beer racket, no one had ever driven a vehicle over the natural berm shielding the bottom of the graveyard from the Mohawk River. He gunned the big engine as the Cadillac passed the last mausoleum, clawed its way through the scrubby foliage and drove up the front of the berm. As the windshield filled with sky and not much else, Benny gripped the wheel tighter and took his foot off the pedal. The heavy Cadillac tipped over the top and shot down the other side, Benny whooping as his stomach hung in the air while the rest of him raced ahead.

The Cadillac bounced and slowed as the ground leveled out. The old stone pump house lay ahead amid the charred ruins of the original mill. Blackened brick and timbers were still scattered about, overgrown with scraggly fall foliage. The river gurgled a short distance beyond.

The pump house was perfect for an illegal brewery. Big enough to accommodate an industrial steel tank, near a source of fresh water, and secluded behind the berm. Once upon a time, it housed the machinery to turn an enormous wheel that generated power from the river's rapid current.

He left the Cadillac in a small clearing and went inside. Cases of malt syrup were stacked against the walls. The tank that Owen Fisher bought with Lido Premium money was full of brew. The crew of Polish workers would transfer it into wooden barrels and smaller kegs and load the trucks. They all jumped up and saluted when they saw Benny. Siwak was there. Benny liked the look of him. Respectful to Benny and tough with the boys, just like Nick.

He went into the office, which was really just a niche in the stone walls, partitioned off with an old door with a desk made out of planks and two sawhorses. Big iron gears protruded from one wall like rusty mammoth tusks. The other walls continually wept moisture that froze into shiny white patches of ice. The place was right out of a Lon Chaney spook show except that it was going to make Benny rich.

Owen was there, bundled in scarf and overcoat. "Do you want to see the books?"

A green ledger as big as the Cadillac waited on the

makeshift desk. "Sure."

Owen nattered about cash flow and staff costs while running his finger down columns of numbers. Benny couldn't make sense out of what he was saying. The only thing that mattered was that the numbers got bigger as the accountant's finger slid down the page.

"Looks good," Benny announced.

He scooped up his cut of the cash, traded a few jibes with the nervous accountant, then set off for Perk's to have a bite until Trixie kicked out her last customer. The diner reminded him of a place in Chicago where some of the North Side gang used to eat. Same rough clientele, same coffee thick enough to stand a spoon in, same rib-sticking grub.

A gust of burned coffee and fried grease greeted Benny as he went inside the diner. He grabbed a copy of the evening *Lido Daily Clipper* from the pile on the counter, tossed down a nickel, and slid into a booth. Ordered coffee and beef stew when Bud ambled over, licking the tip of his pencil before writing Benny's order on a creased pad of paper. Never saw the proprietor of Perk's in anything but a striped shirt and a paper carhop hat. Cigarette stuck in the corner of his mouth. Always needed a shave, too.

Benny spread out the newspaper, in no particular hurry. The front page was gossip about some European royalty visiting unimportant places and Lido doctors attending a medical conference. Benny flipped the page and nearly spit out a mouthful of coffee.

CHICAGO GANGSTERS APPEAR FOR FUNERAL

Parade of Cars Mourn Hymie Weiss, With Official Police Escort. CHICAGO, Oct. 15. -- Between two ranks of police today marched six gunmen, bearing the remains of the lamented "Hymie" Weiss to a hearse. Two hundred persons, most of whom are known hoodlums or beer runners, were at the doors of Sbarbaro's morgue at 708 North Wells Street to view the procession.

A bowl of stew and a spoon appeared on the table, but Benny couldn't pull his eyes off the newspaper. Hymie couldn't be dead. He was Benny's ticket back to Chicago; his partner in the plan to take down Capone.

But the article was the real deal, not the funny papers.

Henry Earl Wojciechowski, aka Hymie Weiss, was shot by gunmen on October 11, 1926. Weiss and four associates had attended the jury selection for the murder trial of Joe Saltis earlier that day. They

parked cars on Superior Street and proceeded on foot to Schofield's Flowers, Weiss's place of business, on State Street across from Holy Name Cathedral. Gunmen hidden in a nearby rooming house opened fire, killing Weiss and associates.

Hymie had been caught in a crossfire from different rooming houses in broad daylight. Only Al Capone and Frank Nitti could have rubbed out Hymie so methodically.

"You must be Mr. Rotolo."

"What?" Benny looked up. "Who the hell are you?"

A fella with jet black hair stood by the booth, cloth cap in hand. Gray tweed jacket buttoned over a thick wool sweater and corduroy pants. Too clean to be a mill worker or a roustabout in the rail yards.

"Gleason's the name. Toby Gleason." A pronounced Irish lilt gave the words a singsong rhythm. Gleason slid into the booth. "I believe we have intersecting business interests."

"Where'd you hear that?"

"We Irishmen have a way of finding each other."

"Chief Doyle." Benny closed the newspaper, wondering if this Gleason fella was some sort of messenger.

Bud sauntered over and poured an extra cup of

coffee without being asked.

"Doyle's protection doesn't come cheap for Italians," Gleason said when Bud moved off. "But it's an essential investment for someone in your business."

"What's this? A shakedown?" Benny stirred his stew.

"It's a business discussion." Gleason unbuttoned his jacket. "You're in the beer business. I'm in the hard liquor business."

"A rumrunner," Benny guessed. The mick had a big revolver under the jacket.

"Rum from the Bahamas, Irish whiskey from the emerald isle. Vodka and champagne every now and then."

"What's that to me?"

"We can be rivals or we can be partners. We serve different customers. There's no need to step on each other's toes."

"You got contacts in Chicago?" Benny asked warily.

"Chicago's not my kind of place."

Then Benny was wasting time talking to this mug. "I don't care what you do, as long as you stay out of my way. I'm building the biggest beer racket east of Chicago. Everybody's gonna buy from me."

"East of Chicago is a pretty big place. Lots of toes

between there and here."

Benny chewed a spoonful of meat and potatoes. "I tell you what, Gleason. I'm planning on opening a real swell speakeasy right here in Lido. Got my eye on a place on Hamilton Street. When my place opens, I'll buy all the rum and whiskey you can sell. But until then, stay out of my way."

"A speakeasy? In Lido? You'd better clear your plans with Chief Doyle."

"My arrangement with Chief Doyle's none of your business." Benny shoved the bowl of stew aside. "You make trouble for me with Doyle, you fucking mick, and I'll make double trouble for you. Got that?"

Gleason's expression didn't change as he slid out of the booth. "A pleasure meeting you, Mr. Rotolo," he said in that Irish way of being polite and lying at the same time, just like Dean O'Banion before he got dead. "Don't let me keep you from your supper."

The stew tasted like dirt. Benny had no stomach for it, anyway. Hymie was dead, throwing a wrench in plans to collar Capone. This Gleason fella was a complication that Benny didn't need but couldn't ignore. The Irishman clearly had an edge when it came to protection from the Lido cops.

The only solution was for the Lido Outfit to be so big that neither Gleason nor Doyle wanted to mess with him. Selling beer to little local places was good money but it wasn't big money. He needed to get rid of the competition and expand.

Benny needed more beer, more trucks for deliveries, more workers who didn't speak enough English to squeal. A swank place where Trixie and the girls brought in top dollar.

Benny needed the Galliano Club.

CHAPTER 20

Questions and cutting

One by one, the crew chiefs were called to Mr. Blick's office during the Saturday shift. Word spread like wildfire that they were being questioned by a detective as to Jimmy Zambrano's disappearance. No one said anything to Karol, but the Italian crew chiefs compared notes after each interview.

Procopio let Karol know it was his turn with a jerk of his chin and a shove on the back. Karol was big and solid enough that Procopio's hand didn't send him sprawling but the acting foreman had slammed smaller men into worktables and support pillars in the short time he'd been in charge.

Karol washed his hands and face, collected his coat, and walked to the office building. A secretary escorted him to Mr. Blick's office and closed the door behind him.

"Ah, Dombrowski." Blick stood, the single blue eye commanding the room. "This is Mr. Avlon, the detective we've engaged regarding Zambrano's disappearance. I'm sure you already know Mr. Fisher, the mill accountant."

"Sir." Karol nodded to Avlon, a slight man in a dark suit sitting in a chair in front of Blick's desk, then to Fisher whom he'd encountered before. The accountant was pinched into a chair by the window with a clipboard on his knee.

Blick indicated that Karol should take the chair facing Avlon.

The detective didn't look old enough to investigate a game of marbles let alone a foreman missing from one of the biggest mills in the country. There was nothing to distinguish the man except for a mop of brown hair and a habit of blinking. He might have been a slightly quizzical undertaker's apprentice.

Avlon scribbled something on a small reporter's pad. "Karol Dombrowski," he inquired. "Is that your correct name?"

"Yes."

The rest of the questions were as easy to answer. When had Karol last seen Zambrano and so forth.

Finally, Avlon pointed his pen at Karol. "You are the only crew chief who isn't Italian. An outsider, so to speak. Do you know what I mean?"

"Yes," Karol replied. "I'm Polish and the others are Italian. It's not a secret."

"What about your worker who quit this week? Broz

Siwak? Another Pole. Only stayed long enough to collect his bonus. Tell me about him."

"Broz is a good man."

"What else do you know about him?" Avlon pressed.

The interview had so far been straightforward but now Karol had a bad feeling. "He's married. Has a few kids. Goes to Holy Angels Catholic Church."

"Have you noticed him meeting up with strangers?" Avlon asked. "Men you don't recognize?"

"No."

"You Polish men stick together, don't you?"

"Broz keeps to himself." It was true now, even if it wasn't a week ago.

Avlon leaned toward Karol. "Zambrano goes missing and Siwak quits abruptly. What do you make of that?"

"It's a coincidence." It had never occurred to Karol that the two were connected.

"Did you get along?"

"Me and Broz? Sure."

"Then why did he quit?"

"He said he got another job."

"Where?"

"He didn't say." Not only was Avlon still too close but Karol felt Blick's eye on him like a searchlight.

"Didn't you ask?"

"I asked him to reconsider," Karol said. "Broz and I worked together a long time. He was my best man on the crew. I told him that I'd talk to Mr. Blick about him staying on. But Broz said he had a better situation."

"That's all?"

Karol was torn between loyalty to an old friend and his innate sense of honesty. "It wasn't a long conversation," he said unhappily.

"How did Broz feel about working for an Italian foreman?"

"He did it for ten years," Karol said. "Guess he didn't mind."

Avlon pursed his lips and wrote in his pad. Karol silently damned Broz for choosing a new career that was going to reflect badly on all the Polish workers at Lido Premium.

Mr. Fisher came out of his corner. "When you saw Zambrano last week, did he have any papers with him? Any account books and so forth?"

Karol shifted to see the accountant better. "Account books?"

"We're concerned about the security of Lido Premium's records," the accountant explained primly. "Industrial spies and so forth."

"No, I didn't see him with anything like that."

Fisher subsided into the background again.

"Do you have any other questions?" Blick asked Avlon.

The detective frowned at Karol as if assessing whether or not the big blonde crew chief was a menace to society in general or just to Italian mill workers. "Not now. No doubt we'll be speaking again as the investigation progresses."

"Thank you, Dombrowski," Blick said in a voice that said the interview was over. "If there's anything you recall that might help discover Zambrano's whereabouts, please let me know."

"I'm taking the police examination next week," Karol said and was gratified to see the smirk fade from Avlon's face. "If I am accepted, I can help the investigation in an official capacity."

"You're applying to join the Lido police department?" A muscle pulsed against the hard line of Blick's jaw.

"Yes, sir."

"Thank you for letting me know." Blick came around the side of his desk, shifting the mood inside the office from combative to something Karol was hard pressed to define. Dismay? Frustration? "Let's move on to the issue of Zambrano's locker."

"Wait!" Fisher exclaimed.

"What is it, Owen?" Blick asked impatiently.

Fisher jumped up and brandished his clipboard. "It's not fiscally responsible to cut open the locker. There will be replacement costs. Work time lost and so forth."

"Ten minutes is hardly a costly work stoppage."

"Wait," Fisher shrilled again. "What if there is something, ah, something embarrassing to Zambrano inside?"

"Such as?"

"Ah, ah, inappropriate literature." Fisher bobbed his head several times. "Yes, what about inappropriate literature? The men will be exposed to unseemly images. Some of them are young. Impressionable."

"I'll make sure they aren't exposed to anything that damages their morals," Blick said dryly.

Clutching his clipboard, Fisher opened his mouth several times, but no more protests came out.

Blick fixed his eye on Karol. "Dombrowski, you're with me."

"Yes, sir." Karol hesitated. "What about Procopio, sir? He's looking for Zambrano's locker key."

Blick made a noncommittal noise and led the group out of the office building. As they rounded the path leading to the mill, the operations manager fell into step with Karol, leaving Avlon and Fisher to bring up the rear.

"Lido Premium would be sorry to lose you, Dombrowski," Blick said. "It's easier to find bodies to put into blue uniforms than it is to find an effective leader of men."

Karol didn't know how to respond. It was a strange feeling to be walking side by side with the intimidating operations manager. They were the same height.

"No doubt you'll pass the examination with flying colors," Blick went on. "But please see me before you make any final decision."

"Yes, sir."

"Thank you." Blick paused. "Now about Siwak."

"I don't know anything about his new job."

"I was going to say that you'll have to replace him on your crew. Do you have anyone in mind?"

Karol was taken aback. Crew chiefs generally didn't get to pick their men. "I was expecting Procopio to assign somebody."

"Give me a name on Monday."

They were at the reception entrance. Karol pulled open the door to let the others in and was surprised when Blick motioned him to follow, instead of circling around the mill to the worker's entrance.

"Go get Virgilio and Lanza and their cutting equipment." Blick named the two most experienced welders. "Bring them to the lockers."

Karol asked around for Procopio as he passed the dipping crew on the way to the welding station. He got shrugs for answers from the men waiting for him to come back. With Broz gone, until Karol was on the line again, the crew was too short-handed to work safely.

The two welders must have known something was up because they didn't question instructions but assembled their equipment. Karol carried the heavy oxy acetylene tank bristling with round pressure gauges, while Lanza brought the hoses and helmet. Virgilio cradled the long brass Harris Calorific cutting torch in both arms.

Back in the long corridor, Blick indicated the foreman's locker door. Avlon and Fisher waited by the shuttered pay window.

"First cut the hinges," Blick said to Virgilio. "Then take out the entire lock."

Removing the door was a statement that Zambrano wasn't coming back. If it stayed off, the status symbol of a closed locker was gone. Would the new foreman no longer have the privilege and stature of a locker door?

Curiosity kept Karol in the corridor as Lanza adjusted the tank pressure, sending a hissing mix of acetylene gas and oxygen through the hoses. Wearing a battered welding helmet, Virgilio wielded the spear-like brass torch as his partner touched a match to its end. The gas ignited and a gout of blue flame whooshed out. A thrumming vibration pulsed through the air. Virgilio adjusted the nozzle and applied the cutting flame to the first hinge.

Heat bit into the metal with loud crackling pops. Sparks sprayed like confetti, only to extinguish against the cement floor.

The sound drew workers from their stations, silent and curious. Procopio was not among them.

The first hinge broke away from the locker frame. Virgilio went to work on the next one. Another umbrella of sparks bloomed around him. Blue flames ate through the third and fourth hinges until only the lock held the heavy metal door in place.

Blick asked Karol to brace the door so it didn't fall on the welder. Karol grabbed work gloves from his own locker and complied. Virgilio resettled his helmet and Lanza lit the torch again. Sparks hissed and spit. The blue flame sizzled as it ate the metal.

By now the entire mill was watching, crowding the corridor. Someone wheeled in a dolly used to shuttle tools around the shop floor. Blick parked it next to the welders.

The lock mechanism fell out and the freed locker door shuddered. Virgilio and Lanza turned off the equipment. Karol let the door tip forward so he could grasp an edge and pull it away from the frame.

Fisher appeared, almost getting in the way as Blick emptied the locker and put the contents on the dolly. An old pair of gloves, a pair of clean socks, an extra shirt, a Polish-English dictionary, a metal mug, and a rock-hard slice of fruitcake in a cloth napkin. The accountant handled each item, almost squeaking with agitation.

Karol decided that Fisher was a strange little man.

A murmur swept through the assembled workers as Procopio barreled his way through, only to stop short at the sight of Fisher with Blick next to the empty, doorless locker. "What's going on?"

"The contents of Zambrano's locker are needed for the investigation into his disappearance," Blick said.

"That's my responsibility," Procopio fumed.

"There's nothing important here at all," Fisher piped up. "The Board of Directors will return them to Zambrano's family."

Karol couldn't help noticing that Fisher and Procopio exchanged looks. The slim, dapper accountant and the bull-necked deputy foreman in stained dungarees made an odd couple. But they obviously had something significant to say to each other.

"Get these men back to work, Procopio." Blick's

voice was as cold as ice.

As the workers headed out of the corridor, Karol lingered at his own locker, wondering what would happen next. Fisher made to follow Procopio but stayed with Avlon and Blick instead.

"Obviously Zambrano was having issues with the Polish workers." Avlon picked up the English-Polish dictionary and showed it to Blick. "Very odd that you're losing another one so soon, too. Do you really believe it's to join the police department?"

Karol didn't hear Blick's reply because Fisher dropped his clipboard.

CHAPTER 21

So blatant, so lacking in subtlety

After church, Owen dropped off Cynthia to attend a bridal shower at the home of a friend, leaving him free to enjoy Sunday lunch at the Bison Club. After the drama of opening Zambrano's locker and his abject relief that the ledger wasn't inside, Owen needed some obsequious tableside service to soothe his nerves.

Hopefully, he could kill two birds with one stone. Many Irish Catholic members ate at the club after Mass at St. Brigid's.

The Bison Club was the most exclusive in Lido, housed in a three-story mansion a few blocks from West Park, Lido's nicest neighborhood. Owen always felt a glow of satisfaction as he drove around the circular drive, past the massive pillars and the pale gray painted brick. The club was ostensibly devoted to charitable works, orphans and whatnot, but more importantly, it was where the elite of Lido relaxed in masculine comfort seven days a week.

Standards were high, although everyone knew loopholes had to be found now and then. For example, last year the chairman of the membership committee, Doctor Brian Lanigan, nominated his brother-in-law Sean O'Malley, a policeman with the manners of a western cowpoke. Given that Doc was a legacy member, respected family doctor, and the police department's medical consultant, not to mention Owen's fraternity brother at Syracuse University, the committee approved O'Malley's nomination. No one could blame Doc for his sister's poor taste in husbands.

Chief of Police Doyle was also a Bison and obviously had a soft spot for O'Malley, which also helped grease the approval process.

The dining room was nearly empty when Owen arrived. He sat alone and enjoyed a nicely underdone slab of roast beef, washed down with a bottle of sparkling grape juice that the West End Brewery marketed as extra dry Champanneto Mum.

When O'Malley and Lanigan walked into the dining room, Owen invited them to join him.

Ties were mandatory at the club. O'Malley looked uncomfortable out of uniform. His suit was barely a step up from secondhand while knotty fingers fidgeted without a nightstick to hold. On the other hand, Doc Lanigan didn't look a day older than when Owen met him during Pledge Week. Clean-shaven, brilliantined brown hair swept back from a high forehead, perfect teeth and a cleft in his chin.

While the newcomers ate, the conversation circled around the upcoming gubernatorial election pitting incumbent Governor Al Smith against the Republican challenger Ogden Mills. Smith was both Irish and Catholic, which meant he had Doc's vote. Owen would never vote for a Papist but would not say so to his friend. O'Malley added darkly that the Socialists were fielding a candidate, too. Some upstart named Jacob Panken who should be in jail and not spouting Bolshevik propaganda. Both Owen and Doc fervently agreed.

The waiter served coffee, giving Owen a chance to shift the conversation. "I wonder if I could talk about a business issue with you," he said to O'Malley.

"Business?"

"Excuse me," Doc said smoothly. "I've just seen someone I need to speak with."

"I'm sure you know that Lido Premium's foreman has gone missing," Owen started when he and O'Malley were alone at the table. "Causing quite a disruption, as you can imagine. Everything has fallen on Henry Blick's shoulders."

"The one-eyed fellow?" O'Malley said. "The mayor's friend. Lost his eye in the war, I heard."

"Yes," Owen said. "One of our most illustrious

Bisons."

O'Malley slurped coffee.

Owen squeezed his hands together. "One of our best workers is a fellow by the name of Karol Dombrowski."

"That's a Polish name."

"Yes, despite his unfortunate origins, Dombrowski is well thought of by Henry, who'd be quite upset to see him leave Lido Premium." Owen paused to make sure O'Malley was following. "I'd like to help Henry and keep Dombrowski from leaving."

"You want Henry Blick to owe you a favor," O'Malley said.

"No, no, not at all," Owen lied. "I'm simply concerned that things will be easier for Henry if Dombrowski stays where he is."

"So?"

Owen hesitated. "Perhaps you could arrange for that to happen."

"For what to happen?"

"For Dombrowski to, ah, not leave Lido Premium to become a policeman."

O'Malley leaned back in his chair. "I'm a wee bit confused," he said. "You mentioned a business issue. But now you want me to do you a favor and sink this fella with the police department. For nothing."

Fisher patted his lips with his napkin to mask his

chagrin. It was just like this large uncouth lout to be so blatant, so lacking in subtlety. "Let's call it a retention bonus," he said. "Should Lido Premium be able to retain Dombrowski, I'll pay you a retention bonus of, ah, let us say, one hundred dollars."

"A retention bonus," O'Malley snorted. "All right, call it what you want. I'll make sure he flunks the exam. But it'll cost you two hundred."

"Two hundred," Owen confirmed. He told himself that it was a small price for the inner circle's gratitude.

Two hundred to Nick, two hundred to O'Malley. It was everyone's favorite amount.

CHAPTER 22

I would be a very cruel husband

Enzo's truck pulled up in front of Mrs. Esposito's and the horn bleated. Luca waved to the kids in the bed of the truck. He was about to join them when Rosaria leaned out of the cab. "Luca! Is that what you are going to wear to meet Annunziata?"

Luca gaped at her. Slowly, painfully, he recalled his promise to meet Al Genovese's sister.

"You forgot," Rosaria accused as Enzo roared with laughter from behind the wheel.

"I remembered," Luca blustered.

"At least bring a clean shirt!"

He ran inside to collect a neatly folded shirt and pressed tie, both still wrapped in butcher paper from the laundry. Rocco and Matilda grinned like little devils as he climbed into the truck bed with the package. Luca distracted them with the counting game as they rode to the farm.

Once there, the children ran off to change clothes and do their chores. Rosaria made coffee and cut slabs of gingerbread to fuel the men for a few hours of work before dinner, all while describing what she'd prepared for the Genovese family. To Luca, it sounded ominously more like a wedding feast than two families sharing a Sunday meal.

After a week of intermittent rain, the day was a memory of summer. Luca and Enzo worked shirtless, suspenders digging into bare shoulders. Sawing wood in the sun to make mangers and stalls was hard work. Luca's arm ached with the repetitive motion of dragging the saw back and forth, forcing it to bite into the thick planks.

By the time the sun cast a belt of crimson across the sky, Luca and Enzo had washed and put on clean shirts. The farmhouse smelled like heaven and was bursting at the seams. The Genovese family included Al, his wife Claudia, three energetic children, and his sister, Annunziata.

Introductions were made in Italian and English. Luca barely glimpsed Annunziata before Rosaria and Claudia chivied her into the kitchen. The men sat on the porch with dandelion wine. The children played tag in the front yard.

It wasn't until the adults were seated in the dining room and the children relegated to a makeshift table in the kitchen that Luca really got a look at Annunziata Genovese. Of course, Rosaria seated Luca across from the girl. Claudia took the chair next to her. Enzo was at the head of the table, with Al in the place of honor at the other end.

Annunziata kept her head down. Now and then she glanced at Luca from under thick eyelashes.

She had dark hair scraped back into a bun like Luca's 60-year-old landlady. Big eyes, dark brows that met over the bridge of her nose, and the hint of a mustache. Her white blouse, ankle length gray skirt, and farm boots marked her as a recent immigrant as clearly as if she wore a sign on her forehead. Her torso was square and thick-waisted. She barely had any breasts.

The antipasto was passed around, each person selecting from the wealth of marinated vegetables, artichoke hearts and olives, as well as sliced salami and three different cheeses. Annunziata made no attempt to help herself when the platter came around but waited for Claudia to put some of each on her plate.

In the kitchen, the children chattered away in English, but the conversation in the dining room was in Italian. A few words in English found their way in when no translation would do. After the antipasto, Rosaria brought out her *prima piatti*. The lasagna was hot from the oven, cheese and sauce bubbling. The scent was heady.

"Annunziata makes lasagna like this," Al proclaimed. "She's going to make some lucky man a good wife, no?"

Luca tucked his napkin into his collar to avoid staining his clean shirt.

"In America, a good Catholic woman is hard to find." Claudia gave Luca a brittle smile. Al's wife was older and flintier than Rosaria, with frizzy brown hair and nervous eyes.

The plates were passed around. Luca complimented Rosaria and meant every word. The sheets of homemade pasta were layered with pork sausage, pepperoni, and slices of hardboiled eggs, plus ricotta thinned with milk and parmesan cheese to balance the heavy meats. Her red sauce was perfection.

For several minutes no one spoke, too busy appreciating the masterpiece of lasagna to do more than eat. Even the children in the kitchen were quiet.

Al finally wiped his mouth with the tail of his napkin and pushed his empty plate away. "Annunziata is happy to be in America," he announced. "Here in America, we make a good life. We gonna build the farm, the biggest dairy farm in all of New York. Be a family of property."

"Did you have a good crossing?" Luca asked Annunziata, loudly enough to cut through her brother's bluster.

The girl looked at Al. Her brother waved a hunk of bread at her. "Go on, answer him."

"I came with my cousins," she said.

"Did you get on a ship in Genoa?"

"Yes." She stuffed a wad of bread into her mouth.

"Did you see the big statue in New York?"

Annunziata looked at her brother again.

"Talk to the man," Claudia said sharply.

"I saw the statue of the lady with the book and the lamp," Annunziata murmured with her mouth full.

"And now she's here to find a husband," Claudia said before the girl could say anything else. "Annunziata needs an older man, someone who can show her how to be a good wife."

"What would you like to do here in America?" Luca directed his comments to Annunziata again. "See the Grand Canyon? Niagara Falls? Go to California where they make the movies? Florida where they have alligators? Watch the New York Yankees?"

"Luca," Rosaria exclaimed as Annunziata blinked in confusion. "You haven't done any of those things."

"But I could." Luca drank some wine. "That's the point."

"Girls in America have crazy ideas." Al shook his head even as he raised his glass. "They get crazy for the dancing and movie stars. Don't know what's good for them. Annunziata's not like that."

"Nobody wants to be told what's good for them," Luca retorted. "Annunziata, you came all the way to America. It's full of opportunity. You can learn things here. Go places. Make things happen."

The girl gaped at Luca as if he was speaking a language from another planet instead of Italian. Half-chewed bread glistened in her mouth.

"Annunziata came to America to be with family," Al said with a snort at Luca's obvious fairy tales. "She's a sensible girl. A good girl."

"Good hips, too," Claudia said. "She won't have any trouble with the babies."

"What do you like to talk about?" Luca asked Annunziata.

"Talk?" Claudia shrilled. "Why does she need to talk about anything?"

Luca resisted the urge to say something unkind and addressed the girl again. "How old are you, Annunziata?"

"She's older than she looks," Claudia said swiftly.

"Fourteen?" Luca pressed. "Fifteen?"

Rosaria kicked Luca under the table. "That's enough, Luca," she muttered under her breath.

"Fourteen," the girl said.

"Fourteen." Luca exclaimed and was rewarded with

a second kick. "Don't you want to do something before having babies?"

"What's wrong with babies?" Claudia demanded.

"Little girls don't get married and have babies in America," Luca said. "In America, girls go to school. Learn about the world. Learn mathematics and economics and how to think for themselves."

"Think?" Al boomed. "Her husband can tell her what to think."

Rosaria was red-faced with embarrassment. Enzo kept his eyes on his plate.

"See?" Claudia said in triumph, although it wasn't clear what she'd won.

"Not now, Luca," Rosaria pleaded under her breath.

Luca fought down a sharp retort and mopped up his last bit of sauce with a bite of bread.

He wasn't sure which was worse; the scheme to rope him into marriage with a child half his age or Annunziata's placid acceptance of everyone else's plans for her life. Clearly, Claudia intended to get her sister-in-law out of the house and Rosaria wanted to help a friend, but the girl was not ready to get married. She was like a cow. Big eyes, constant chewing, no thoughts of her own.

When the Genovese family left, Luca would make Rosaria and Enzo understand that he didn't want a cow or a child. He wanted a woman like Tess Kennedy.

Tessa.

A full-grown woman who looked him in the eye and had interesting things to say. Luca reveled in the challenge of catching her attention, of matching wits with her cleverness. Someone who forgave his sins and made him laugh. *A baseball mustache. Nine hairs on a side.*

"Annunziata's going to make a good wife." Al pointed his fork at his sister. "A good worker. She cooks. She cleans. She sews. Took care of our mother, God rest her soul, until she went to her eternal rest."

"I'm sorry about your mother," Luca murmured, but Annunziata didn't acknowledge him. Perhaps she was accustomed to being talked *about* rather than talked *to*.

"She's strong enough to pull a plow," Al kept on, now aiming at Luca. "I'll give you a share in the dairy business and five acres as her dowry. What do you say?"

"She's a virgin, too," Claudia whispered, leaning sideways toward Luca as if to shield Annunziata from the facts of life. "But if a man dabbles with a more experienced woman every now and then, she won't complain."

It was the last straw.

Luca yanked the napkin out of his collar and threw

it on the table. "Look at me, Annunziata," he ordered.

The girl raised her head from her plate, brow furrowed in concern.

"I'm not going to marry you." Luca spoke slowly and deliberately. "I would be a very cruel husband and you would be very unhappy. Go to school and learn to read. Get married after you grow up. Don't let anyone sell you for cows or a house."

"How dare you!" Claudia practically threw herself across the table in an effort to slap him. Luca caught her arm and stood, levering the irate woman back into her seat. Al stayed where he was, slack-jawed with surprise that anyone dared to cross his wife.

"My apologies," Luca said stiffly to Rosaria. "But this was your idea, not mine."

He collected his cap and mackinaw and left the house.

It was still warm as he trudged along Bell Road in the gathering dark. No vehicle came by to pick up a solitary hitchhiker. His stomach growled as he crossed the bridge and picked his way over the railroad tracks. It hurt to think that he was missing Rosaria's veal and peppers, not to mention cake and coffee and six kinds of cookies.

Luca was almost to Hamilton Street when Enzo caught up to him in the truck. The headlights stabbed yellow cylinders through the gloom.

Instead of inviting him to hop inside the cab, Enzo thrust a pail out of the driver's window. "Here," he said. "Rosaria's sorry."

Luca grabbed the heavy tin pail by the handle and inhaled the rich sauce of Rosaria's *secondi piatti* through the dishcloth covering the contents.

"Rosaria should have known better," Luca said.

"She just wants you to be happy."

"She thinks I'd be happy married to a child?"

Enzo sighed. "It's best if you don't come around for a few weeks," he said and drove on.

Chess with Karol that night was in Luca's room. Karol had seen the newspaper articles about Bolsheviks and had a disturbing conversation with a private detective to relate, as well as gloomy speculation about his friend Broz being in trouble. Jimmy Zambrano's locker had been cut open but yielded no clue as to the foreman's disappearance.

Every move on the board was accompanied by speculation that Bolsheviks were haunting Lido in an effort to ruin American industry and what Karol would do once he passed the upcoming police examination and proudly wore the blue uniform.

Luca lightened the mood with the debacle of meeting Annunziata Genovese. The two friends shared side-splitting laughter at his description of Claudia.

Loath to invite *malocchio* by talking about her, Luca said nothing about meeting Tess Kennedy.

Tessa.

CHAPTER 23

Ruthie June's big night

Ruth pulled the quilt up to her nose as O'Malley rolled out of the bed. Wearing socks and a thermal undershirt, he reached for the cotton boxers lying across the chair in front of Ruth's vanity.

"There now, Ruthie June," he said, buttoning the fly. "We had ourselves a big night, didn't we?"

"You got what you came for," Ruth said, her words muffled by the sheet.

"Less of that attitude." O'Malley hauled on his trousers. "I brought you a rose, now didn't I? You've got no cause to be snotty."

He showed up at eight o'clock, just as Ruth was hoping he had lost his nerve. O'Malley wore his police uniform, cheeks chapped from the cold. He held out a single red rose bearing a ribbon from Fulton Florist, the nicest in Lido. The rose was such an incongruous gesture that Ruth could only gape as O'Malley thrust it at her.

They playacted for a while, pretending he wasn't there upon the threat of blackmail, but courting like a young man with her father's permission. O'Malley looked at the pictures in her parlor and told her the settee was comfortable. Ruth mentioned talking to Detectives Schultz and Dooley on Friday.

The charade lasted an excruciating hour before O'Malley led Ruth into the bedroom and clumsily helped her out of her clothes before dropping his pants.

It wasn't good, but it wasn't the worst, either. O'Malley didn't humiliate or hurt her. He didn't care when Ruth closed her eyes and let him get on with it as he panted like a racehorse.

"I'll see myself out, Ruthie June," O'Malley said. He flipped up his suspenders and bent to watch himself in the mirror vanity as he buttoned his tunic.

"Stop calling me that," Ruth said.

Now fully dressed, O'Malley came to the bed. "On second thought," he said. "You should walk me out like a real lady would do."

"I need to wash first," Ruth said.

O'Malley chuckled and went into the parlor.

Ruth crept out of the bed, slipped on her flannel dressing gown, and picked up the tall perfume atomizer from the vanity. It was lead crystal, nearly as big as a milk bottle, and filled with drugstore scent.

She tiptoed to the doorway and peered into the parlor. O'Malley's back was to her as he stood by the settee, examining the picture of the cast of *Little Johnny Jones*.

Ruth rushed forward; the atomizer poised to strike. O'Malley flinched away and grabbed her wrist. They wrestled but his weight and the pressure of his thumb was too much. Ruth's hand opened and the heavy crystal bottle thudded onto the carpet.

Instead of slapping her, O'Malley grabbed her by both shoulders and kissed her hard enough to bruise, mouth snarling and wide as his fingers dug into her shoulders. When Ruth tried to pull back before she suffocated, he pitched her into the armchair with graceless strength.

"You got spirit, Ruthie June," he said and ran the back of his hand over his mouth. "Makes a man build up an appetite. Next Sunday, make some supper afterward."

"I can't afford to feed you." Ruth's eyes burned and her lips stung.

O'Malley made a production out of extracting a money clip and thumbing off a few bills. He dropped them onto the carpet next to the perfume bottle. "I like a nice roast chicken for my Sunday supper."

"You think I'm going to cook for you?"

"See you next Sunday, Ruthie June," O'Malley said. "Don't forget about my chicken now, you hear?"

Ruth closed her eyes.

The apartment door banged. Loud whistling accompanied O'Malley's footsteps as he descended the stairs. The tune was *Yankee Doodle Dandy*, the signature song from *Little Johnny Jones*.

Ruth opened her eyes after she heard O'Malley shut the street door. The crumpled bills on the floor mocked her. Far from climbing her way up, she had fallen even lower than before.

She was no better than a prostitute.

CHAPTER 24

The spitting image of his father

Luca made sandwiches as Guido cleaned the front window with vinegar and newspaper. Someone came and slammed the front door closed behind them. An unwelcome draft swirled around the pony wall and blew into the saloon. Luca looked up to see a blur of navy wool and red-faced fury throw a looping punch at him across the bar.

The fist grazed his chin, whipping his head to the side. Luca automatically countered with a blow to the jaw that sent his assailant staggering backward into an empty table. It overturned, dumping a tangle of arms and legs on the floor. The card players protested as chairs skidded by.

"*Oddio*," Luca exclaimed, thoroughly confused.

He'd struck Sonny Zambrano, Jimmy's oldest child.

Luca vaulted over the bar top and yanked Sonny upright by the front of his navy pea coat. "What the hell's going on, Sonny?"

The teen was the spitting image of his father. Compact and wiry, with the same Roman nose and deep-set eyes.

Sonny twisted himself out of Luca's grasp and dug a handful of dollar bills out of his coat pocket. "Take it," he shouted, thrusting the money at Luca. "You wanted your money back, so here it is. Take it and stay away from my mother. Talk to her again and I swear I'll kill you."

But the fight was out of him, and tears streamed down his face. As Guido began putting the saloon back to rights, Luca propelled the kid down the hall, away from the curious stares of the card players.

Luca pulled Sonny into the tiny library and planted him in a chair. "I gave your ma some money to keep. Why would you think I wanted it back?"

"The men you sent," Sonny said miserably.

"I didn't send anybody."

"Three men came to the house. They said stuff about an account book, then money. Ma thought they were asking about Pa's account at the club. You said that's where the money came from."

"I didn't send anybody," Luca said again. He had a very bad feeling. "Then what happened?"

"Ma said she didn't have it, but they stampeded through the house anyway. They searched everywhere. Opened every drawer, dumped everything out. They broke Ma's china. Threw it on the floor. Even ripped up the mattresses."

Jimmy was dead, now strangers had ransacked his house. *Bolsheviks.* It was as if Luca's conversation with Karol on Sunday night had conjured them out of their hiding hole.

"Did your ma ring for the police?" Luca pressed.

"No, she was scared." Sonny's eyes filled. "Ma couldn't even give them the money if she wanted to. She put it in the bank as soon as you gave it to her. It's all she's got to keep us going. That and Pa's bonus."

"Then what's this?" Luca pointed at the wad in Sonny's hand.

"My college money." Sonny's face crumpled.

"*Oddio,*" Luca swore. He needed time to figure out what to do. "Did you eat today?"

Sonny shook his head. One cheek was bright red and would probably be purple by morning. "Ma hasn't cooked anything since Pa disappeared."

Back in the saloon, Luca swiftly assembled another special of the day: crusty bread loaded with soft mozzarella and razor-thin *prosciutto di parma* drizzled with a figgy balsamic vinegar.

"Here, eat this." Luca slid the plate to Sonny just as the mill whistle blew.

The teen's eyes nearly popped out of his head at the size of the sandwich. "Thanks, Luca."

Luca gave him a glass of lemon-lime rickey and paced behind the bar, trying to figure out who had been to the Zambrano house. He paused in front of Sonny as the kid inhaled another mouthful of bread, cheese, and ham.

"Did you recognize any of the men who came to the house?"

"No." Sonny was certain. "They weren't Italian."

"Irish?"

"No, they didn't speak English very well at all."

The door scraped open, and a crowd of workers trooped in, shedding coats and hats.

"They looked like that," Sonny said. "Rough. Like they'd worked all day and didn't wash. They smelled bad. One of them was a big guy, bigger than you, with a scar on his lip."

"Rough men who didn't speak English or Italian." Luca absorbed that fact as the workers recognized Sonny and came over to the bar to offer him words of encouragement. *Your pa will turn up. Too scared of your ma to stay away for long. Fall fishing trip, everybody knows your pa likes his fishing. First vacation in 20 years, that's all. You see him, tell him to get back to work.*

Watching Sonny, Luca knew that as much as he wanted to stay away from the police, he couldn't. He fished the business card out of the cash register, got his coat, and told Guido to go behind the bar.

Luca walked Sonny all the way to the small police station next to the courthouse and made him repeat the story to Detective Dooley.

"Mother Mary, pray for us," the detective muttered. His pale red hair was neatly parted in the middle as he sat at his desk scribbling furiously. "Sounds like Bolsheviks to me."

"Do you think they kidnapped Pa?" Sonny asked.

"Sure could be, kid," Dooley said. "Maybe we'll get a ransom letter."

Luca hated the way Sonny's face lit up with hope. Perhaps Dooley saw it, too, because he directed Sonny to the office door. "Lemme talk to Mr. Lombardo here for a minute, kid."

Alone with the detective, Luca cursed himself for being a Good Samaritan.

"Thanks for bringing the kid in," Dooley said, taking his chair again. He wore a plain gray vested suit with a skinny striped tie.

"Seemed like the right thing to do."

"Anybody hanging around the club that don't belong?"

"No." Luca took a deep breath. "These Bolsheviks. Do they throw bombs like the anarchists?"

"Sure, they could do anything."

"What else would they do? Shoot or . . . or strangle a man?"

"Wouldn't put anything past them." Dooley frowned. "What have you heard?"

"Nothing," Luca said hastily. "Just wondering about Bolsheviks if Jimmy wasn't kidnapped. If something worse happened."

Dooley picked up his pencil again. "What about Officer O'Malley?"

"The policeman who patrols Hamilton Street?"

"Yeah, him. Saturday night? Was he walking his beat?"

"Yes."

"Did he come by the club?"

Luca almost replied yes. Just in time he recalled that Vito had told O'Malley that no one else was there. "Not when I was there."

The answer seemed to satisfy the detective and Dooley threw down his pencil. "Thanks for coming in. Me and Schultz will be around if we have any more questions."

Confused and uneasy, Luca collected Sonny and left the police station. Why would one policeman ask questions about another? Was O'Malley a suspect? Was he involved with Bolsheviks?

The policeman was tall and strong enough to have strangled Jimmy.

"You okay, Luca?" Sonny asked.

"Sure." Luca brought himself back to the present, walking down Union Street toward the intersection with Hamilton, with the son of a dead man. "Sonny, do you need a job?"

"Yes," Sonny admitted. "Ma's going crazy wondering where the money's going to come from."

"How about working at the club? Washing dishes, sweeping up, clearing the tables. After school and on Saturdays. Say, five dollars a week?"

"It's a deal," Sonny said.

"You can start tomorrow. I'll fix it with Vito. Mr. Spinelli to you."

"Thanks, Luca. You're the best." Sonny threw his arms around Luca.

Guilt nearly sent Luca to his knees. "None of that. You're a working man now."

Having Sonny in the club was going to be a constant reminder of Jimmy.

A constant penance.

CHAPTER 25

Your truck looks off

Benny was feeling pretty good as he drove back to Lido in his newly acquired Penguin Ice truck with his newly acquired inventory of Canadian beer. The trip up north had worked out even better than anticipated. The competition that sold beer to the Galliano Club was out of business. Nick might think he was a big deal, ordering mugs around in that sweatshop of a mill, but Benny was the brains of the family.

Sal and Milo Antonelli lived on a farm in Ontario. Half a dozen cows, a field of hops, another of barley, and a barn outfitted like a brewery. Their dear old pop, who didn't speak a word of English except "No, no!" was the brewmaster. Guess they never figured the competition would come over the border because Benny drove right up with a carload of Polish thugs and sawed-off shotguns.

After a certain amount of Chicago-style persuading, the Antonelli brothers joined the Lido Outfit. Whatever they brewed now belonged to Benny and they were going to brew double what they had before. Pops got a broken arm in the persuasion phase of the visit, which helped speed things along.

Benny made them sign a paper to finalize the new partnership. Had it in his pocket for Owen Fisher. The Antonellis would get their percentage from the accountant from now on.

Instead of the Cadillac, Benny had driven one of the Outfit's trucks on the rough roads north to Canada. Broz Siwak drove it back while Benny handled the Penguin Ice flagship. The Polack was turning into a top lieutenant. The plan was to meet at the pump house.

The country road was nice and quiet. Dusk was falling and the steeples of Lido were in view. Benny was thinking about taking Trixie dancing, maybe at the Candyland Supper Club, when a siren blared. A police car forced him to swerve to the side of the road.

Benny cut the engine and touched the Colt Pocket Hammerless hidden under his overcoat. He was confident he wouldn't need it. After all, he was paying three hundred a week to keep Lido's cops in line. Still, maybe he should have told Siwak to stay close.

"Hiya, officer." Benny swung out of the truck cab. "Nice night, ain't it?"

"I've seen this truck before," the policeman said. "Guess you get around."

"Sure, everybody needs ice." Benny grinned. "My

name's Rotolo."

"Truck is riding low like you've got a load."

"Full of ice." Didn't the cop know who Benny was? "Rotolo. Guess you've heard my name before."

"Can't say that I have." The cop squinted at Benny. "Most ice trucks load up in the morning. By evening they're empty."

"Yeah, well, I deliver when my customers want it."

"They want ice delivered at dinner time?"

"My name's Rotolo," Benny said again, getting hot under the collar. Did this cop expect to get a piece of the action? "Ring a bell?"

"Like I said, can't say that it does."

The conversation with that mick rumrunner in Perk's Diner took on fresh meaning. "Did Gleason put you up to this?"

"I don't care who your friends are, buddy. Your truck looks off."

Maybe the copper didn't know Gleason but he sure as hell knew his own boss. "My next delivery is to Chief Doyle," Benny said. "He ain't gonna like it if I'm late."

"No kidding." The cop still acted like he didn't know nothing. "Delivering ice to Chief Doyle's house."

"Sure, they're regulars."

"What's the address?"

"West Park," Benny guessed.

"You're pretty dressed up to deliver ice," the cop said but didn't challenge the West Park answer.

Benny made a show of brushing his coat lapels, his hand teasing the hidden Colt Pocket Hammerless. "Taking the missus to the moving pictures when I get off."

"New Buster Keaton picture?"

"Sure, that's the one."

No other traffic came by as the cop circled the truck. Dusk spread shadows over the fallow fields stretching away from the road in both directions. It was a real quiet spot. Benny blew on his fingers to warm them.

"Yeah, okay, looks good," the cop finally said. "Sorry to have stopped you."

"No hard feelings, officer." Benny tugged on the brim of his fedora. "Just doing your job. You have a nice evening."

The cop opened the door of his car with the yellow Lido Police Department shield painted on the side, then closed it again. Gave Benny a hard look then walked all around the Penguin Ice truck a second time and stooped to look underneath.

"Ice melts," the cop said. "A truck full of ice drips all the time. How come yours isn't dripping?"

"Too cold out," Benny said but the explanation was slow in coming.

"Open up the truck," the cop ordered. "Let's see this ice."

Benny stayed where he was by the cab door. "Look, officer. If I'm late with the ice, Chief Doyle's gonna be mighty mad. I'll have to tell him who made me late."

"Or maybe there's something else in there besides ice."

A nice crisp ten-dollar bill fluttered out of Benny's pocket. "Bet you've got a missus who'd like a nice night on the town. Buster Keaton and dinner on the square."

The cop didn't take it. "You aren't trying to bribe an officer of the law, are you?"

"What's a sawbuck between friends?"

"Open the back," the cop said grimly.

Benny slipped the bill under one of the truck's windshield wipers like he once saw Hymie Weiss do in Chicago when a union official wouldn't take the payoff direct, and winked at the cop. All he got back was a big blank nothing.

Twilight blurred the edges of the dark blue uniform. The brass buttons stood out like beacons. Benny backed away and went to the rear of the truck.

"Here we go." Benny jingled his keys. Let them slide out of his fingers, then bent and pretended to look for them under the license plate. "Damn it. Dropped the keys. Do you see them?"

When the cop came to help, Benny plugged him twice in the heart with the Colt Pocket Hammerless.

The cop windmilled backward as the recoil shook the air. Benny thought the fella was going to hop a jig all the way to Hamilton Street, but he only got as far as the police car before falling against the yellow shield, one hand groping for the door handle. Gurgled and hissed and thrashed until Benny shot him again.

Those brass buttons made a dandy target.

The blue uniform flopped flat on the ground and didn't move again. The cop's eyes were open. Benny kicked him to make sure he was dead. He was. Served him right, working for a double-crosser like Chief Doyle.

Back at the truck, Benny plucked the tenner off the wiper, scooped his keys off the ground, and started her up. Swung wide to get around the police car and the stiff lying there studying the stars. The police must have the Penguin Ice truck pegged. Another thing to dump in the river.

Blood fizzed in Benny's veins as he hammered the accelerator. Hymie would have been damn proud of him for luring that cop into a trap.

Lido was getting to be more like Chicago every day.

CHAPTER 26

Asking permission

Sonny caught on quickly and made himself useful in no time. When Ruth's class ended Thursday evening, Luca introduced Sonny to Tess before letting the young man take over the bar for an hour.

The night was unexpectedly balmy, and stars winked against an indigo sky. Tess was in her sailor trousers again and readily agreed when Luca proposed a walk. She took his arm again, as if it was the most natural thing in the world to do. Pride and protectiveness rose in Luca's chest.

Hamilton Street was quiet, but it was a good quiet, the kind of quiet that said people were in bed and the city at rest. They strolled slowly, peering into shop windows. Luca translated a few signs, but Tess already knew many words, such as *panetteria* which meant *bakery,* and *pesce* for the fish sign in front of Fiori's.

They didn't talk about the investigation into the missing mill foreman or Bolsheviks but teased each other with number puzzles and shared little secrets about themselves. Luca told her about studying Latin with ancient Father Caviglia in Serra San Bruno, that his parents died when he was very young, and how his grandparents objected when he said he was going to America instead of becoming a priest. Tess revealed that her father had been her first teacher, encouraging her to study math and science as he worked in his laboratory. She never attended a real school until she came to live with her aunt in Lido.

"I used to wear trousers all the time," Tess laughed, then grew serious. "Your young helper was scandalized by a woman in trousers. But you haven't said a thing."

Luca smiled, recalling Sonny's pop-eyed reaction. "My mother wore trousers."

"In Italy?" Tess exclaimed. "She must have been a very modern woman."

"I don't think so. She never even learned to read." Luca's memories of his mother were hazy now. For some reason he could recall more about his father. "But she loved when my father read out loud in the evenings. She said we traveled the world when he read to us."

"What happened to your parents?"

"It's not a nice story."

Tess tugged gently on his arm. "I'd still like to hear it."

"My father was an educated man," Luca began slowly. "An army officer from the north, near

Switzerland. The army sent him to Abyssinia. He ran away and came to Serra San Bruno, in Calabria where he met my mother. The army caught up with him and executed him for being a deserter. When my mother protested, the officer in charge of the firing squad killed her, too." He stopped before he told Tess about killing Orsini.

"How old were you?" she asked softly. They were walking very slowly now, their heads close together.

"Five or six. I didn't learn about my father's military career until much later."

"I'm sorry," Tess said. "I'm sorry for all the hard things that have happened to you. Losing your parents. Losing your wife."

"But now good things are happening," Luca replied. "I'm in America. Here in Lido. I met you."

Tess smiled, the green eyes radiating warmth behind the spectacles. "This is going to sound odd but thank you for telling me about hard things. I'm not a child or a woman given to the vapors who has to be shielded from bad news or difficult decisions. Thank you for trusting me."

"I'd like to see you again, Tessa," Luca said as they reached Saint Rocco's and began retracing their steps. "How do you say it? Formally."

"Are you asking permission to court me?"

"Yes, if that's the right way to say it."

Tess glanced up at him. "You need to ask my aunt."

"Not you?"

"Well, yes." She was obviously pleased. "My permission comes first."

Luca paused. "Is that how two becomes one in America?"

"Yes, I believe it is."

Thanks to a streetlight, he saw color flood into her cheeks. They kept walking, something bigger and sure and exhilarating sparking between them. Luca wanted to leap into the air, shout the news the length of Hamilton Street.

Tess tugged on his arm. "Aren't you going to ask me?"

"Now?"

"Why not?"

"Not in the middle of the street," Luca said.

"Are you an old-fashioned man?"

"Asking in the middle of the street would show a lack of respect."

Tess laughed and the night brightened. "You're not like any other man I've ever met, Luca. You never talk down to me. I like you very much."

"I like you very much, too." *More than you know.*

"Come to supper on Sunday," she said. "I can't wait

for you to meet Aunt Evelyn."

When she finally drove off, Luca stood on the sidewalk on the quiet street in front of the club. There were stones in his heart but there was room for Tess Kennedy, too.

Tessa.

CHAPTER 27

A pillar of America

The first thing that Karol saw when he entered the courthouse was a vaulted ceiling with light streaming from the cupola.

The second thing were the words etched across a marble wall.

THE DUE ADMINISTRATION OF JUSTICE IS
THE FIRMEST PILLAR OF GOOD
GOVERNMENT
– GEORGE WASHINGTON

Karol straightened his tie, took off his hat, and approached a big semi-circular reception desk. A hard-eyed policeman in a blue uniform asked his business.

"I am here to take the police examination," Karol announced.

"Name?"

"Karol Dombrowski."

"Dombrowski?" The officer consulted a clipboard.

"*Ja.*"

The officer wrote on a slip of paper and handed it over. "All right, Dombrowski. You're on the list. Take this to Room 12." He pointed toward a corridor branching off the vast lobby. "Good luck. We could use some fellows your size."

Room 12 was crowded with men sitting at desks like overgrown schoolchildren. Karol handed his slip to the officer at the door. A woman with gray hair, spectacles and a watch pinned to her sweater introduced herself as Mrs. Clancy, "Secretary to himself." She assigned Karol to a desk where a pencil and booklet sealed with a wax stamp awaited him. Karol dutifully wedged himself into the seat.

He didn't know any of the other men. All were quietly well dressed. None had work-calloused hands. No one spoke.

After ten minutes of restless fidgeting, an officer with an impressive amount of gold braid on his uniform marched in and announced from the front of the room that he was Chief of Police Gerald Doyle. Clearly, from the rapt expression on Mrs. Clancy's face, this was "Himself." Doyle had an impressive belly, a red nose, silver hair, and a foghorn voice that bade them to stand, face the flag, and recite the Pledge of Allegiance. Along with the rest, Karol clapped a hand to his heart and spoke the words from memory.

Once everyone was seated again, Chief Doyle let them know that the very few who passed the test and became a policeman in Lido would have the privilege of wearing the blue, carrying a callbox key, and taking orders from Himself.

With a final warning that Lido took only the best, Chief Doyle barreled out. Mrs. Clancy instructed the candidates to open their booklets. Once everyone had broken the wax seal, she consulted her watch and said they had two hours to complete the examination.

Karol skimmed the booklet before answering the questions. The first part was a section to provide his name and address, his wife's name if married, and his parents' address as well. All the jobs he'd held for the past 5 years, and his school certificates, if any.

He puzzled over a particularly odd question.

Have you ever before made application for employment for a position requiring a physical examination? Were you accepted or rejected?

No one gave him a physical examination before he went to work at the mill. Jimmy Zambrano had simply made him pick up eighty pounds and read a paragraph from the *Lido Daily Clipper* to test his English.

Karol wrote *No* in the space provided.

Have you ever been discharged or suspended from any situation? No.

Have you now or have you ever had any civil litigation?

His secondhand copy of *The Civil Government of the United States* was peppered with phrases like *civil litigation*. When he first encountered it, the concept was nothing short of unbelievable. Poland had been overrun, partitioned and remade so many times that no one had ever experienced such a thing as civil litigation. Again, Karol wrote *No* in the space provided.

The next section was all about the state of New York. Karol happily filled in the blanks. The state capital was Albany, the governor was Al Smith, and the lieutenant governor was Edwin Corning.

Other questions weren't so simple.

New York has many canals. Land for canals is acquired by: _____.

Karol smiled to himself and wrote *The right of eminent domain.*

After a few more obscure questions about the state,

Karol arrived at the last section and felt a rush of excitement. Twenty questions and he knew the answers to all of them.

Q: The highest tribunal in the land is:
A: The Supreme Court

Q: A written accusation against some person, charging him with a crime is a:
A: A bill of indictment

Q: How many men serve on a jury in the United States?
A: 12

The rest of the questions were equally straightforward. Anyone who'd read the section entitled "The Judicial Department" in *The Civil Government of the United States* couldn't help but get them all correct.

Karol rechecked that all the questions in the booklet were complete and legible, before sitting back to survey the room. All the other men were still hunched over their booklets, some even nervously chewing the erasers on their pencils. Surely, they had all studied, just as he had. Why were they taking so long to complete the questions? Karol flipped open his booklet again, wondering if he'd missed a section. But no, his test was complete, and he was positive that his answers were correct.

After two hours, Miss Clancy collected all the booklets and gave them an hour for lunch. Once outside the courthouse, despite biting cold, most of the men lit cigarettes and milled around, commiserating with each other. Karol walked briskly to the drugstore a block away and ordered a sandwich at the lunch counter. He wolfed sauerkraut and corned beef on pumpernickel bread before rushing back.

Mrs. Clancy was at the door to Room 12. Consulting a clipboard, she allowed some of the test-takers back in. Others were sent home.

"Go ahead and take a seat," she said when Karol gave his name. "Wait to be called for your interview."

Eight men remained in the room. A few exchanged whispers as they waited.

Mrs. Clancy reappeared. "Mr. Mulligan, this way please." A man in the front row collected his coat and hat and followed her out.

Fifteen minutes later, she summoned Mr. O'Reilly. The next to be called was Mr. O'Hara. The string of Irish names continued until Karol was alone.

"Mr. Dombrowski, this way please."

Chief of Police Doyle, two other uniformed officers, and a man in a white cotton coat sat behind a table. A single chair faced them.

"Have a seat, Dombrowski," Chief Doyle said.

"Thank you." Karol sat down, his coat and hat on his lap.

Chief Doyle didn't introduce anyone facing Karol but tapped an examination booklet labeled DOMBROWSKI in thick black grease pencil. "You did very well on the examination, Dombrowski. Very high marks."

"Thank you."

"Why do you want to join the Lido police department, eh?" Chief Doyle settled comfortably against the back of his chair. "Says right here in your application that you already have a good job."

Karol had rehearsed his answer for a week. "I believe in America's laws, sir. Where I come from in Poland, the laws are not fair like in America. But fair laws mean opportunity. I want that for all the citizens of Lido. Opportunity, I mean."

"You're Polish," Chief Doyle pointed out. "The Poles in Lido are mostly law-abiding. We don't need police in that section of the city."

It hadn't occurred to Karol that he'd be confined to policing the Polish population. He wanted to do the same job as every other policeman in Lido. As every other policeman in America.

"President Washington said that due administration of justice is a pillar of good government," he said, with a burst of inspiration. "I will be a pillar for America."

All four men across the table burst out in hearty guffaws. Karol smiled at the response, but he hadn't intended to make a joke.

"I guess you think you're pretty smart?" Chief Doyle snorted.

"I studied very hard, sir," Karol said, realizing that they meant to make fun of him.

Chief Doyle stood, prompting the others to spring to their feet, too. Karol did the same.

"Officer O'Malley," the chief addressed one of the policemen. "You and Doc Lanigan see if Mr. Dombrowski is fit to join the department." He raised bushy gray eyebrows at Karol. "Good luck, Mr. Dombrowski."

Karol's hope returned. He was sure that he was fitter than any of the other candidates. Perhaps the rough reception was part of an initiation rite.

Chief Doyle and one of the other uniformed officers walked out, leaving Karol's test booklet on the table. There was a scribbled notation on the cover: *100%*.

The man in the white coat introduced himself. "I'm

Doctor Brian Lanigan, Mr. Dombrowski. I'll be doing your physical."

He brought Karol to a corner of the room and made him sit on a stool, then proceeded to look at his throat and peer into his ears. Next Karol had to stand on a chalk mark and correctly read letters on an eye chart.

From there Karol was steered to a scale. A long measuring stick stood against the wall next to it.

"One hundred and eighty-four pounds," Lanigan announced as Karol stood on the scale. "Let me write that down. Officer O'Malley can check your height."

The doctor sat at the table to write on his clipboard, his back to the examination area. Officer O'Malley shoved Karol against the wall next to the measuring stick.

"Looks short to me," O'Malley said and whipped a fist into Karol's stomach.

An acid mix of bile and sauerkraut surged into Karol's throat as he doubled over. O'Malley kicked him in the side of a knee, grabbed his hair, and slammed his head against the wall. The room spun. Karol sagged dizzily, suddenly in danger of heaving up his lunch.

"Five feet, six inches," O'Malley sang out.

The officer moved away. Karol stumbled forward, sucking in air. His head cleared slowly, although his throat burned so badly that he was afraid to speak. The door to the room slammed. The paper eye chart fluttered in the draft.

"You can go now, Mr. Dombrowski," the doctor said without looking up. "I'm afraid you don't meet the police department's height requirement."

CHAPTER 28

What Jimmy left behind

Luca read the article in the morning edition of the *Lido Daily Clipper* aloud to the regulars. A policeman was found dead with three bullets in his chest next to his police car on the outskirts of Lido. There were no witnesses or clues as to the identity of the killer.

The article linked his death to the disappearance of Lido Premium's foreman, although the murdered policeman was not assigned to the investigation. But the killing was a second indication of Bolshevik activity in upstate New York.

"Bolsheviks," Tony Bilotti sputtered. "What does a Bolshevik look like?"

"Bolsheviks blow things up," someone else said. "Remember the big scare back in 1920? Bombs going off in New York City?"

"Crazy bombers who wanted to overthrow the government," Tony agreed.

"That's what anarchists want. No government."

"Bolsheviks are different," Luca cut in and read the rest of the article to them.

According to the *Lido Daily Clipper*, the Bolsheviks were infiltrators from Moscow, bent on destroying American government and industry. They were the Reds who defeated the good White Russians after the fall of the Tsar and subverted Russia into the Union of Soviet Socialist Republics. Josef Stalin was the country's new leader, gathering his populace into "collective" farms and purging those who weren't Red enough.

Lido was a Bolshevik target because it was a model American city, the article claimed. Lido Premium was one of the most productive and successful industries in the Northeast. It also operated without a union. Bolsheviks were spreading influence through labor movements like unions and particularly hated successful non-union manufacturers and service providers.

Cripple America's industry and cripple America herself.

Luca gave the newspaper to Tony. Karol was taking the police test today. News of a murdered officer was an unwelcome coincidence. Lido was no longer a refuge. Bolsheviks were plotting just outside the club's door. Killing Jimmy, tearing up the Zambrano house, infiltrating the mill where his friends worked.

Had he and Vito unwittingly helped the Red effort

by hiding Jimmy's body in the river? Would Bolsheviks strike the banks? Was Tess safe?

Outside the sky was the color of dirty laundry. Everyone who came in shivered and predicted an early snowfall.

Vito came in. Thrashed around in his office. Luca heard the safe clang shut. The boss stomped through the saloon with his coat on and muttered something about going to the bank.

Luca knew the boss was out of whiskey and on the prowl for more.

By noon the sky was delivering another round of cold rain that threatened to become sleet. Guido spent most of the day sitting on his stool in the vestibule, staring absently through the glass at Hamilton Street.

Undaunted by the weather, Sonny came after school. Luca fixed him Genoa salami and roasted peppers on a hard roll and sent him to the far end of the bar to do his homework. The stack of dirty dishes could wait.

Luca was checking his orders for next week when Al Genovese ducked into the vestibule, rain gleaming on the shoulders of his barn coat, and murmured something to Guido. The doorman hooked a thumb over his shoulder toward the bar.

Maybe he had come to clear the air about

Annunziata.

"Hey, Al," Luca said when the man came up to the bar. "What brings you in?"

Al's gaze landed between Luca's third and fourth shirt buttons, his eyes admitting defeat before the battle was even joined. "Hello, Lombardo."

Luca pushed his paperwork aside. "What can I get you?"

"You got any of that electric coffee?" Al asked.

"Sure." Luca set out a clean mug. "Sandwich? Or a sinker to go with that?"

Al eyed the glass cake stand with the last remaining donuts of the day. "Sure, I'll take a sinker."

Luca poured two cups of coffee and kept one for himself. "Look, Al. No hard feelings about what happened at Enzo's, right? Me and Annunziata? It just wasn't going to work out."

Al eventually pushed the empty plate and cup toward Luca and clambered off the stool. "You got someplace we can talk private?"

"Sure," Luca said unhappily. "We can go in the office."

He could understand Al not wanting to flap dirty family laundry all over the saloon but didn't see how discussing it further was going to make a difference. Even if she was the sort of girl Luca wanted to marry,

Annunziata was too young. All the cows in the world weren't going to change that.

Sonny replaced him behind the bar and Luca led Al down the hall. The other man plodded along the way he'd come into the saloon, head bent low with an unseen weight. Of course, if Luca was married to Al's shrew of a wife, he'd probably have all the fight knocked out of him, too.

With the door closed, Luca leaned against the desk and folded his arms. "What did you want to say?"

Al glanced around the room. His eye lingered on the safe next to the Chesterfield. "This is nice. Vito's office?"

"That's right," Luca said.

"I talked it over with Annunziata," Al said, squeezing his cap in both hands. "She says she'll still have you."

Luca gave a laugh. Al didn't reply.

As the silence stretched out, Luca realized that the other man was completely serious. *Oddio.*

"Look, Al," he began. "I'm not going to change my mind. She's too young to get married. Too young for me, too young for anybody. Let her grow up before you sell her off."

"Listen here." Al twisted the cap into a spiral of pilled tweed. "If my sister says you're the one she wants, then you're the one she gets."

"Maybe in the old country," Luca said. "But this is America. Grown men don't marry children."

"Ten acres," Al pleaded. "I'll give you ten acres, a house, and seven cows. That's a big share of the farm. You'll be a man of property. The dairy business is good."

Luca stared at him, anger mounting. "I don't want to be a farmer and I'm not going to marry your sister. She's only fourteen. Keep your cows and your land and let your sister grow up."

"She's been crying like a gypsy over you!" Al burst out. "The girl thinks she's in love. My wife is going to stab me in my sleep if I don't get Annunziata settled. So, you have to marry her."

"Al, for the last time. I'm not going to marry your sister."

Al moved restlessly around Vito's office. He fingered the 1925 Lido Industrial League pennant, examined the framed picture of the late Ciro Spinelli, and tapped his thumbnail against the stack of ledgers on the desk.

"What if I told you that on a certain Saturday night, I saw Vito Spinelli's Packard drive off Bell Road and head down to the riverbank?" Al asked. "In the middle of the night. Came right across the field and into a grove of trees along the riverbank."

Luca felt himself turn to stone.

Al went on. "It was the same night Jimmy Zambrano went missing."

"Are you accusing Vito of something?" How close had the Packard been to Al's land? What did the farmer really see?

"You and Vito," Al corrected him. "Everybody knows he doesn't do a thing without you. Jimmy Zambrano went missing after being here. I think something went wrong and you and Vito tossed him into the river."

"Everybody left. We both went home. End of story. Vito wasn't anywhere around Bell Road that night."

"I saw what I saw," Al said stubbornly. "Spinelli's Packard was there."

"The police have been here," Luca pointed out. "They talked about Bolsheviks. Didn't you see the newspaper today? A policeman is dead."

"I don't care what the papers say. Marry Annunziata or the police are going to hear about it."

"You're crazy, Al." As dangerous as the situation was, the absurdity was not lost on Luca. "You accuse me of murder, but you want me to marry your sister?"

"That's her problem," Al said, and his face reddened. "Claudia wants you to talk to Annunziata.

Bring flowers."

"Forget it." Luca was done with the conversation. He needed to find Vito and make sure the boss kept quiet. "I'm not marrying your sister."

"Either you marry Annunziata," Al said obstinately, "or I go to the police."

"Get out, Al, before I throw you out."

Luca watched as Al shuffled down the hall and passed through the saloon without acknowledging Sonny. Once the other man was gone, Luca shut the office door and dropped into Vito's desk chair, his legs too rubbery to hold him up. He closed his eyes against a rush of guilt.

They should have given Jimmy to the nuns. Claimed to have found him in the middle of Hamilton Street or on the railroad tracks. They'd been too frightened, too desperate, too sure that Vito was being framed. Luca dropped his head into his hands, wishing he could crush his thoughts into sawdust.

He was still sitting like that when Vito lumbered in. The pockets of his overcoat bulged. "The kid's behind the bar again. What's going on?"

Luca forced himself out of the boss's chair. "Al Genovese was here. Says he saw your Packard Saturday night by the river."

"*Madonna santa*," Vito swore as he extracted two

bottles from each pocket. "What did you tell him?"

"I told him you went home." Luca studied the bottles, which were old and scarred. The labels were reduced to scraps of paper and remnants of glue and the necks were grooved from homemade capping techniques. Who knows what they contained.

"Did he believe you?"

"No. He says that unless I marry his sister, he'll go to the police."

Vito worked the cork out of one of the bottles and sloshed a generous portion into a glass. Tossed it down and gave a slight shudder. "Poor Jimmy, God rest his soul. He doesn't deserve a legacy like this."

"You went home Saturday night. I walked back to Mrs. Esposito's. Nothing else happened. Have you said anything different to anyone?"

"No." Vito shook his head, mustache drooping.

"I'd better get back to the bar," Luca said. "The place must be filling up."

Vito slumped into the chair Luca had just vacated.

Luca hated to see the boss like this. Vito had aged ten years in two minutes. The boss was no longer the shadow mayor of East Lido but a lost child needing someone to pin a note to his coat so he could be found again.

With Al Genovese's threat hanging over their heads,

as soon as Luca was out of sight, the blue dog came out of hiding. It was another evening of covering up; making excuses while trying to prevent a drunken rant.

Tony Bilotti was the last person to leave the saloon that night. "Goodnight, Luca," the old man croaked as he shuffled to the door.

"Good night, Tony." Luca looked at the frail old man with the crabbed hands. "Are you going to be all right walking home alone? Sidewalks are icy."

"I'll walk with him," Sonny said.

"*Oddio*," Luca swore. "I sent you home an hour ago."

"I had homework to do. It's quieter here than at home."

Luca sighed. "Go on, get out. Both of you."

The teenager shifted his books to one arm so he could open the door for Tony with the other. They passed in front of the big window, Sonny matching his stride to Tony's slow shuffle. Jimmy Zambrano had raised a good kid.

Jimmy had been right about beer and the bonus payout. Members were drinking more beer than usual. The club was a good business but the mortgage on the building held by the First National Bank of Lido was a hungry beast, plus Vito paid for the annual Christmas party, bocce tournaments, baseball team uniforms and special events. Hopefully they'd make a good profit from Toby Gleason's whiskey.

He finished his calculations. The light was on in the office when Luca came to store the account books in the safe. Vito was sound asleep on the Chesterfield, his mustache fluttering with every exhale. The club's membership ledgers were piled on the desk.

Luca spun the dial, heard the click of the release and opened the door. The new bottles of whiskey were inside. A messy collection of envelopes were scattered over the bottom of the safe. They held Vito's important papers including insurance policies, the deed to the club building, and the telegram informing Ciro Spinelli's parents that their son was dead. As Luca gathered them up, he saw a small ledger hiding underneath. It was new, or nearly so, with an unbroken spine and leather corners.

"What's going on?" Vito blinked blearily and sat up, swinging his feet to the floor.

"I was putting the account books away and found this." Luca held up the small ledger.

Vito's expression changed from sleepy to shocked. "*Madonna santa*," he breathed. "It belongs to Jimmy."

"Jimmy Zambrano?" Luca nearly dropped it.

"The night of the big celebration he asked me to put it in the safe and not say anything to anyone about it. I forgot it was in there."

"Is it his shift log? Some sort of mill account?"

"I don't know. I didn't ask and he didn't say." Vito passed a trembling hand across his mouth. "*Madonna santa*. Take it and burn it."

"It has to be something important if Jimmy asked you to keep it in the safe."

"You think I don't know that? But do you think we can afford to be caught with something belonging to Jimmy with the police coming and asking questions? Get rid of it. Put it in the furnace."

"I'll take care of it, boss," Luca said.

Vito collected his coat and hat and staggered out. Luca heard the back door slam. A moment later the Packard rumbled away.

Luca locked up. He slipped the ledger under his shirt, where it pulsed against his chest all the way to the boarding house.

Once in his room, he braced a chair against the door. The small bedside table lamp threw oval shadows across the bedspread.

Luca opened the front cover.

WATERMARKED QUALITY LEDGER PAPER
Royal Vernon Line,
New York, N.Y. Elizabeth N.J.

This fine quality paper was selected for strength, to resist age, to permit numerous erasures and continuous handling.

No. 1424 Account Book
Single entry ledger.
180 pages
Made in America, U.S.A.

The pages had big numerals in the top outer corner. The paper was ruled with fine blue lines and striped with red accounting columns. The first 50 pages were filled with numbers written in a clean, precise hand. The rest of the ledger was blank.

Unlike the club's account books, in which everything was labeled, the columns had nothing to indicate what was being recorded.

Luca studied a few more pages but a pattern refused to emerge. He idly flipped to the flyleaf and discovered a title and three signatures.

THE LIDO OUTFIT

Benito Rotolo, President
Nicola Procopio, Vice President
Owen Forbes Fisher, Treasurer

CHAPTER 29

Swell place you got here

When the doorbell rang, Owen was reading the evening edition of the *Lido Daily Clipper* and puffing on a pipe packed with Prince Albert tobacco.

"Darling, you'll have to get it," Cynthia called from the kitchen as she washed the Limoges. At dinner, he'd promised that she could buy the matching soup tureen and invite the Rutherfords to dinner to show it off. Now he was *darling*.

Owen had high hopes for later.

"I'll get it," he called and left the newspaper on his chair.

He opened the front door to find Benny Rotolo on the porch, looking smart in a pearl gray overcoat and a black fedora cocked over one eye. That flashy V8 Cadillac was parked on the curb.

"What are you doing here?" Owen blurted. Neither Benny nor Nick had ever come to the house, and it was a shock to think they'd have the audacity to try. "My wife is here."

"About time I met the missus." Benny shouldered

past him, tracking slush into the living room. "Swell place you got here, Fishy-boy."

Owen shut the front door. "What are you doing here? Is there some kind of trouble?"

"Worst kind," Benny said gravely, then his face split in a grin. "Empty pockets."

The water in the kitchen stopped flowing.

"The Outfit's pockets." Benny took off his hat and overcoat, revealing a bold houndstooth check suit and a red tie. Rather than waiting for his host to offer the closet, he flung the outerwear on the arm of Cynthia's white sofa with the mint green piping. "We need some cash."

"How could our pockets be empty? We made eight deliveries last week."

"I just bought out the Antonelli brothers." Benny cruised the room, examining the china pug dogs and leather-bound books on the mantel, even fingering the silk draperies. "Next up is the Galliano Club."

"You want to launch a business takeover?" Owen said, lowering his voice.

"I like it when you use them two-dollar words, Fishy."

"We're not ready." Owen used a finger to steer a paperweight away before Benny left greasy Italian fingerprints on the tiny glass dome. "We haven't established a steady growth trajectory. For a successful takeover, you need an established foundation, not just a few weeks' worth of erratic income. We have to plan for this sort of thing. Calculate the cost, determine what percentage of profits can be put aside--"

"We expand the beer racket, and the dough will take care of itself," Benny interrupted in the same testy tone Cynthia used when Owen didn't understand why she needed Limoges tureens and Gorham meat forks. "Another tank. Coupla more trucks. Drivers. I figure ten grand will do it."

"Ten thousand dollars?" Owen was caught unawares. "How did you come up with that figure?"

Benny made a face at one of the china pugs. "I'll give you four, five days to raise the dough."

"Where am I supposed to come up with ten thousand dollars?"

"Same place you got the other money."

"It's impossible." Owen was aghast at the prospect of embezzling more money from Lido Premium while Henry Blick and that nosy Detective Avlon turned the place upside down searching for Zambrano. "Everyone at Lido Premium is on high alert since the foreman disappeared. There's a private detective there now. Roaming at will, sticking his nose into everything."

"A private detective?"

"He reports to Henry Blick. I refuse to do anything to attract the man's attention. It'll ruin everything. We're doing fine now. We shouldn't try to grow too fast. If you plan your takeover carefully--"

Cynthia walked into the living room, trim and lovely and blonde in her peach-colored crepe dress and long rope of pearls. Benny's eyes raked her from head to toe. Owen's heart surged into his throat.

"Owen, you should have told me that we had company." Cynthia held out her hand to Benny. "I'm Cynthia Fisher. Welcome to our home."

A refined visitor would wait for a proper introduction but to Owen's spiraling horror, the gangster took Cynthia's hand and actually kissed it. "A pleasure, ma'am. I'm Benny Rotolo. Here to talk a little business with your husband."

"I'm sure Owen can help. He's a business genius. Why he just got a huge raise at Lido Premium." Cynthia gave Benny the brand of smile Owen hadn't seen since their honeymoon.

"Could I impose on you for some coffee?" Benny asked.

Owen silently damned the man to hell.

"Why, of course." With another dazzling smile at Benny, Cynthia went back to the kitchen.

"Fishy," Benny drawled, after they heard cups rattle

in the kitchen. "You got yourself one hot tomato."

"I'll thank you not to talk about my wife like that," Owen whispered furiously.

Benny spied Cynthia's silver calling card case and extracted a card. "Mrs. Owen Forbes Fisher," he read. "Nice."

"Put that down." Owen lifted the man's fedora and overcoat from the arm of the sofa in a signal surely even the most obtuse visitor must recognize. "Go home, Benny."

"How soon can you get me the money?" Benny resumed his idle inspection of the living room. Nudged the needlepoint footstool. Scuffed the fringe of the Persian carpet, which Cynthia always combed flat. Took down a small gilt-framed oil painting they had purchased in Syracuse a few weeks ago. It had been expensive, even more than the future tureen. According to Cynthia, it was French and therefore worth every penny.

"I can't magically find you ten thousand dollars," Owen said stiffly, offering Benny's outerwear like an English butler.

"You did it before."

"I told you; things are different now. Everyone's suspicious. We're all being watched."

Benny held up the painting. "Is this worth ten

grand?"

"No, of course not. Five hundred to the right art dealer, perhaps."

"Peanuts," Benny said contemptuously and dropped it on the sofa. Then to Owen's speechless horror, he opened the front closet and gave a low whistle. "Now here's something I can use." He took out Cynthia's mink jacket.

"You can't have that." Owen dumped the coat and hat and made a grab for the mink.

Benny held him off with one hand. His suit jacket fell open to reveal suspenders that matched his tie and a large gun tucked into the waistband of his trousers.

"See how this works, Fishy? The Outfit needs ten grand. What have you got that comes to ten grand? House? Maybe. That tomato making coffee? Definitely."

"Cynthia doesn't have a job," Owen said in confusion.

Benny's grin widened into a frightening leer. "Dame's a looker. Bet she's got pep, too. The missus could earn ten grand on her back in two weeks."

Owen reeled backward.

Benny snorted and finally took his hat and coat, although he hung onto the mink. "You come up with ten grand or I'll put the missus to work."

"This is not how partners treat each other," Owen gasped.

"It is in Chicago," Benny said.

CHAPTER 30

Nothing friendly about it

Karol stood at the bar in the Warsaw Club with an untouched glass of root beer. The familiar cadence of the Polish language massaged his sore pride.

He was wedged into the corner where the end of the bar curved into the wall, not that the long, narrow place was big enough to hide. There were a few tables at the back for cards or chess, but mostly the Warsaw Club was a place to stand, drink, and exchange gossip.

The place was smaller and rougher than the Galiano Club where Luca worked. The Polish community in Lido could barely afford cabbage, let alone club dues. Anybody who spoke Polish and didn't mind the occasional fistfight was welcome.

Karol had broken up more than one free-for-all between men whose allegiance to the German or Russian divisions of the old country was more important than having a full set of teeth in the new country.

Yet that policeman had gotten the drop on him, sure that any idiot who claimed to be a pillar of America would not retaliate against a blue uniform.

"Look who's at the Warsaw Club looking sharp today." Anton the bartender was a big raw-boned man from Slupsk who was the center of information for Lido's Polish community. An hour at the Warsaw Club was better than a year of the *Lido Daily Clipper*. "Getting married?"

"I was at the courthouse," Karol said by way of explanation for the suit he was still wearing. He left it to the other man to come to his own conclusion. Marriage, citizenship papers or criminal charges were the only reasons to be at the courthouse unless you were an idiot who thought memorizing the *Civil Code of the United State*s made you a policeman.

Anton wiped the bar with a towel. "Bad news?"

"Nothing important." Karol moved away from the bar with his drink, silently thanking the Blessed Madonna of Częstochowa for keeping his mouth shut about his plan to become a policeman. Besides Mr. Blick and the others in his office the other day, Luca was the only person who knew. If the Polish community learned what happened, he'd be a laughingstock.

He squeezed past the mill workers in rough clothes, repeating the same oblique words about being at the courthouse when someone commented on the suit. Maybe he could find a chess partner in the back.

Instead, he saw Broz Siwak at a corner table wearing a spotless three-piece suit and a watch chain looped across his vest. Three men were with him. All looked to be recent immigrants. Rough woolen jackets, worn leather boots, shaggy hair. They all needed a shave, too, a rarity when there was a barbershop on every street corner in America.

Their conversation was quiet but obviously intense, all hunched forward, gestures made with short, jerky movements. One of the men, a tough customer with a scar sliced through his upper lip, spread his hands and shook his head as if to indicate that he didn't have something that Broz wanted. The other two evidently agreed.

Broz reluctantly pulled out a wad of bills, peeled off a selection and handed the money to the scarred man. More conversation ensued before the three left Broz's table. When they passed the bar, Anton gave them a nod but there was nothing friendly about it.

Drink in hand, Karol walked over to Broz. "Hey, Broz. Been awhile."

"Well, look at you," Broz observed coolly. "Karol Dombrowski dressed to kill. Been to a funeral?"

"I could say the same about you," Karol said. "Looking real sharp."

"Goes with the job."

Karol took the opposite chair. "Who are your new friends?"

"New friends?" Broz leaned back, pretending not to understand.

"The three who just left," Karol said and raised his glass in the direction of the door. "They looked new to Lido."

"Oh, them." Broz shrugged and lifted his glass of beer. "Couple of fellows looking for a place. I told them to go to Holy Angels and talk to Father Nowicki."

Karol drank some root beer, mainly to hide his surprise at the ease with which Broz had just lied to him.

"How's it going at the mill?" Broz asked.

"Blick hired a private investigator to look for Jimmy Zambrano," Karol said.

"No kidding? Having any luck?"

"The detective questioned all the crew chiefs. He asked me questions about you. Said it was suspicious that you quit right after Zambrano went missing."

"Let him ask. I don't know what happened to Zambrano."

"He asked if you and Jimmy got along."

"What are you getting at?" Broz demanded. "You think I rubbed out Zambrano and stuffed his body in a closet?"

"Just letting you know that they're nosing around. His name is Avlon. He suspects that the Polish community knows something about Zambrano."

"So?" Broz spoke with a belligerence he never had before. "I'll tell him the truth. I don't know what the hell happened to Zambrano."

"They want to know where you're working now."

"What did you tell them?"

"Said I didn't know. They didn't believe me."

"Did they talk to Procopio?"

"Procopio?" Karol frowned. "Sure. They talked to him and all the crew chiefs."

"What did Procopio say about me to the detective?" Broz leaned forward.

"I don't know. Why should he say anything about you?"

"Because I'm somebody now." Broz relaxed and settled back in his seat again. "I'm making three times what I made in the mill."

"What do you have to do to make that kind of money?" Karol asked evenly.

"Nothing you want to hear about." Broz laughed. "People choose to buy beer, or they choose to buy trouble. I just help them decide."

"You and your new friends?"

Broz emptied his glass before replying. "I told you

they were looking for the church."

Maybe it was none of his business, but the dismal outcome at the courthouse had Karol unwilling to let the lie pass. "You aren't a good liar, Broz. You handed over more than a hundred dollars to them. Why?"

"Keep your nose out of my business, Karol."

Every nervous whisper at the mill, every shrill article in the *Lido Daily Clipper*, every moment of his uncomfortable interview in Mr. Blick's office pointed to just one thing. "Are they Bolsheviks?"

Broz laughed. "Grow up, Karol. There's no such thing."

"If you know something--"

"Shut up, Karol," Broz interrupted, standing and swiping dust off his trousers. "I'm not going to rat anybody out because we used to be friends."

Karol stayed at the club, nursing root beer and gloomy thoughts until closing time. On his way out, Anton motioned him over to the bar.

"Stay away from Broz," the bartender said quietly. "He's in with a bad crowd."

Karol leaned closer. "Those three who were in before with him. What do you know about them?"

"Newcomers," Anton said. "Off the boat from Gdansk. Broz has hired at least a dozen newcomers lately."

"Hired? What for?"

"Beer. But you already knew that, didn't you?"

"Who is Broz working for?

Anton gave a harsh laugh before his mouth twisted into a grim scowl. "Things are happening in Lido. Some good. Some not so good. Keep your eyes open and your mouth shut. Like the rest of us, eh?"

Back at Mrs. Esposito's, Karol wearily plodded upstairs to his room. *The Civil Government of the United States* was still on his desk. Pages full of promise, yet so detached from real life.

CHAPTER 31

And in this corner . . .

A maid answered when Luca rang the doorbell.

"You must be himself come to dinner," she said in a thick Irish brogue. She was a tiny thing in a high-collared black dress and a white cap on a tangle of gray hair. "Come in out of the freezing cold."

She held the door so Luca could enter a spacious hall, feeling big and clumsy in his rubber galoshes. The box of roses under his arm nearly stabbed the woman in the shoulder as he edged past her. Nearly four feet long, it boasted an embroidered ribbon from Fulton Florist.

"Put that on the table there while you get out of your coat." Eying the distinctive box, she pointed to a marble-topped console table and waited impatiently as Luca shed his outerwear.

She made him leave his galoshes in a copper tray by the door but put his coat and hat in a closet the size of Vito's office.

"Now then, are these roses for Miss Evelyn?" the maid asked as Luca retrieved the precious box, which had cost him a week's salary.

"Yes."

"Don't think you can buy her with fripperies, but she does like roses." The maid tipped her head and her expression drilled right through Luca's good suit and clean shirt. "I'm Annie Harper. Been with Miss Evelyn since before Miss Tess came to live with her. She looks out for Miss Tess, you know, and I look out for her."

Luca accepted the challenge. "Anything else I should know, Miss Harper?"

"Call me Annie and keep those Eye-talian bedroom eyes to yourself." She took the box of roses from him. "I'll take this in. A gentleman caller needs his hands free. No patty-fingers, mind you."

Luca had never heard the expression before, but he got the meaning. The tiny woman marching ahead was much more than a maid.

She led him across a marble checkerboard floor to a set of double doors that slid open into pockets on either side, revealing a vast parlor divided in the middle by a grand piano with the lid propped open to show the soundboard. Swathed in cream silk and black tassel trim, a row of tall windows flooded the room with afternoon light that bounced off the prisms of twin crystal chandeliers and highlighted the ceiling's plaster relief trellis and vine motif.

"Luca!" Tess rose from a cream-colored sofa, her face shining with pleasure. Her long-sleeved dress was olive-toned, a quiet counterpoint to the cool drama of the room.

"Tess," Luca said formally. He was farther away from Hamilton Street than a brisk 30-minute walk would suggest.

She put a hand on his sleeve and drew him past the piano to where a slender woman with faded red hair sat with her legs crossed and a book on a table next to her. "Aunt Evelyn, may I introduce Gianluca Lombardo? Luca, this is my aunt, Evelyn Kennedy Thompson."

Evelyn unfolded herself from the chair, wrapping a long white sweater around a black dress at the same time. The buttons on the sweater looked like diamonds and matched the rings on long, slender fingers.

"Mr. Lombardo, thank you for coming." Evelyn wasn't very old, but she was worn out. Bone thin, with skin the color of parchment.

She extended her hand and Luca pressed it briefly. It was like holding a featherless bird. "Thank you for inviting me," he said.

"Mr. Lombardo brought these." Annie brandished the box from Fulton Florist.

"Oh, Luca," Tess exclaimed. "How thoughtful."

"You go ahead and open it, dear." Evelyn sat down

again, as if standing was an effort.

Tess set the box on a low table, carefully untied the ribbon, and set the lid to one side. Luca watched her face light up as she lifted out a pink rose and inhaled the perfume.

"Oh, Luca, they're beautiful. Thank you." Tess brought the rose to her aunt. "They have the loveliest scent."

Evelyn sniffed appreciatively. "Thank you, Mr. Lombardo, your roses will make us forget the dreary weather today. Annie, why don't you put them in the Tiffany crystal vase? Leave them on the sideboard in the dining room to enjoy while we eat."

"Cook's making you a lemon tea," Annie said. "I'll fetch it directly after I do the roses."

Tess made a little gesture to the other end of the sofa as Annie bustled out with the blooms. Luca waited until Tess sat before joining her.

"I trust you found the house without any problem?" Evelyn asked.

"Yes, it was very easy to find," Luca said.

West Park was a circle of green that interrupted Lido's orderly grid of streets to create a hub of wealth and seclusion. Brick mansions ringed the park, detailed with soaring white columns and cedar hedges that afforded a scrim of privacy. Some homes had stables in the back and covered drives originally designed for the coach and horses of years gone by. Now the drives were occupied by Franklins and Cadillacs.

"It's going to snow soon," Tess said.

"It snowed well before Halloween last year, if I recall correctly." Evelyn opened a box on the table next to her and took out a cigarette. Luca leaned across the space between sofa and armchair and lit the cigarette with a faceted obsidian lighter that matched the box.

Up close, the nailbeds of her fingers were tinged with blue.

The squeak of rolling wheels traveled from the hall. Annie pushed a wooden cart draped with a linen cloth and gleaming with a silver tea service into the room and frowned at Evelyn. "Cook says you're to keep your appetite sharp. She's laid on a real feast, so she has."

Evelyn smiled crookedly and idly waved away a stream of cigarette smoke.

"I'm sure it will all be delicious," Tess said and took charge of the teapot.

Her natural exuberance was still there, but below the surface, pushed down by concern for her aunt's wellbeing. Luca found himself drawn to her even more strongly than before.

"Tess tells me you're from Calabria, Mr. Lombardo," Evelyn said. "That's an agricultural region, isn't it?"

She all but shouted *cafone*, accusing him of being an itinerant farmer. "Yes, it is," Luca said, sitting stiffly upright.

Tess held out a cup and saucer, clinging to the china until his fingers brushed over hers. The forces for and against him were evenly divided.

"We had a wonderful time in Italy last year, didn't we, Aunt Evelyn?" Tess put her aunt's tea on the table next to the cigarette lighter.

Evelyn blew out more cigarette smoke and bestowed a brittle smile upon her niece.

It was a relief when Annie announced that dinner was served. Evelyn stubbed out her cigarette in a china ashtray. "I'm sorry we can't offer wine with your meal," she said to Luca. "Unfortunately, Prohibition has reduced us to lemon water. I know how much Italians enjoy their wine."

If anything, the dining room was more daunting than the parlor.

Luca's roses were in a tall glass vase on a carved mahogany sideboard nearly as long as the bar in the Galliano Club. Dozens of prisms from yet another magnificent crystal chandelier cast diamond-shaped shadows against wallpaper patterned with blue and green fans. Heavy blue draperies, topped by yards of damask, were swagged to either side of the windows with tasseled ropes.

Three place settings took up one end of a table long enough to seat an entire orchestra. Luca pulled out Evelyn's chair at the head of the table, then did the same for Tess. The chairs were elaborately carved with ribbons and scrolls and anchored by bulbous ball and claw feet. The seats were padded and embroidered with green shamrocks, although Luca doubted the intention was to have guests linger in comfort.

Now wearing a starched white apron, Annie ladled soup from a tureen into shallow bowls rimmed in gold.

"Our cook makes an excellent *vichyssoise*," Evelyn said.

The fancy soup with a French name wasn't much more than chicken-flavored cream. Three spoonfuls and Luca's bowl was empty. Evelyn sipped a quarter of a teaspoon and inquired if Mr. Lombardo went to Saratoga for the horse racing this past summer.

Mr. Lombardo did not.

The *prima piatti* was a small trout, filleted and arranged on wafer-thin slices of lemon. Luca looked around for the bread. Annie served him a couple of crackers from a basket using silver tongs.

Evelyn picked at the fish and asked if Mr. Lombardo played duplicate bridge.

Mr. Lombardo did not.

"Aunt Evelyn, I'm sure Luca would be interested in the book you're reading," Tess said brightly.

Luca ate his fish as Tess and her aunt discussed a book by someone named Baroness Orczy. It was called *Unraveled Knots* and was quite as thrilling as *The Scarlet Pimpernel*.

"We saw *The Scarlet Pimpernel* on Broadway," Tess said. "He kept saying 'Sink me!' in this very plummy English voice. It was terribly clever."

"Have you ever been to a Broadway play, Mr. Lombardo?" Evelyn asked.

Luca put down his fork. "No, but I was once in a fistfight on 42nd Street."

"Did you win?"

"I always do," Luca said.

"*Touché*, Mr. Lombardo," Evelyn said.

Annie collected the fish plates. The *secondi piatti* was roast beef, candied carrots, and a doughy beige slab. Luca prodded at the foreign block of goo with his knife.

"Yorkshire pudding," Tess murmured. "It's one of Cook's specialties."

It was indescribably bland, as was everything else on his plate. Neither Tess nor her aunt noticed the appalling lack of flavor.

The conversation ground on, goaded by Evelyn's patronizing questions and countered by Tess's sweet determination.

"Tess, could you fetch my shawl?" Evelyn asked when they finished the last course. "Mr. Lombardo and I will have a chat in the library. Please tell Annie we're not to be disturbed."

Even by you. The unspoken words hung heavy.

Luca came around the table to pull out Tess's chair.

"I'm sorry," Tess breathed and left with a soft rustle of silk.

The library was smaller and more welcoming. Luca was mesmerized by the sheer number of books that flowed from floor to ceiling along two walls. A polished wooden ladder slid along a brass rod so book lovers could reach the volumes on the top shelves. Canary yellow draperies framed the only window. Two plush armchairs were arranged invitingly in front of it, near a cabinet decorated with marquetry woodwork.

"I have some medicinal brandy in that cabinet, Mr. Lombardo," Evelyn said. She dropped into one of the armchairs and the fabric molded itself around her thin body. "*Spiritus frumenti*, the doctor calls it. Won't you pour each of us a glass?"

Luca found snifters and a full bottle of Hennessey cognac. He poured a finger's worth in both glasses and handed one to her.

"Please accept my apologies for speaking so bluntly to you," Evelyn said when Luca was seated in the other armchair. "But what I am going to tell you may change your obvious intentions toward my niece and it's best to tell you as soon as possible." She paused. "You see, Tess has no money of her own."

"She works in the bank," Luca said, confused.

"I'm not talking about her salary."

"I don't understand."

Evelyn sipped the cognac as if to fortify herself. "When my husband died, I did not inherit his shares in the railroad he founded with his partner. The only thing he left me was dividend income from a certain percentage of shares he held. The railroad owns this house and I maintain it on the company's behalf. Upon my death, everything reverts to his partner's children. All interest in the Adirondack and Western Railroad, including dividend income and this house."

Luca waited.

"When my brother died, Tess became my ward." Evelyn took another sip before continuing. "My late husband's partner saw no reason to change my husband's will to accommodate my orphaned niece."

"Tess, you mean."

"Yes, Tess. Despite appearances, she is not wealthy.

She inherits nothing upon my death."

Luca let the cognac spread some warmth before he spoke. "I'm sorry that you are ill."

"Are you a doctor, Mr. Lombardo?"

"No, but I have eyes."

The tension in Evelyn's posture seeped away; the pretense of good health could be dispensed with. "Tess must provide for herself when I'm gone."

"She will," Luca said. "You raised her to think."

"It's my understanding that your culture doesn't prize female education." Evelyn paused. "Or independent thought."

"That is, er, how do you say..." One of Ruth's vocabulary words came to mind. "A stereotype."

"Let me be honest, Mr. Lombardo," Evelyn said icily. "Right now, Tess sees you as an exotic specimen. A handsome man with a charming accent from a place she associates with gondola rides and the Colosseum."

"A specimen?" Luca thought the word had a scientific meaning.

"Forgive my poor choice of words," Evelyn said. "I should have said souvenir. Tess has no interest in a life of immigrant poverty. It's important for you to understand that my niece's infatuation with you will end as quickly as it began."

Luca drank his brandy. "I think you are very

wrong."

"Do you really think you know my niece so well?"

"I intend to," Luca said. Now more than ever, he wasn't going to be turned away. "May I have your permission to court her?"

Whatever Evelyn had expected him to say, it wasn't that. She lifted her snifter in a weak toast to his fortitude. "You remind me of someone I lost long ago," she said. "Very sure of himself."

"I am sorry for your loss," Luca said, because it was the polite thing to say, "but I would like an answer to my question."

"Tess came to me after my brother died," Evelyn said. Her spare frame sank even further into the chair cushions. "He gave her a very unorthodox upbringing, you see. She was angry that not only had she lost her father, but she'd lost the freedom to be a tomboy. Saying the first thing that popped into her head was no longer acceptable. She was rebellious. Headstrong, with her father's Irish temper."

"I am not afraid of Irish tempers," Luca said.

"What I am trying to convey is that it has been a difficult learning process for Tess, but she finally understands that there are rules for a young woman who must think about the future. She must make a match that comes with financial security. You are a momentary distraction from that goal."

"What about a match that makes her happy?"

Evelyn brushed his words away with a weary wave. "You bring nothing. Your background would be a burden to her."

"You think that I'm poor?" Luca hitched himself to the edge of the seat, out of patience. "Maybe before but not now. I was an orphan in Italy. Expected to become a priest because I was not allowed to inherit land. I'm not poor now because I know how to work."

"Very admirable--"

"You want Tess to be with some boy who has money today but doesn't know how to work? Who doesn't know how to provide for his family no matter what happens?" Everything Luca had swallowed since the minute he walked into Evelyn Thompson's frosty palace of social superiority bubbled up. "I see men like that all the time. The family gives them money and they gamble it away or take up with loose women. Meanwhile, the wife sits at home with only pennies to feed her children. With a man like that, Tess will have nothing in five years, because her husband will spend it all and his father won't give him more."

Evelyn raised her eyebrows but otherwise sat quite still, both hands clasped around the snifter.

"You think I would let that happen to Tess?" Luca

made no effort to disguise either his scorn or the heat surging through his veins. "A woman who is smart and has more interesting things to say than ten rich men? Tess is precious to me. My dream is to make her dreams come true, whatever they are. I will give her everything because I know how to work."

He stopped talking, suddenly aware that he was gripping the delicate glass hard enough to squeeze it into dust. It took a massive effort to relax his hand. The room was silent except for Evelyn's uneven breathing and a muffled rustle by the door.

"Well," Evelyn said at length. "You certainly aren't what I expected, Mr. Lombardo. I do hope you never challenge me to a fistfight on 42nd Street."

"I made two hundred dollars for winning that fight," Luca replied.

Evelyn put her head back and gave a peal of laughter that bubbled from somewhere deep inside her disease-riddled frame. "All right, Mr. Lombardo," she said with a certain amount of reluctant admiration. "You have my permission. Provisionally. Don't make me regret it."

After coffee in the living room, Luca and Tess strolled around the park. The air was cold enough to turn their breath into frosty spume, but they walked slowly, the metal clasps on their rubber galoshes chiming in time with their steps. Tess wore a fluffy raccoon fur coat and a pink cloche hat the same color as the roses from Fulton Florist.

Trees dotted the park inside the traffic circle. Grass twinkled as evening dew rapidly turned to ice. Gray clouds scudded past a hazy moon, propelled by a wind that had yet to touch the ground.

The rim of the circular park was the most well-lit place in Lido. Electric streetlights glowed above the sidewalk and in windows of the mansions ringing the park. Most of the houses had two or three automobiles parked in the drive.

"Your aunt gave me permission to court you." Luca was wound up by his triumph, as evidenced by Tess's arm through his.

"I guessed," Tess said with a smile in her voice.

"Has she been sick for a long time?"

"Six months or so," Tess said. "The doctors say there's cancer in her lungs. She didn't tell me until she simply couldn't hide it anymore. Said she waited for my own good. God, how I hate that phrase."

They strolled past a house with flickering gas lights atop brick columns flanking the drive.

"Maybe she didn't tell you because she was afraid."

"I know." Tess blew out a plume of white breath. "She was afraid of how I'd react. But I'm strong. I can handle bad news. I can handle anything except being treated like a child."

A narrow alley lined with privacy hedges branched off the circle. In years past it had probably been used for delivery wagons catering to the wealthy West Park neighborhood.

Luca tugged Tess to a stop across from the mouth of the alley. The jingle of their galoshes quieted. "What's on the other end?" he asked.

"Jay Street," she said.

"What's on Jay Street?" Away from the lampposts that dotted the park, the alley unspooled before them like a black ribbon of privacy.

"Perhaps we should find out," Tess said softly.

They proceeded down the alley, the fog from their breath dissipating into the cedar hedges on either side. A handful of snowflakes swirled in the air, mixing with the stars above.

Enclosed by the cedars, the kiss came easily and naturally. Hat in one hand, Luca held her against him, fur coat and all. Tess's mouth was warm, and she responded with an intensity to match his. Luca forgot about the stinging cold. Nor did he hear the occasional rumble of a car driving around the circle.

Snow frosted their coats and Luca's bare head.

Tess gripped his shoulders like she was never going to let go. And she didn't, not for a long, long time until her gloved hands gently dusted the snow off his hair.

"Do I have your permission?" Luca asked.

"Only if you can tell me the solution," she said. "Seventy-three. Fifty-nine. Forty."

"Too easy." Luca grinned, his mouth lingering close to hers. "The solution is one."

She grinned back. "You win the prize."

Luca kissed her again.

CHAPTER 32

Thrifty is such a low-class word

"We need the Italians to muscle the materials," Doc reflected. "Poles to shovel the boilers and the Irish to keep them all in line."

"And we aim to keep it that way," O'Malley said with a smirk.

"Hear, hear," Owen said absently.

Full of members escaping their wives for yet another leisurely Sunday lunch, the Bison Club dining room was buzzing with speculation about the upcoming gubernatorial and senate elections. Owen had O'Malley's two hundred in his pocket and the sure knowledge that Dombrowski would be staying at Lido Premium. Henry Blick was pleased and had said as much to Owen. Avlon, the detective, had grudgingly admitted that Dombrowski appeared to be clean as a whistle and in no way connected to Zambrano's disappearance.

The problem was that once Owen paid O'Malley, the Fisher household would be in temporarily straightened circumstances. As a result of Benny's horrid visit, Owen raised ten thousand with a loan against the house and had to start payments immediately. He'd use his share of Lido Outfit beer sales, of course, but Owen no longer had that lovely extra, just his partner's share. And his pitiful salary from Lido Premium.

The worst part was that Benny had stuffed Owen's ten thousand dollars into a paper sack without so much as a thank you.

Cynthia didn't know, of course. She bought that damned tureen and a sterling silver ladle the size of a mixing bowl, sending their account at Nelson's Department Store into the red. Cynthia would not get a maid or another mink jacket any time soon.

After church on Sunday, Owen gave Cynthia the weekly housekeeping money. He wondered if he might need to say something about being a bit thriftier. But *thrifty* felt like a low-class word. Lido's inner circle recoiled from *thrifty*.

The pocket ledger was still missing, too. Owen worried about it so much that his stomach was upset all the time. Maybe he was developing an ulcer. At least if he did, it would be an excuse not to go to Buckner's again.

The club's signature scalloped potato casserole tasted like paste as Henry Blick came into the dining room with none other than his uncle Nathan Packham, the owner of Lido Premium. The two were accompanied by Blick's brother-in-law Jack Rutherford. The heir to Lido Lumber, Rutherford ran the Lido Chamber of Commerce and was the current president of the Bison Club. The group was escorted to the table in the bay window reserved for the club's more illustrious members.

Blick nodded to Owen as they passed, in a way that was courteous yet managed to convey that intruding on a private lunch would not be appreciated. Owen gave a nod in return as he manfully attempted to swallow the mouthful of ham-flavored glue.

The apple cobbler looked promising as far as dessert went, but Owen had barely dug in when a mountain of a man with a ruddy nose approached their table. O'Malley jumped to his feet. Doc stood, too. Vaguely recognizing the man, Owen followed suit.

"Good day to you, Chief Doyle, sir," O'Malley said.

"A fine day, a fine day." The booming voice matched the man's corpulence. "Doc, O'Malley."

Introductions were made. The man with the foghorn voice was none other than Lido's chief of police, Gerald Doyle, who pumped Owen's hand hard enough to steal his vote.

"Lido Premium, eh?" Chief Doyle proclaimed to the

dining room. "Backbone of Lido's business community."

"Yes, well--"

Doyle dropped Owen's hand as his attention swung to O'Malley. "Well done the other day, laddie. Kept the riffraff off the force yet another year. Damned jumped-up Poles should know better. Bad enough we've got Schultz but at least he knows his place. I can't abide those Slavic types. Worse than the Italians. Sausage eaters, all of them."

Owen clutched the edge of the table to keep from keeling over.

O'Malley preened. "Looking out for the force, sir."

Chief Doyle clapped Doc on the shoulder. "Well done to you, too, Doc. I hear you sent the fellow packing with a minimum of fuss. He'll think twice before getting above himself again. In our department, a physical means more than an eyc chart."

The police chief gave a heart guffaw. Owen was amazed to see Doc and O'Malley share the laugh.

"Fine job, both of you. Ended up with a solid slate of fine Irish boys." Chief Doyle rubbed his hands together. "Enjoy your lunch, I've got to pay my respects to Mr. Packham."

The man barreled across the room to the private table by the window. Owen watched, openmouthed, as the police chief leaned over the table to shake Mr. Packham's hand.

When lunch was over, Doc went to the restroom. Owen and O'Malley went into the foyer and gave their chits to the coat check girl. Owen was so full of righteous indignation he was ready to explode.

"The police department was never going to hire Dombrowski," he whispered furiously to O'Malley when the coat check girl went to get their coats. "You knew that the whole time. You led me on."

"I was the one who made sure," O'Malley replied. "So, I'll take that bonus. Now. And be quick about it. I got things to do today."

"How dare you?" Owen sputtered. "Dombrowski didn't have a hope. I was worried for nothing, and you knew it. Our arrangement was made under false pretenses."

O'Malley accepted his overcoat and fedora from the girl. "We had a gentlemen's agreement," he said.

"I consider it null and void," Owen declared. "Gentlemen do not mislead each other."

O'Malley flung out an elbow, catching Owen in the chest and dumping him against the wall. The next thing Owen knew, the policeman was counting money.

"You have no right," Owen gasped.

O'Malley put the money in his own pocket. "Got

every right. I'm a copper."

The coat check girl held out Owen's things. He tipped her a dime and staggered out.

He was done. First Procopio, then Rotolo, and now O'Malley. One after another, they'd taken advantage of him, belittled him, tricked him, and then held out their hand to be paid.

Well, Owen Forbes Fisher was done being their patsy.

CHAPTER 33

Let blue fire scorch her palm

On Sunday night, O'Malley brought Ruth a music box. It was a little black cylinder on gold filigree legs with a peaches and cream cameo fastened to the lid. He wound it, smiling like a suitor. A tinny rendition of *Camptown Races* filled the parlor.

O'Malley played the song several more times, apparently delighted with his gift. Ruth sat in the armchair gritting her teeth. They both knew why he was there. She didn't understand his approach. First a rose, now a music box? Was he attempting to assuage his guilt? Pretend that she enjoyed his attention?

He didn't expect to win her over, did he?

After the fifth rendition of the tune, O'Malley took her into the bedroom. Ruth lay beneath him, as unresisting and unresponsive as before. Her thoughts flew far away from the grunting and panting man, all the way through the pages of *National Geographic* to Paris and Athens and the marvelous Panama Canal. By the time he was done, she was on her way to Rio de Janeiro.

Afterward, Ruth sat at the table in her dressing gown and watched him demolish roast chicken and potatoes.

"You're not a bad cook, Ruthie June," O'Malley proclaimed with a satisfied burp. "What's for dessert? How about some coffee?"

Ruth took his empty plate into the kitchen. She filled the coffee pot, lit a wooden match, and turned the stove valve. The gas hissed. She applied the match to the burner ring. Blue flames appeared with a *whoosh* and raced around the iron circle. Ruth extinguished the match in a dish of sand but didn't set the coffee pot on the flame.

The flickering blue was mesmerizing. Rising warmth caressed her face. A strange impulse to burn seized her. The fire would take away the chill that ached in her bones.

Once upon a time Ruth had been excited about the next show, the next town, the next song-and-dance man who might be Him. Now she felt only cold disappointment with her life. She was a scandal, a whore of a woman submitting to a blackmailer.

She held out her hand. Let the blue heat scorch her palm and smolder in her body. Maybe if she was ugly and maimed, men would leave her alone.

"Hey!" O'Malley shoved her away from the stove. "You almost caught your sleeve on fire."

Ruth gaped at him as good sense rushed back with a force that nearly floored her. "I'm tired," she said.

She fed him apple pie and a cup of coffee before he got ready to leave. O'Malley pressed a couple of dollars into her hand. "Get some steak for next week, Ruthie June," he said. "I like a good piece of meat now and then."

"I'm not running a restaurant for you," Ruth said angrily.

O'Malley gave her a bruising kiss, holding her upper arms and pinning her to his chest. Before he left, he gave her breast a squeeze. Ruth locked the door and sank into the armchair, both hands holding her dressing gown closed. The policeman's footsteps scraped on the stairs going to the street door. She was too exhausted to follow and lock the street door behind him.

The music box was on the table next to the chair. As if to punish herself, Ruth wound it with swift, jerky movements. *Camptown Races* rolled merrily out of the cylinder.

As the tune plinked on, Ruth forced open the window, the wooden sash swollen with condensation and sticky with ice. Just as O'Malley emerged from the street door, she hurled the music box to the sidewalk. It smashed into flying fragments of metal and porcelain right in front of him.

Almost too late, Ruth realized she should have barricaded the door. She quickly shoved the armchair against it.

When O'Malley didn't come back, Ruth sank into the chair, giddy with meaningless victory.

CHAPTER 34

It's a good offer

Benny stuffed a two-dollar bill into Fatso's hand and walked into the Galliano Club with a paper sack under his arm. On an afternoon like this, the place could be printing money off booze and girls, but only a dozen or so men were there. Oldsters playing cards and chess, others eating sandwiches. Folks played pool in another room; Benny heard laughter and the clack of balls.

Old man Spinelli was behind the bar, a sheet-sized apron around his tubby middle. Some kid learning the ropes was with him. No sign of Sheik.

"Hey, Pops." Benny swaggered up to the bar. "How's business? Looks kinda lousy to me."

The old man was surprised to see him. "Rotolo."

"You ain't buying my beer, but hey, no hard feelings." Benny rested his foot on the brass rail.

"Good," Spinelli said. "East Lido's too small of a place for that."

"Where's Lombardo today?" Benny asked.

"Out."

Up close, Spinelli looked bad. Bloodshot eyes,

shaky hands. Prohibition sure wasn't keeping him from getting his.

Benny took off his hat, all friendly-like. "How about a cup of coffee for old times' sake?"

"Sure," Spinelli said. "We got good coffee."

The kid grabbed a big electric percolator and poured a mug full of steaming brew. "I'm Sonny Zambrano," he said and set the mug in front of Benny. "Haven't seen you in here before."

"I'm a businessman, kid." Benny tipped him a nickel. "Don't have a lot of time to waste sitting around."

Benny sipped coffee and saw the potential in every corner. His place would be the best of the best. Capone in Chicago would be green with envy when he heard about the Galliano Club. Rothstein and Luciano in New York City would come north just to take a gander. Even Hymie would hear about it as he shoveled brimstone for all eternity.

"Where did you say Lombardo was?" Benny asked.

"He took Tessa to lunch," Sonny said. "He does that sometimes."

"Tessa? That his girl?"

"Sure, she's real nice."

Benny recognized a good opportunity when it bit him. Spinelli was drunk. Lombardo was away, probably lifting some dame's skirt in a cheap hotel.

"You're the one making decisions, right?" Benny snapped his fingers at Spinelli. "Forget the business about the beer. I'm making a straight-up offer to buy you out. Twenty thousand dollars. Cash on the barrelhead."

Spinelli blinked. "For what?"

"I'm buying your club."

"But the Galliano Club is not for sale," Spinelli sputtered. "This is my business."

"Look, old man," Benny said impatiently. "You're out of step with the times. Ten years ago, a club like this was a moneymaker, but not no more. People want night life. Girls, music, dice. Another year like this and you'll be bankrupt."

He opened the paper sack and dumped out the money. Bound packets of twenty-dollar bills fell every which way on the bar top. "Twenty thousand cash. You ain't gonna get a better offer."

"Jesus." The kid's eyes bugged out.

Spinelli's mustache fluttered hard enough to take off. A shaky hand reached for the money with reverence.

"What's going on?" a voice demanded from behind Benny.

It was Lombardo, his Valentino looks tight with

suspicion. Benny had been so focused on Spinelli that he didn't see the man come into the saloon.

"Hey, Sheik." Benny eased off the bar stool and held out his hand. "Doing some business with the boss."

"What kind of business?" Lombardo kept his hands in his coat pockets.

Benny didn't care for the snub. "Yeah, well, it's business between me and your boss. Nothing to concern you."

"He says he wants to buy the place," Spinelli croaked. "Twenty thousand dollars. Cash. Look."

Instead of ogling the cash, Lombardo gave Benny a stare like Douglas Fairbanks about to run his sword through a silver screen rival. "The club's not for sale."

"It's all here, Luca," the kid piped up. "Twenty thousand dollars."

"Go do your homework, Sonny," Lombardo ordered. The kid backpedaled to the other end of the bar.

"The kid's right." Benny cocked his thumb toward the pile of cash. "Go ahead. Count it."

Lombardo shook his head. "The club isn't for sale."

"Okay, Sheik. Twenty-two grand. How does that sound?"

Spinelli made a sound, but Lombardo didn't bend. "The Galliano Club is not for sale."

"Ain't you the one holding the deed to the place?" Benny focused on Spinelli. "Twenty-two thousand, Pops. Let's do it."

"No, no, I can't sell." Spinelli reluctantly clasped his hands together.

Benny was done being a nice guy. He swept the money back into the paper sack. "Between the two of you, there ain't half a head for business. You won't take beer on credit and now you're turning down my offer to buy the place. Don't you see that this is more money than you can make from this dump in a hundred years?"

Now that Lombardo was there to lean on, old man Spinelli toughened up. He folded his arms over straining vest buttons. "Even if I was going to sell, it would never be to a Procopio."

"Trashing my family now? That's the kind of talk that gets people killed."

"You should go now," Lombardo said.

"Nobody talks to Benny Rotolo like that," Benny shouted, hand reaching inside his jacket for the Colt Pocket Hammerless.

Everybody in the place stood up. Mill workers. Shopkeepers. Ditch diggers. Farmers. They didn't look friendly and there were more of them than rounds in the Colt Pocket Hammerless.

Benny left the gun where it was and tucked the sack

of cash under his arm again. Furious, he walked the gauntlet of unsmiling faces, Lombardo on his heels.

"The Galliano Club's not for sale," Lombardo repeated when they were on the sidewalk. "Don't ask again."

"You got the right look for the place I got in mind, Sheik," Benny said. The outside air cooled him off enough to size up the other man's usefulness. Clearly, Lombardo held sway over both the boss and the customers. Maybe Benny had been too quick to write off the bartender as nothing more than a pretty face. "Put you in a penguin suit and the dames will fall over themselves trying to get in. Get the old man to sell, and I'll give you a bonus. Keep you on at a hundred a week, too."

"Forget it," Lombardo said. "You aren't ever going to own the Galliano Club."

"You think about it, Sheik," Benny called over his shoulder. "This offer's got a time limit. Tick tock, tick tock."

CHAPTER 35

A third off the top, then divide by four

Luca didn't join the crowds that lined the streets to view the mournful funeral procession for the slain policeman, which was bigger than Lido's Independence Day parade. Chief of Police Doyle led a procession from the Lido green all the way to Saint Brigid's church in West Park.

The *Lido Daily Clipper* continued to publish headlines linking the policeman's murder and Jimmy Zambrano's disappearance to Bolsheviks intent on destroying American industry. Mill workers were cautioned to report strangers in their midst. New York state troopers were called in to help search for the villains.

Nervous residents of East Lido stayed close to home, rarely straying into other parts of Lido. Several shop owners confided to Luca and Vito that non-Italian vendors refused to do business with them until the crisis was over.

Karol reported a near-hysterical reaction in the Polish community. Father Nowicki at Holy Angels cautioned his flock that a foreign language speaker could be mistaken for a Bolshevik and set upon by an angry mob.

The saloon was crowded every night. Heated talk ranged from Procopio's heavy hand running the mill as acting foreman, to plans to tackle the Bolsheviks when they finally showed their faces. The bonus money was spent on beer and whiskey. Trips to the brothel near the railyards, too, if the sly talk was true.

More than once, Luca was tempted to ask one of the workers at Lido Premium who'd been friends with Jimmy, like Frank Conti or Gio Tulipano, if they knew anything about the pocket ledger with the leather corners and the so-called Lido Outfit headed by Rotolo, Procopio, and Fisher. The question of why Jimmy asked Vito to lock it up, and whether or not it was connected to Jimmy's murder gnawed at him. But Al Genovese had reignited the fear of being blamed for the foreman's death. Luca kept his mouth shut and the ledger hidden in the treasure box.

The days grew shorter. The maple trees lost their last scarlet leaves. O'Malley continued to come by to be paid, ensuring that he continued to ignore members with liquor on their breath. Luca helped Sonny with his Latin homework, handled Vito's blue dog days, and made sandwiches. He barely saw Ruth anymore and missed their Wednesday morning lessons.

But mostly Luca thought about Tess Kennedy.

Tessa.

With her red hair and spectacles, she was striking and modern and thoroughly American. Above all, Tess was smart and witty. Nothing needed to be explained to her. She had a wide range of interests, as if ready to grasp everything America had to offer, taking Luca far beyond even the most articulate conversation in the Galliano Club saloon. Every time they were together, Luca was desperate to impress her, make her smile and be proud to be with him.

They met for lunch at McSweeney's, coffee at Bella Napoli, a dance at a sports club and lectures at the public library. Luca discovered an entire room there with newspapers and magazines that anyone could read for free. Mathematics, science, faraway places, the origin of words, new inventions. His English vocabulary grew by leaps and bounds.

Tess lent him books, too. He rediscovered Dante, Seneca and Marcus Aurelius; the works his father had read aloud a lifetime ago.

The ledger was in his coat pocket as Luca waited in front of the Strand Theatre, under the marquee announcing *Battling Butler*. His heart nearly burst when he saw Tess approach. She wore a bright blue hat and a tan trench coat that showed off the hem of a pleated knit skirt. Everything around her receded, unable to match her brilliance.

"Luca!" Tess's eyes danced under the narrow brim of the blue hat. "You look very serious."

"Do I?" Luca tried to lighten his expression. "I was thinking how nice you look."

"Thank you. Do I have a red nose from the cold?"

"A little," Luca admitted.

"That's what I like about you," Tess said with a laugh. "You're honest."

She slid her gloved hand through the crook of his elbow, and they went to the ticket booth. Luca paid for two seats, wishing he could trumpet to the entire theater that Tess Kennedy, *Tessa* Kennedy, was there with him.

The theater was crowded. They sat near the back. Tess produced a paper twist full of red licorice vines.

The short was *Dog Gone*, the latest silly animated film based on the Mutt and Jeff newspaper cartoon. Down in the orchestra pit, the organist kept up a lively accompaniment. As he chewed the sweet raspberry licorice, Luca watched Tess more than the screen. She knew and winked at him.

Battling Butler did not disappoint. They both howled at Buster Keaton's stone-faced antics as a weakling who pretends to be a boxer to win his true love.

When the theater went dark after the first reel, to the accompaniment of flapping celluloid from the projection booth above them, Luca leaned over the armrest. Tess met him halfway for a long, luxurious kiss tasting of sugar and raspberry that made his head swim. They hastily broke apart when the screen blossomed with the second reel but held hands for the rest of the film.

Keaton won the girl. The theater lights came up as the organist churned out a carnival tune.

They went to Bella Napoli in Tess's green Ford. A table in the back was the perfect spot to sit close enough to touch. With coffee and cannoli on the table in front of them, Luca took the ledger out of his coat pocket.

"My boss found this," he said. "He told me to throw it away but I thought it might be something important. Could you look at it? I don't understand this type of accounting."

"Of course."

Tess took her time studying the ledger pages. She adjusted her spectacles, ran her finger down the columns, flipped pages, made a little humming noise. Luca sipped coffee. He could almost hear the gears spinning in her head.

Finally, Tess looked up. "If I had to guess, I'd say

it's a very long divvy sheet."

"Divvy sheet?"

"Dividing the spoils from an illegal business." She showed him two different pages, flipping back and forth to make her point. "Whoever is keeping this account is making it needlessly complicated, but I think it's recording income or maybe just projections for growth because the increases are absurdly optimistic. No business earns that much that fast. Another interesting thing is that in every scenario, a third is carved out and calculated to grow at four percent interest."

"The same rate the bank offers for savings accounts," Luca said.

"Exactly. I wonder why interest is calculated only for this third."

"What else?"

"I can't be sure, of course, because the divvy is terribly complicated, but it would appear that the remaining amount is divided into fourths."

"The amount that's left after a third is subtracted?"

"Yes, exactly. Frankly, I don't see how anyone could be expected to follow such erratic accounting for very long. But my best guess is that it's a long divvy sheet with a third skimmed off the top before payment is made to four partners. Plus, lots of calculations as to growth rates or additional income, something like that. It's quite messy."

"Five partners in total?" Luca asked, thinking of the three signatures on the flyleaf.

"The one-third off the top goes to one partner or syndicate or whatever," Tess said. "Four divide what's left. When all these speculative percentages are swept away, that's the basic divvy. So yes, five."

Luca was struck by her clear grasp. "How do you know about divvy sheets?"

"The most interesting thing I've done so far working at the bank was to assemble evidence for a trial of someone accused of fraud." Tess closed the ledger. "He was cheating his business partners and used an account at our bank for part of it. I got to comb through the files and submit the findings to the state Attorney General's office. The accountant there called it forensic accounting. He said it's how they'll put away gangsters one day, but I wonder."

"Do you want more cannoli?" Luca asked.

"My reward?"

"Yes."

When Luca came back with two more pastries on a plate, Tess had opened the ledger again and was studying the signatures on the flyleaf. "Owen Forbes Fisher," she said. "Did you know that he's the accountant at the Lido Premium mill?"

Luca nearly dropped the plate. "Are you sure?"

"He was just in the bank," Tess said. "He took out a loan for ten thousand dollars, using his house as collateral."

"A loan?"

"I'm sure that this is his handwriting. I handled the loan paperwork and he had to fill out some very long forms."

Tess bit into the pastry, but even the sight of her licking her lip didn't slow the connections and theories racing through Luca's head.

A third off the top. Four divide what's left.

Had Jimmy been part of that equation? Is that why he gave the ledger to Vito to keep safe?

Jimmy had always struck Luca as a straightforward person, nothing more and nothing less than what he appeared to be, but maybe he succumbed to temptation in order to send Sonny to college.

Had Jimmy been a partner without signing the flyleaf? Were other workers at Lido Premium involved? Was that why Rotolo kept showing up at the club? Was the bootlegger casting a net over both the mill and the club?

Or did Jimmy stumble on the ledger and his murder had nothing to do with it?

Bolsheviks.

"Do you recognize the other names?" Tess asked when she finished the pastry.

"Rotolo is a bootlegger," Luca said, keeping his voice low and a hand on the ledger. "He and Procopio are cousins. Procopio works at Lido Premium, too."

"But if Mr. Fisher is a bootlegger, why would he need to take out a loan against his house? Even if he's only getting a fourth of the leftovers, look how much money that is."

Luca had no answer. If Fisher was working with Rotolo, he should be walking around with a paper sack of cash, too. "That's a very good question."

"I know I shouldn't say this, but isn't it exciting?" Tess whispered, leaning close. "A bootlegger's account book! Maybe you should give it to the man from the Attorney General's office, the one who is so interested in forensic accounting."

"Maybe," Luca said.

Her green Ford was parked in front of the Galliano Club, now closed. They stopped by the corner of the building where the night hid everything under a cloak of shadow and kissed until they were both panting with desire.

When Tess drove off, Luca wanted to run after her, all the way to a conversation with Evelyn Thompson in the house on West Park Circle. But he needed more than his paltry salary before asking the dying woman for her niece's hand in marriage.

The ledger, Jimmy's murder, Rotolo's vow to buy the club, even Al Genovese's threat. None of it mattered as much as his future with Tess Kennedy.

Tessa.

The next morning, Luca walked to St. Brigid's and left a message for Toby Gleason.

CHAPTER 36

Lido's newest made man

As twilight fell, Benny left Railroad Street and drove slowly through the cemetery. The latest snowfall had melted but the air was moist with the promise of more. The fading light played tricks on his eyes, throwing shadows over the cracked and tilted headstones.

He'd sent a telegram to Arnold Rothstein in New York City, inviting the famous gambler to partner with him in the Galliano Club, New York's newest and finest speakeasy. Benny figured it would take a day or so before Rothstein replied.

The gambler was known to have interests in Saratoga resorts that reeked of money and luxury, not to mention rumors of fixing the 1919 World Series and the 1921 Travers Stakes horse race. With Hymie gone, Rothstein would be Benny's new ticket to the kind of wealth and prestige that would pound nails in Al Capone's coffin. Of course, the telegram omitted the fact that Benny didn't own the Galliano Club yet. He would soon. Real soon.

He tipped the Cadillac over the berm, swung the wheel as the downhill momentum bled away and brought the car to a halt near the pump house. His boys got out, taking their shotguns and ball bats with them. Broz Siwak followed him over the berm, driving a second car loaded with sluggers.

Inside the pump house, Nick was counting cases of malt syrup as a couple of the Polish boys filled the new second tank with filtered river water.

"Is Fishy here?" Benny asked Nick. "The boys gotta get paid."

"In the office."

Benny sent Broz to collect the pay for the sluggers. They'd done a good job. All the saloons in Utica were now buying beer from the Lido Outfit.

"You buy the Galliano Club yet?" Nick asked.

"Not yet," Benny said. "I offered Spinelli twenty thousand in cash. Dumped it right on the bar. No dice."

"Where did you get twenty thousand in cash?"

"Where do you think I got it? I ain't squirreling away my share under the mattress like you." Benny paced in front of the stacked boxes before swinging around on Nick. "Say, what's old man Spinelli got against you? Said he'd never sell to a Procopio."

"Kicked me out of his club last spring."

"You never told me that."

Nick shrugged. "We was playing pinochle. Spinelli accused me of cheating at cards. I wasn't going to stand for that."

"Were you?"

"Was I what?"

"Cheating."

"Spinelli's such a drunk he doesn't know one card from another."

"You took advantage?"

"Hey, if a man's not sober enough to see straight, that's his problem."

Benny laughed.

Broz came out of the office area, delivering Polish faster than a machine gun. A couple of his boys on the receiving end didn't look happy.

"What's going on?" Benny asked.

Broz switched languages. "I told them not to go to the Warsaw Club anymore."

"Why not? Ain't we supplying beer to the joint?"

"Yes, but Anton says somebody was asking questions."

Nick muscled his way into the circle. "Who's been asking questions?"

Broz jammed his hands in his coat pockets, clearly reluctant but smart enough to know which side the bread was buttered. "Karol Dombrowski."

"He's a big wheel at that club?" Benny asked.

"Dombrowski works for me," Nick said.

"That settles it." Benny laughed and clapped Broz on the back. "Go home, Broz, problem solved."

"Thanks." Broz collected his sluggers and left.

Without so many people bustling around, the pump house was quiet. Nick walked around the big tank, checked the pressure gauge.

Benny waited until his cousin was satisfied before prompting him to tell the rest of the story. "Go back to this business with Spinelli. He said you cheated at cards. Was there a fight?"

"Didn't last long enough to be a fair fight," Nick growled. "Lombardo took me down with a baseball bat. The crowd was all for him, too. Even Zambrano. I told him that Nick Procopio doesn't forget. I'd make Spinelli regret the day he kicked me out of his fucking club."

"Hey," Benny said, alarmed. "Don't get any ideas about burning the place down. That's my speakeasy we're talking about."

"I already got him good," Nick said. "I dumped Zambrano behind the club, right next to Spinelli's car. Like a fucking gift."

"Zambrano, the missing mill foreman?"

"Yeah, Zambrano. Fought like a stuck pig but he

was dead as a doornail when I left him there."

"You killed him and left him behind the club?" Benny was astounded. Nick was strong enough to twist horseshoes, but it took a lot of Chicago-style moxie to snuff somebody then frame somebody else with the stiff. His cousin soared in Benny's estimation.

Nick swiped at his face with his ever-present red kerchief. "I wanted Spinelli to get sent up the river for doing Zambrano."

"How come you're just telling me now?" Benny grabbed his cousin by both shoulders. Nick had softened up Spinelli for Benny and didn't even know it. "Jesus, Nick, you're a made man now! Buy a new suit or something. In Chicago we'd be passing the word and standing you drinks to celebrate."

Nick blinked. "Never thought about it like that."

There was a soft choking sound and Owen sidled out of the office niche.

"Hey, Fishy." Benny gave Nick a last thump of approval. "Mcct Lido's newest made man. Did in that mill foreman and never said a peep until now. Got the cops running around looking for crazy Bolshies, too."

"I heard." Owen's voice wasn't much more than a squeak. "Is that true, Nick?"

"You bet," Nick said, real belligerent-like. Throwing it in the accountant's face because Fishy would never do nothing as bold and they all knew it.

"To get the foreman job?" Owen quavered.

Nick snorted. "Sure, why not."

"Never thought for one minute that's what happened to the fella," Benny said in admiration. "All the talk about Bolsheviks and all."

"But if you left Zambrano behind the Galliano Club, why did nobody find him?" Owen's chin dimpled as if he was about to cry.

Nick scowled. "Yeah, Spinelli never got arrested. Maybe Lombardo took care of Zambrano."

Benny paced again. "No, Lombardo's too much of a straight arrow." He thought about his so-called weekly donations to Chief Doyle and how Toby Gleason the mick rumrunner claimed that the cops in Lido were only concerned with protecting the toffs in the city. Nobody was more important in Lido than the owners of the Lido Premium mill.

"It was the cops." Benny snapped his fingers. "That's who took care of the stiff. A dead foreman would be a problem for Lido Premium, so they swept him out with the trash. Better to be missing than to give the owners a black eye. Hell, they probably started the talk about Bolsheviks themselves to throw dogs off the scent. Zambrano is under ten feet of cement right now, courtesy of Chief Doyle and friends."

"Oh my God." Owen was as pop-eyed as if he'd just invented dames. "Chief Doyle was talking to Mr. Packham at the Bison Club. He went over to their private table. I know, I saw them."

"See, Nick?" Benny said. "You're in the clear. A made man now, partner in the best beer racket in New York. Quit that mill job whenever you want. I get that speakeasy up and running and we'll be printing money."

Owen coughed. "Did you ever kill anyone, Benny?"

"Well, I shot a couple of mugs a couple of times, but I never stuck around to ask after their health." Benny whacked Owen on the back and laughed uproariously. "You're in the big leagues now, Fishy. What did I tell you? Just like Chicago."

By the time they were ready to go, the new tank was full. The pumphouse smelled sour and yeasty. The accounting was divvied the way it should be in four equal shares. One share each to Benny, Nick, and Owen. The last share to Broz to be split among the brewers, drivers, and sluggers.

"I'll walk out with you," Nick said to Owen. He cranked an arm around the accountant's neck, pulled him close, and they left the pump house together.

Made man and the money man. Benny liked to see people get along.

CHAPTER 37

Running Rum Row

The Lido Premium whistle blew and blew and blew. Against every instinct that told him to remain perfectly still, Luca forced his eyes open. Four silver dots slowly resolved into the tines of a fork hovering about an inch from his eyeballs.

"*Oddio*," Luca rasped and scrambled backward. His head banged into something, and fireworks exploded behind his eyes. The whistle went on and on.

"Does he speak English?" a woman shouted, adding to the mayhem.

"Jesus wept, woman," a familiar voice replied. "Of course, he does. Did you think I learned to speak dago?"

Luca gingerly pressed his hands to the sides of his head to keep it from flying apart. The fork still confronted him, clutched in the fist of a chubby toddler improbably dressed in a blue sailor suit. The whistle slowly faded.

"Leave the poor man alone, Patrick." A dark-haired woman scooped up the child, rested him on her hip, and commandeered the fork. She wore a floral apron over a plum-colored dress. Her eyes twinkled in frank amusement.

"Where am I?" Luca asked weakly.

"He doesn't know where he is," the woman shouted over her shoulder. Her Irish lilt was unmistakable.

Luca realized he was lying on a carpet, with a blanket over his legs and his wool mackinaw balled up for a pillow. He levered himself into a sitting position and waited until the sparkles faded from his vision.

The room smelled like coffee. His stomach rumbled.

Trousers and work boots swam into view. "You've got no head for the whiskey." Toby Gleason's voice was loud enough to crack bones.

"*Oddio*." Luca squinted up at him. Last night floated by in a hazy patchwork of vignettes. Toby picking him up in a lumber truck on Hamilton Street after the Galliano Club closed. A long drive. Sitting in a barn, trading a bottle of whiskey back and forth.

"Barely a mouthful and you passed out like a girl." Toby hauled Luca to his feet. "Come on now, it's past four in the morning. Time to get going."

Luca sluiced his head under freezing water from a pump at the kitchen sink and joined Toby at the table. The child was in a highchair, feeding himself small chunks of apple with pudgy fingers.

"Mary Kate, meet Luca Lombardo, king of the

Galliano Club." Toby caught the woman around the waist as she carried an enamel coffeepot to the table. "This is my Mary Kate, the love of my life. Our boy is Patrick."

"I apologize for shouting," Luca said awkwardly. "Thank you for letting me sleep on your floor."

"Aren't you a polite one." Mary Kate gave him a devastating grin and filled a white china mug. "Here, drink this and I'll fetch the oatmeal."

"What my Mary Kate meant to say," Gleason said, "is that you're a wee bit of a disappointment. Having to be carried in last night and after I told her you were a tough Eye-talian."

He went to the stove with his wife and murmured something that made her laugh.

The coffee was boiling hot. Luca gulped it down and felt himself come to life. The kitchen was warm and inviting, with a black and white range on curved legs and a tall cupboard with glass doors showing off brown transferware. The night sky was a purple haze in the window over the sink.

Little Patrick stared at him intently. Luca put his hands over his eyes, then opened them like wings. "Aaahh, boo."

Patrick chortled. Luca did it again.

Mary Kate ladled out big portions of oatmeal along

with thick rashers of bacon and more hot coffee. When they were done, Toby kissed his wife and child. "We'll be back in three days," he said. "Four at the most. Take care of Patrick."

"Hardboiled eggs and apples." Mary Kate handed Toby a basket. "You come home to me, you crazy man."

"I always do." Toby kissed her again, tousled the boy's hair.

Luca followed Toby out of the two-story clapboard house set on the edge of a rolling meadow. Two trucks waited inside the big barn with spare tires belted to the front fenders. Toby showed how each truck had a false rear panel covered with the sawed-off ends of pine boards designed to make them look as if they were hauling lengths of cut lumber. Even up close, the ruse was perfect.

The rural landscape was still cloaked in velvety darkness as Toby took the lead. Luca tucked in behind him. The two trucks blended with early morning traffic through Utica, then on to Ilion past the Remington Arms factory.

Dawn burned away. They traveled through little towns Luca had never seen before. Springfield. Cherry Valley. Carlisle. Duanesburg, where they stopped for fuel and food.

It was noon when they hit Albany and turned south toward New York City.

The day stretched on and on, lonely, tedious, and uncomfortable. The empty truck bounced like a gorilla over indifferently paved country roads where speeds rarely topped 45 miles per hour.

Billboards along the way advertised American Automobile Association clubs, Lucky Strike Cigarettes, and Franklin cars with their innovative air-cooled motors. Luca thought about Tess. What if he drove up to 112 West Park Circle in a Franklin? Swooping black fenders, a long sleek hood, burled wood dashboard, and wheels with shiny yellow spokes. Tess would look like a queen in a Franklin.

Painted on the side of a barn, a sign for Celotex Building Products swept by. Luca exchanged the Franklin for a house full of books. A Victrola in the parlor. Tess making messes in the kitchen. Children.

Seeing Toby and Mary Kate in their home had wakened a longing for a home of his own. Never in a million years had he envisioned the scheming Irish rumrunner in a peaceful farmhouse with a wife and child. Luca liked him even more.

Ahead of him, Toby signaled with an arm out the window. They stopped at a roadhouse near West Point. Luca was so stiff and sore from the battering he was taking with every mile that he nearly fell getting out of the truck.

"We've got another six, seven hours to go." Toby eyed Luca over a plate of fried chicken. "You look pretty rough."

"I'm fine," Luca said, wishing he could put his head on the table and go to sleep. "Can you?"

"Sure, but I don't have a holy mother of a hangover."

A hot meal helped, as did a packet of licorice flavored Black Jack gum, although he nearly choked on the wad as they crossed the Hudson River on the new Bear Mountain Bridge. Luca was petrified to drive off *terra firma* as wind forced him to strain every sinew to drive straight. The bridge was a narrow strip of road hanging over both river and green treetops. Cables rose on either side like thick white cords. Rectangles of steel at the other end gave his eye something to focus on, but it was still a nerve-wracking ordeal.

They continued south along Route 9 on the other side of the river, passing through more towns with unfamiliar names. Croton-on-Hudson. Ossining. Sleepy Hollow. Billboards touted Octagon Soap in a *New Puffed Form* and Gulden's Mustard, *Delicious With Hot Meats* although Luca knew it was tasty on ham sandwiches, too. Everyone needed Interwoven

Socks for men and a Hohner Harmonica for *Fascination, Education, Musical Accuracy, and Entertainment.*

They fueled up in Yonkers, then pushed on to New York City. Despite the crush of evening traffic in the sprawling city, Luca's thoughts strayed to the past. He was a long way from Mulberry Street now. Hunched over the wheel of a rumrunner's truck, he was determined to make enough money to marry an American woman and step into her world.

They reached Long Island in the dark. Cold air seeped through every seam of the false lumber truck, chilling him to the bone.

"One hundred and eighteen miles to go," Luca said out loud to himself as they passed a sign for Montauk. With luck, they'd be there before midnight, three hours before the rendezvous with Toby's contact. If they missed him tonight, they'd return tomorrow, same place, same time.

Toby led him through small coastal towns. Merrick, Amityville, Islip, Sayville. Rippling against the night sky, the ocean beckoned through the passenger side window when the road dipped close to the coast.

A lighthouse sent a reassuring beam into the dark sky, but otherwise Montauk was a spit of nothing poking into the Atlantic Ocean. A few houses hugged the road before it petered out. They hid the trucks in a ramshackle garage. Toby tucked a big revolver into his belt, and they set out for the rendezvous point on foot.

"I told you I don't know anything about boats," Luca warned as he and Toby sat on the beach with a lantern, not far from where a metal spike was sunk into a hardened pool of cement. It was cold but they were both dressed for the temperature in mackinaw jackets, corduroy trousers, and wool caps.

The packed sand was dotted with low grassy shrubs. Beyond the makeshift dock, the ocean was black and restless. Hanks of seaweed undulated with the current. The air smelled like an open tin of Sicilian sardines.

"It's a good spot," Toby said. "Deep. Keeps us away from the Shagwong reef, too."

"Where's that?"

Toby waved a hand at the darkness. "Over there. To the north."

The drive had taken them nearly 18 hours, not counting stops to patch tires, buy gasoline, and eat. Luca stretched out on the prickly ground to rest his eyes. The hungry slap of the waves and the damp chill coming off the ocean would keep him awake.

"Did you shoot him here or in Italy?" Toby asked.

"What?" Luca's eyes popped open.

"The man who killed your parents. Did you do him

in Italy or here?"

Oddio, how much had he told Toby last night? Had he blabbed about putting Jimmy in the river, too? Luca struggled to sit up.

"You don't remember anything about last night, do you?" Toby snickered. "Go on, was it here or in Italy?"

"In Italy," Luca said warily.

"Does your girl know? Tessa?"

"No."

"Does she know about this trip?"

"No."

"You're going to marry her with a head full of secrets?"

"What's it to you?" Luca shot back, feeling bolder now that Toby did not appear to know anything more damning.

"Just offering a wee bit of advice." A match flared as Toby lit the lantern. "It's better to be honest. If you like her, that is. Lots of men don't like women but they marry them anyway."

"Did you tell your wife that you were a rumrunner before you married her?"

"My Mary Kate already knew what I was when she lifted her skirts for me. A cocky Dublin thief living by my wits. When she got pregnant, I knew they'd send her to the nuns. Treat her like a slave and give our baby away. I robbed a gambler who had more than he needed, and we ran away to America."

"Did he follow you?"

"No. Never knew it was me."

"You were lucky."

"A man makes his own luck. We've got everything we never had in Ireland. Land. A proper home. Enough money under the mattress to pay the taxes for twenty years and nobody saying they'll take my boy away because me and Mary Kate sinned against the Church."

The faint thrum of an engine mixed with the slap of water against the improvised cement pier.

"It's them." Toby swung the lantern.

A boat nosed into the shallows. The engine throttled back to a faint growl. Toby caught a rope that snaked through the air and fastened it to the metal spike.

Luca followed Toby onto the boat. The wooden craft was sleek and minimal, with a sheltered cabin in front, bench-like teak wood lockers along the sides and a pile of fishing nets that covered the deck in between.

"Luca, this is Mac," Toby said by way of introduction. "He's the shrewdest captain along Rum Row. Mac, this is Luca. Runs a place upstate called the Galliano Club." No one shook hands.

"Welcome to the *Shirley Jo*," Mac said. The captain was a small man in a lumpy coat and a billed seaman's cap. His face was so creased and weathered that it was impossible to guess his age. "Built for the job. Thirty feet long and the fastest Liberty engine working Rum Row."

"Sounds fast."

"Forty miles an hour on a good night." Mac gripped a boy of about twelve or thirteen by the shoulder. "Here, meet my new deckhand."

"I'm Henry," the kid announced, nearly invisible in a knitted watch cap and dark coat.

"Where's Hogan?" Toby asked.

"Took off on me," Mac said. The idling engine gave a throaty rumble. "Let's get going."

Henry hopped over the side and cast off the boat, nimbly scrambling back in with the length of rope.

The *Shirley Jo* growled backward, swung wide and picked up speed. Luca and Toby sat on the lockers, careful not to get feet tangled in the netting so carelessly strewn about. In less than a minute, they were flying through the black night pressing in on all sides. The deck throbbed. Henry braced himself against the doorjamb of the cabin as Mac stood inside at the wheel.

"How old are you, Henry?" Toby asked the boy.

"Old enough. I've been sailing Montauk for ten years."

Luca grinned at the obvious exaggeration.

"You know what happened to Hogan?" Toby asked.

Henry shrugged. "Just what Mac told me."

"Look sharp, boy," Mac snapped, leaning through the open cabin door. "Or I'll heave you over the side."

Luca was fairly certain the man would make good on this threat. Henry barely reacted.

It wasn't long before Luca saw pinpoints of light in the distance. The *Shirley Jo* aimed straight ahead, and an entire city of light emerged out of the night. Streets and cars and skyscrapers all bobbing and blinking on the undulating ocean.

"Rum Row ahead," Toby said. "A dozen mother ships waiting for babies like us to suck booze out of their tits."

"How do you know when they'll be here?"

"They're always here. Used to be three nautical miles was far enough. Now it's twelve. International waters. They come in with loads from Nassau in the Bahamas." Toby grinned, his teeth flashing white in the dark. "Nassau is the biggest liquor warehouse in the world."

"What about the Coast Guard?"

"Not a problem until we're inside the twelve-mile limit with the booze."

The whine of the engine changed, and the *Shirley Jo* slowed. A dwarf in comparison, the boat cruised along the line of tall Rum Row ships. Banners hung from their hulls advertised the prices per case of whiskey, rum and wine as brazenly as if they were advertising Coca-Cola or Orange Crush in ribbed bottles. Small boats bobbed alongside, loading purchases. Mac shouted greetings here and there and got shouts and waves in return. A party atmosphere was palpable along the line of ships, yet a sense of urgency prevailed.

They bumped against the side of the last ship in the floating city. Henry made the *Shirley Jo* fast to the larger vessel. A short rope ladder clung damply to the hull. A sign boasted prices for genuine whiskey, cane sugar rum, and sloe gin.

"Showtime," Toby said. He swung himself over the edge of the boat and climbed up the rope ladder to the deck of the big ship.

Luca felt a pang of unease as Toby disappeared from view.

Mac left the cabin and lit a cigarette. "You armed like Gleason?" he asked Luca.

"No."

"You're a wop." Mac sucked on the cigarette.

"That would make you a mick," Luca replied.

"Nothing worse than a wop with a smart mouth."

Toby reappeared at the top of the ladder. "Let's get loaded."

Henry pushed the fishing nets aside and opened a hatch which had been hidden underneath. The *Shirley Jo's* hold was a deep cavern. Toby handed down heavy wooden cases, stenciled with names like Old Bushmills and Boodles. Luca hefted them into the hold. Henry made sure the load was balanced.

Stretching, lifting, bending, stacking. They worked like machines until the hold was full. More bottles were stowed in the lockers, cleverly packed in burlap bags and cushioned with salt.

"In case we meet any thirsty friends between here and Montauk," Toby murmured. Sweaty from the work of wrestling the heavy cases, he extracted a couple of bottles from a locker and stowed them in a niche concealed behind the round lifesaver.

At last, Toby thumped on the hull of the mother ship and Henry cast off. Luca dragged the heavy fishing nets over the deck to hide the hatch. Back in the cabin, Mac swung the wheel. They retraced their route along the line of Rum Row ships riding at anchor.

The floating city of Rum Row rapidly receded until Luca could no longer distinguish between stars and ship lights. The boat left behind a churning wake as they sped across the water. Luca couldn't help grinning. He was cold and edgy but exhilarated, too. This was the adventure of a lifetime.

A searchlight blazed out of the night. A klaxon horn blared. "This is the Coast Guard. Cut your engine."

"Business as usual," Toby said and buttoned his coat to hide his revolver.

Luca understood. This was a shakedown, no different than O'Malley holding out his hand after the Galliano Club closed.

The engine went silent. The *Shirley Jo* rocked with the current. The Coast Guard boat came alongside, alike enough to be *Shirley Jo's* twin.

A sailor grappled the boats together. A big man in an officer's cap clambered aboard. "Good haul tonight, Mac?" he asked.

"I'm just the driver," Mac replied. "Talk to Gleason."

Toby went forward. "Lieutenant Carter, as I live and breathe."

"Gleason. My favorite Irishman." There was nothing warm or friendly in the Coast Guard officer's voice.

"What a marvel." Toby indicated the ocean all around them. "Two little boats on the sea of Ulysses."

"Always with the fancy talk." Carter's glance circled around the boat, taking in Luca and Henry before coming back to Luca. "Riding low tonight," he said. "Eighty cases?"

"Sixty, I swear on my sainted mother's grave," Toby replied. "A dollar a case, of course."

The transaction went down quickly. Sixty dollars and two bottles of Old Bushmills in exchange for allowing the *Shirley Jo* to proceed on her way. The Coast Guard boat quickly disappeared into the night. The throb of its engine was lost in the slap of the water against the *Shirley Jo's* hull. The heap of fishing nets undulated gently as the boat rocked.

"Let's go home, Mac." Unbuttoning his coat again, Toby left the cabin and collapsed onto the locker opposite Luca. "See, some of the Coasties aren't above doing a wee bit of business."

The engine made a throaty grinding noise. The boat jerked forward, sending the nets sliding over the deck, but didn't continue. It rocked silently, the water sloshing dangerously close to Luca's head as he sat waiting.

"Something's fouled the propeller," Mac called from the cabin. "Lotsa garbage in these waters. Gleason, you'd better have a look."

"Jesus wept," Toby muttered and clambered to the stern.

The inky night embraced them in every direction. Luca went to help. Henry brought a kerosene lantern, holding it high as he edged around the pile of nets covering the hatch. Toby stretched over the gunwale next to the big engine, his torso parallel to the surface of the water.

Luca grabbed the back of Toby's coat and braced himself with one foot on a locker, allowing Toby to inch out a bit further. Henry swung the lantern as far as his arm could reach.

"Nothing," Toby grunted.

"Nothing," Henry relayed to Mac.

Without warning, the engine bellowed. The *Shirley Jo* leaped ahead. The lantern sailed out of Henry's hand as Toby catapulted over the side, the coat peeling off his back like a banana skin. He hit the water, throwing up a geyser that rapidly disappeared in the *Shirley Jo's* wake.

The breath was knocked out of him as Luca tumbled onto his back with Toby's coat still clenched in his hand.

"Man overboard," Henry shouted.

The *Shirley Jo* continued to run hard, the Liberty engine howling like a banshee. Luca sucked in cold air and scrambled to the cabin on all fours. "Mac! Stop! We have to turn around. Gleason's in the water."

Hands on the wheel, Mac didn't respond.

"Gleason's overboard. Go back!" Luca forced himself upright, gripping the cabin entrance, and saw an ugly black revolver leveled at his chest.

"Nobody's going back for Gleason," Mac snarled. "Open the hatch and bring those cases up on deck."

"You can't leave him," Luca said. "He'll freeze."

A light appeared on the horizon.

"You see that, wop? Do what I say if you want to see land again."

Luca stumbled back to Henry across the pitching deck and pulled the netting off the hatch.

"Pirates," Henry breathed.

Luca understood immediately. Get Toby to pay for the booze, then hand it over to the pirate boat in return for a juicy bounty. Mac had meant to toss Toby off long before they boarded the boat in Montauk. No wonder Mac had asked if Luca was armed.

Now the question was whether or not Mac would leave any witnesses.

Henry stared at Luca, a corner of his mouth trembling. Obviously, the boy had come to the same conclusion. The cargo was more valuable than their lives.

The approaching light blinked in a sequence obviously meant to signal the *Shirley Jo*.

Luca stared at the stacked cases in the hold, calculating a new counting game. Speed of both boats, angles of the shifting deck, the probability of Mac's skill with a gun.

"Do you like baseball?" he asked Henry.

"Sure, everybody likes baseball."

"Who's your favorite player?"

"The Babe, of course."

"What about Lou Gehrig?"

"He's okay, I guess." Henry glanced nervously at Mac at the wheel.

The engine's tempo decreased to a purring idle. The *Shirley Jo* slowed to a drifting stop. The other boat was close enough to see that it was a similar single-engine craft. Its engine thrummed loudly. Mac called a greeting across the water to someone named Hogan, giving Luca further insight into their predicament.

Former crew member. Current partner in piracy.

"Gehrig plays first base." Luca lifted out a case. "I play first base, too. Upstate, in Lido."

"Okay," Henry said doubtfully.

Luca reached into the hold again, bringing his mouth close to Henry's ear. "I'm going to get Mac out of the cabin. You grab the wheel. Bring us behind the other boat. Fast as you can."

Henry mouthed *okay* and crawled forward. Luca extracted a bottle from the hiding place behind the lifesaver.

The other boat closed in. Henry crouched by the

cabin.

"Gleason!" Luca shouted. "Look, it's Gleason! Hang on, we're coming!"

"Gleason?" Mac came out of the cabin. "Where?"

Luca threw hard, but the *Shirley Jo* lifted on a swell at the same time. The bottle missed Mac by a good six inches and smacked into the doorframe. Glass sprayed everywhere. Mac fired into the dark, but Luca was already upon him. The *Shirley Jo* rocked madly as they wrestled across the deck. Excited shouts came from the boat closing in.

A shot zinged past Luca's ear. Adrenaline surged through his veins. He got a grip on Mac's coat collar with one hand and the loose cloth of a trouser leg with the other and heaved the smaller man over the side. Mac screamed, bicycled through the air and landed spread-eagled on the prow of the other boat as his gun plopped into the water. The *Shirley Jo* bucked with the sudden shift in weight even as the engine gave a roar. Henry brought the boat around, heeling on its side. Luca toppled to the deck. Bullets thudded into the gunwale. Splinters rained down.

"Stay down," Henry shouted. Slithering along the deck, Luca raked the netting into his arms. As the *Shirley Jo* circled the pirates, Luca dumped the mass of rope and cork over the side. The fishing net billowed out like a hungry octopus only to be sucked toward the pirate boat. Then the *Shirley Jo* was running over the water, alone in the dark night.

Henry gave a whoop. Luca sat on the deck and sucked in air, each breath a tiny explosion of burning pain. All he heard was the throaty song of the Liberty engine and the froth of water left in their wake.

"You knackered their engine," Henry shouted. "Look!"

Luca levered himself onto a locker and looked back. Three bobbing points of light marked the wildly rocking silhouette of the pirate boat. It wasn't chasing them. The lights grew smaller and smaller.

He found the last bottle of Old Bushmills tucked behind the lifesaver, pried off the cork and slugged down a mouthful. The liquor cleared his head. How long had Gleason been in the frigid Atlantic? Ten minutes? Fifteen?

"Can you take us back to where Gleason fell in?" he called to Henry.

"Maybe the Coast Guard picked him up," Henry said dubiously.

Luca bargained with the only thing he had. "Ten cases of whiskey if we find him."

"Deal."

A few minutes later, Henry throttled back the

engine. Luca swept the ocean with Mac's flashlight, wishing they still had the big lantern.

"Gleason!" he shouted over and over. "Gleason."

"There are sharks in these waters, you know," Henry said.

"Make a circle," Luca said.

"We might not have enough fuel to make it back to Montauk."

Black sky faded to dirty gray. Luca shouted himself hoarse. They were on the third circle, and he was exhausted beyond belief, when he saw a motionless lump bobbing at the ocean's whim.

"Gleason!" There was no answering shout as Luca threw out the lifesaver. It slapped against the water at least ten feet short. He pulled in the rope and tried again, this time hitting the object before the lifesaver slid away.

Henry brought the boat alongside. Luca nearly wept as he saw a waterlogged chunk of driftwood.

"Over here." The voice was so faint as to be an illusion.

"Cut the engine," Luca shouted to Henry.

The sudden silence was broken only by the slap of water against the wooden hull.

"Gleason!" Luca shouted. "Gleason!"

There was no answer. The sky was measurably

clearer now, but the ocean was still a mysterious abyss. A faint splash disturbed the surface. "Gleason!" he shouted again.

"Over here."

Luca threw the lifesaver with the force of a Greek discus thrower and was rewarded. As dawn finally filtered across the horizon, he pulled in his prize like a man possessed.

Toby tumbled over the side and onto the deck; teeth chattering, hands shaking. His lips were blue. Luca shucked off his own coat, wrapped it around Toby and forced him to swallow a mouthful of whiskey. Henry brought rain slickers from the cabin to serve as blankets.

"I lost my gun," Toby croaked, shivering uncontrollably under the pile of rain gear. "What happened to you?"

Luca looked down at himself. There was a hole in the side of his canvas work shirt. Mystified, he pulled it aside to see a similar hole in his woolen long-sleeved undershirt. Both layers were soaked and discolored. He peeled wet wool away from his ribcage.

"*Oddio*," Luca swore in amazement. "I think I've been shot."

"Jesus wept. I can't leave you alone for five minutes."

Thirty minutes later, Luca was drunk enough not to quibble as Henry's mother dug the slug out of his ribs. She stitched him up with quilting thread, just below the scar left by Orsini's blade so long ago. To finish the job, she sloshed a thimble of whiskey over her handiwork. It had an instant sobering effect.

All Luca could do was press a hand to the bandage and gasp as the room swung around him. Henry's mother unceremoniously shoved a wash basin under his chin in case he threw up.

Luca and Toby left Montauk as soon as the false lumber trucks were loaded with the whiskey. The stitches in his side had cost them precious time. Either Mac and the pirates or Prohibition Bureau agents could be hot on their trail.

The drive back was a grueling marathon. The smoother ride was a godsend, due to the heavy load, but the tires suffered more punctures. Changing them on the side of the road became a recurring nightmare of cold metal and searing pain.

Thinking about the money kept Luca going. Not only would the club make a handsome profit from the cases Vito had contracted for, but Luca's cut from Toby was enough to build a real future.

With Tess.

Tessa.

CHAPTER 38

When in doubt, consult a fraternity brother

"I wanted to bring my mink," Cynthia said with a sniff.

Owen kept both hands on the steering wheel. "I told you, it's at the cleaners, darling. There was a spot on the lining. Your mother would have noticed it right away.'

"I didn't notice it," Cynthia pouted.

"Well, I did." Owen attempted a reassuring smile.

They were driving to his mother-in-law's house in Syracuse. The truck ahead was hauling bales of hay and slowly getting on Owen's nerves.

He'd convinced Cynthia to stay with her mother for almost two weeks. Enough time to sort things out.

"If I'm going to be with Mother, I should be wearing the mink." Cynthia fussed with the handbag in her lap.

"I paid for that mink," Owen snapped as annoying whisps of hay floated past the Ford's windshield. "I should be able to take it to the cleaners if I think it needs to go."

Cynthia lapsed into sullen silence with her chin held

high. She dabbed at her eyes with a handkerchief as she stared out the passenger window.

Guilt and fear washed over him. Owen was doing all this for Cynthia, to make her happy and ensure she never left him.

"I'm sorry, darling," he said. "I didn't mean to hurt your feelings."

She sniffed again. Pressed the hankie to her eyes.

They passed a sign for Chittenango.

"Shall we stop for coffee?" Owen asked.

It took donuts, a souvenir postcard, and endless primping in the ladies' lounge before they were lovebirds again. Owen stayed a decent interval with his mother-in-law before being allowed to kiss his wife goodbye.

"The fiscal year, you know," he explained with an air of overwork-induced exhaustion, managing to imply that he'd be burning the midnight oil for days to come while Mr. Packham lashed him to the adding machine. He promised to return for Cynthia in ten days and gave her twenty dollars for fripperies.

Once on his own, Owen drove across Syracuse, a city he knew well from his days at the university. Nibsy's Pub on Ulster Street was a frequent watering hole for Owen, Doc, and the rest of the Delta Kappa Epsilon fraternity brothers as were the hotels and restaurants on South Clinton. Known informally as "Deke" and founded at Yale, the fraternity was one of the oldest and most prestigious Greek societies in America.

His closest Deke connection was Doc Lanigan who got him into the Bison Club. It was time to call on another Deke brother, one who almost certainly had experience with Owen's particular situation.

He parked on East State Street around the corner from a commercial garage with *Empire Automobile Sales* painted across the front. A Model T was parked sideways under the lettering, ostensibly as an advertisement.

The place was more like a hastily built barn than an automobile showroom. Beams crossed overhead. Raw pine board walls gave off the aroma of woody bacon. Two vehicles waited for buyers.

The place was empty except for a short man in a bowler hat who stopped Owen from taking more than three steps forward. "Can I help you?"

"I'm a friend of the governor," Owen said, hoping it was still the right thing to say.

"Are you now?" The man tipped his bowler, suddenly suitably officious. "Come along and watch your step."

He led Owen through a door set into the rough

paneling so cleverly that it was indistinguishable to the uninitiated. A short hall, two more doors, around a corner and Owen was deposited in the office of Ted Lansbury.

"Hey, Owen!" Ted came around the side of an ornately carved desk. The man's dark hair was combed in a distinctive pompadour. He wore a fawn-colored suit and an eye-watering yellow tie. His handshake was robust enough to dislocate a shoulder.

"Nice set-up," Owen said. "Sold many cars?"

"You're a card, Owen." Ted beamed with the same intensity in his eyes that had unnerved Owen in their college days. The man never changed; he was still sleekly handsome and addicted to gambling for fun and profit.

He took Owen by the elbow, propelled him across the hall and threw open another door. "What do you think? Two automobile shops, a tire repair garage, and a place to have a party every night."

"If I didn't see it, I wouldn't believe it," Owen said.

The back of Empire Automobile Sales was a genuine speakeasy. Owen counted two dozen tables, upholstered benches, and a bar that ran the length of one wall. There was no décor to speak of besides dark blue velvet wallpaper, but it was hard to tell because of all the activity. Workmen were installing shelves above the bar. More men stacked crates full of clinking bottles. Leggy girls in skimpy spangled costumes practiced a dance routine. They waved at Ted when they spotted the proprietor. Ted waved back. Owen was sure that Ted had carnal knowledge of all of them.

"Filled every night," Ted said proudly. "Here. A souvenir of the best joint in New York."

He scooped a dark blue matchbox off a table and tossed it to Owen. *The Empire Lounge* was written in fancy script. The tips of the matches were dark blue, too.

Everything about the place said high class and deep pockets. Owen murmured his compliments as they went back to the office. Ted closed the door, shutting out the sounds of hammering and tap shoes.

"Now." Ted returned to his desk and offered Owen a cigar from a box of *cubanos*. "Tell me about the little problem you mentioned on the telephone."

Owen accepted a light and inhaled the rich scent of tobacco, gathering his thoughts. "Well," he said with a sheepish chuckle, "I've gotten myself into a bit of a pickle."

"Pickles are my specialty." Ted leaned back and puffed on his cigar. "Tell me all, Owen my boy."

Owen left Empire Automobile Sales three hours later with more than a book of matches. He had some unexpectedly valuable information, a snub-nosed revolver, and a plan.

CHAPTER 39

Always a two-man job

The scream was so piercing that it galvanized Karol into action before there was time to think. He yanked on the red rope by his station to ring the emergency bell. Another bell pealed at the same time. Soon bells were ringing across the mill floor.

"Safety protocol!" Karol bellowed as he snatched up the cigar box full of first aid supplies kept by the bell pull. "Now! Now!"

The conveyor that moved sheets of copper to the dipping vat stopped with a sudden *thunk* and the screech of metal-on-metal. His crew immediately began the safety drill.

The dipping and wire crews were on the same end of the mill. Beyond the chemical vats, the size 3 wire roller was still clattering, extruding warm wire but the iron spool was not in position to catch and wind the wire. In another minute, loose loops of copper would be inextricably tangled in the gears and pistons of the trolley-sized machine.

Ferlo, one of the youngest workers, swayed white-faced up on the catwalk used by the spool changers. He held his left wrist as blood spouted out of the remnants of his glove.

Shouting for someone to telephone Mr. Blick's office, Karol made it to the narrow catwalk just in time to catch Ferlo as the young man's knees buckled and Frank Conti, the wire crew chief, slammed a hand on the emergency button to stop the machine. The din from the wire roller ebbed, but it took precious moments until it was quiet enough to hear what Ferlo was saying.

"It slipped," the youngster said through chattering teeth as Karol whipped off his own belt and used it to make a tourniquet around Ferlo's arm. "The new spool slipped off the hook. I unlocked the brake and tried to center it in the cradle, but it tipped off the hook and fell on my hand."

The massive iron spool was just inches from Karol's head. It was caught at a precarious angle with one circular flange propped on the brake bar. Half of Ferlo's glove was caught underneath, dripping blood like a stuck pig. Ten feet below, the cement floor was sprinkled with red.

If the massive spool fell out of control, it could take out the catwalk as well as dozens of workers and their stations on the shop floor below.

"I knew this was going to happen." Tulipano, the

crane operator, raced up the catwalk stairs. With three men up there, the catwalk was at maximum capacity. "He's been up there alone all day."

"Alone?" Changing the spools was always a two-man job.

Workers switched out the spools standing on the skinny catwalk rigged to the side of the roller. Either empty or full of wire, each iron spool was so heavy it had to be moved into place on top of the roller apparatus with a crane. To remove a spool, workers chained it to the crane hook above them, unlocked the brake on the cradle mechanism, and sent the spool on its way. Then the crane boom brought a fresh spool, and the process was reversed.

It took both men to guide a spool in or out of the cradle as it dangled from chains attached to the crane hook. To keep it from careening like a wrecking ball, one man worked the brake that stabilized the cradle and the other steadied the chains.

Ferlo nodded convulsively. "Mr. Procopio said I had to work alone today."

"I heard that Procopio and Conti had a big blowup over it," Tulipano said out of the side of his mouth to Karol.

Using the small scissors from the cigar box, Karol carefully cut away what was left of Ferlo's left glove to reveal his butchered hand. White bone and strands of ligaments were all that were left of three fingers.

Tulipano held Ferlo steady. Karol tore open a packet of sulfa powder and sprinkled it over the mangled hand, then gently wrapped it in a bandage padded with cotton wool. Ferlo whimpered but managed to climb down the catwalk stairs afterward. His arm was still squeezed by Karol's belt tourniquet.

Emergency bells had stopped ringing and all the roller machines were silent. Karol watched Ferlo be delivered into the care of an ambulance crew before clambering down the catwalk steps. He immediately collared Conti, who'd watched the first aid effort from the base of the catwalk stairs. "Why was he up there alone?"

"You think I don't know somebody should have been up there with him?" Conti was just as upset. Older than Karol, the wire crew chief was a no-nonsense type with a barrel chest. He was one of the few Italians who didn't give Polish workers a cold shoulder. "DiCastro is out today. I wanted to slow the shift, make sure we had two up there all the time. Procopio said no."

"That station is never manned alone," Karol fumed.

"Don't you think I said that? Procopio doesn't care." Conti clenched his fists, emanating both anger at Procopio and deep concern for Ferlo's fate. "He and I had words last week about cutting corners like this. Not one safety check since Zambrano went missing. This was Procopio punishing me for speaking up. Ferlo got caught in the middle." He let out a stream of Italian invective.

"That spool's gonna fall and kill somebody," Tulipano observed.

The air pulsed with tension. The wire crew milled by the roller, sullen and angry. Through no fault of his own, the youngest member of the crew had been injured beyond any hope of working again. Although they were accustomed to changing the spools, Karol knew that not one of the men was going to volunteer to retrieve the dangling hunk of iron.

Whoever did go up on the catwalk had to untangle the spool chains, hook them to the crane, and somehow avoid being clocked by the spool as the crane pulled it away from the brake bar. One wrong move and a man could lose more than just a couple of fingers.

"I'm not asking for volunteers," Conti said loudly. "This is my responsibility. I'll do it."

"It's a two-man job," Karol said. "I'll go with you."

Up close, the empty iron spool was a deadly cutting machine with two circular blades. Blood dripped steadily from the pieces of Ferlo's hand still caught under it. No longer buffered by adrenaline flowing through him like liquid fire, Karol's stomach clenched at the smell of raw meat.

"The brake is open," Conti said, squatting to examine the spool's position. "The cradle isn't going to be stable as we try to raise the spool. But we got a bigger problem."

Not only were the remains of Ferlo's hand trapped, but so were the chains strung through the spool's hollow core. To make matters worse, the roller's guide arm, which normally enabled wire to fill the spool as neatly as thread on a sewing machine bobbin, was tangled in the warm wire which had streamed out of the cutters before the machine was shut down. Now cool, the wire had hardened into a spider's web, ensnaring the side of the spool hardest to reach from the catwalk.

Conti produced a pair of cutting pliers, reached out and began carefully snipping wire, while Karol did his best to steady the cradle. Ten snips and the spool abruptly canted toward the catwalk. With a deafening crack, the cradle support shattered like cheap pot metal. Complete with loose chain, the spool crashed through the brake bar.

Karol caught the massive chunk of iron before it sailed off the catwalk. The impact sent him to one knee. The remains of Ferlo's hand plopped onto the floor below.

"Get the hook," Karol gasped.

His arms were breaking, and his legs were trembling by the time Conti managed to attach the crane hook to the chains. The crane took the weight, and the iron spool flew over Karol's head, trailing a garland of copper wire.

"You all right?" Conti bent over, hands on knees trying to catch his breath. "I never saw anybody lift one of these things, much less catch it like a ball."

Karol examined himself, surprised to see he was unharmed apart from a few cuts on his forearms. "I'm okay."

"You're a good man, Dombrowski." Conti extended his hand.

Procopio was waiting when they climbed off the catwalk. "Whose crap is this?" He upended the cigar box. Sulfa powder sprinkled out like snow. The remaining bandage snaked to the floor. Karol caught the bottle of mercurochrome before it smashed on the concrete.

"You two thought you'd be a couple of heroes, did you?" Procopio went on angrily. "Which one of you gave the order to shut down?"

"I did," Karol said before Conti could speak. "Ferlo lost half his hand working a two-man job."

"Serves him right. Kid's a sloppy worker."

"I told you there'd be trouble," Conti retorted. "You knew that was a two-man job. We never work that station with just one man."

Procopio scowled. "Run your crew like you're supposed to and keep your mouth shut."

"That station requires two men," Conti insisted.

"That's enough," Procopio bellowed. "I'm busting you down, Conti. You're reassigned to the boiler crew."

"I got seniority," Conti exclaimed.

"Not today."

The lunch whistle blew, drowning out anything else Procopio planned to say. The big foreman shoved past and disappeared into the rush of men going to the lockers.

Conti swore and ran after him.

Mr. Blick was in the mill for the rest of the day. Half the machines remained shut down as safety protocols were reviewed. The mood was tense. Everyone was wary. Karol didn't see Conti again.

Procopio caught up with Karol by the lockers at the end of the day. "You asked Blick for Carbone to replace Siwak," Procopio said. "You ain't getting him."

"Why not?" Carbone was a floater, filling in as needed until he got a permanent assignment.

"Run your crew with what you've got."

"There's no reason to run my crew with a man short.

Carbone filled in when I had leave and did a good job. Somebody gets sick and we've got the same problem that cost Ferlo half his hand."

"Carbone stays where he is. Ferlo's accident was his own fault."

"How would you know?" Karol charged. "Where were you when it happened?"

Procopio came nose-to-nose with Karol. "Gave you the chance to play hero, didn't I? Everybody's talking how you saved his fucking arm or whatever, then went up on the catwalk with Conti. Half the men think you're wearing a crown, the other half want to put a halo on you."

Taller by at least three inches, Karol didn't budge. "This is about working with full crews. All the new men are getting assigned to crews that don't need them. You can spare Carbone."

"Forget Carbone, Polack," Procopio snarled. "I saw you with Blick helping to cut up Zambrano's locker. How come? How come you was so interested in Zambrano's locker? It was none of your business. Makes me kind of suspicious about you. Maybe you're one of them Bolsheviks everybody's worried about. That detective sure seems to think so. Asking questions about why you go to the Warsaw Club, too. Better stay outta that place, Polack, unless you want me to talk to him about you."

Procopio's breath smelled like beer.

CHAPTER 40

A chat with Detective Dooley

Luca told everyone, including Tess, that he was moving stiffly because he fell down the cellar stairs at the club.

It was a miracle he didn't, given the number of cases he stored there from the Montauk haul. The whiskey was hidden behind gallon jars of roasted red peppers. Luca worried that Vito would drink it all before they saw a profit, but the investment was recouped in a single Saturday night when everyone drank to forget a bad accident at the mill.

Two days later, Detective Dooley showed up.

"Hey, Lombardo." The stocky man tossed his hat on the bar and ran a hand through his shock of pale hair. "Got a minute?"

"Sure."

"Say, kid." Dooley lifted his chin at Sonny who was at the end of the bar with schoolbooks spread out and a pencil in his hand. "Your ma doing all right?"

"She's fine, sir," Sonny replied. "Thank you for asking."

"No more strange visitors at the house?"

"No, sir."

"Good." Dooley rubbed his chin. "You hang out here?"

"Sonny works here," Luca cut in. "Does odd jobs. When it's quiet, he does his homework."

"Still hunting Bolsheviks?" Sonny asked.

"Looking at all the angles, kid." Dooley picked up his hat and pointed it at Luca. "When Schultz and I were here, we never looked in the back. Take a walk with me."

This was it, then. Cold fear made Luca fumble as he untied his apron and left it behind the bar. He grabbed his mackinaw from the hook in the hallway and followed Dooley out the front door.

A narrow path ran between the Galliano Club and Panetta's Hardware, intersecting with the alley behind the club. Dooley didn't hesitate but led the way, suggesting that the detective was familiar with the landscape.

The day was clear and crisp. Dry leaves crunched underfoot. All too quickly, they emerged from the path onto the gravel. Vito's Packard was in its usual spot.

"Must be pretty dark out here at night," Dooley said. His voice made it a question.

Luca jammed his hands in his pockets and tried to

think of a safe answer. "No reason to be out here at night."

The detective gazed up at Ruth's window. "Miss Cross lives up there. Bit jumpy."

"She's a nice lady," Luca said.

Dooley crossed the alley and went as far as the bare and bleak line of maple trees. "What's over there?"

"Handball and bocce courts." Luca came to stand by him. "The shed where we keep sports equipment."

"Zambrano could have come this way that Saturday night," Dooley said. "Cut across the bocce courts on the way home to Fourth Street."

"Jimmy went out the front door." Luca wanted to run but his feet had taken root. Did Dooley know that Jimmy was killed behind the club? "Makes more sense for him to walk down Hamilton Street and turn at the corner. There are streetlights on Hamilton."

"What about Officer O'Malley?" Dooley asked. "When I asked you about him before, you said he was around."

"Sure. Hamilton Street is his responsibility."

"Ever see him back here?"

"No."

"You sure? Think about it. He ever show up at the back door?" Dooley gestured to the back porch.

"No." Luca wished he knew what the detective was

thinking. Did he suspect O'Malley of murder? Or was this about O'Malley taking bribes?

Dooley recrossed the alley. Walked around the Packard like he might buy it before shaking a cigarette out of a crumpled pack and lighting it with a match struck against the sole of his shoe. Flicked the spent match into the gravel and gave Luca a long stare. "A fellow came into the station the other day. Swears he saw this Packard on the riverbank in the wee hours the same night Zambrano went missing. You know anything about that?"

Luca heard the traffic on Hamilton Street. The wind scuffing up leaves. His own uneven breathing.

The only way out was the truth. Just not all of it.

"Genovese," Luca said. "Was his name Al Genovese?"

"The very same."

"Al Genovese wants me to marry his sister. He said he was going to go to the police with a story about seeing Vito's Packard at the river unless I agree to marry her."

"He's trying to blackmail you with a story about your boss so you'll marry his sister?"

"Yes."

"A phony story?"

"Yes."

"Can you prove it?"

"Go to his house. Ask him about his sister."

Dooley sucked on the cigarette. "He's taking a big risk, coming to the police with a phony story."

Luca shrugged. "He's desperate. The wife can't stand the sister. He actually said his wife is going to stab him in his sleep if he doesn't get the girl out of the house. Offered me cows and a house to take her. I said no thanks and kicked him out of the club."

"Can anybody vouch for your version?"

"There were lots of people in the club when he came in."

"So, no truth to Spinelli being at the river in the middle of the night about the time Zambrano went missing?"

"You saw the boss," Luca said. "Vito Spinelli is a broken old man. He goes from home to the club and back again. Mass on Sunday. On Armistice Day he goes to the cemetery where his kid isn't buried."

Dooley threw down the cigarette butt and ground it into shreds under his heel. They walked back to Hamilton Street.

"What's wrong with her?" Dooley asked when they were in front of the Galliano Club.

"Who?"

"Genovese's sister."

"She's fourteen."

"Some men would jump at that."

"I'm not that kind."

Dooley resettled his hat on his head and winked. "Gleason told me you were all right. Hope you heal fast. 'Course, don't think either of you are going back to Montauk any time soon."

The detective strode down the street, evidently pleased with how his day was going. Luca went inside and downed a slug of Old Bushmills.

CHAPTER 40

If you want beer in this town

Benny drove the Cadillac with two Polish boys in the back, sticking tight to Sal and Milo Antonelli and another slugger in an unmarked delivery truck. They crossed the bridge with the big lighted sign, gained Hamilton Street and coasted around a corner. A moment later, the truck lights winked off. Benny hit the lights on the Cadillac, too, and stayed on the truck's rear end through the narrow alley.

Two stories of solid brick rose on his right. The truck crunched onto gravel, swung parallel to the alley, and stopped. Benny brought the Cadillac to a halt between the truck and a Packard parked next to the building and got out. Couldn't resist the urge to look around. Nick musta left Zambrano right here.

Two men emerged from the shadows. Benny easily recognized Spinelli and Lombardo. The old man swiped at his mustache in agitation. Lombardo moved slowly. No pep. Something wasn't right with him, which was just fine.

"Hey, Sheik," Benny called. "Nice to see you

again."

"Rotolo." Lombardo's gaze passed over Benny and settled on the Antonelli brothers as they got out of the truck. "What's going on?"

"Sal and Milo are working for me now," Benny said.

Lombardo ignored Benny and grabbed the front of Sal's coat. "What's going on?"

"Sorry, Luca," Sal mumbled.

Benny swaggered over to Spinelli. "You say you won't sell the club. Here's how things are gonna go until you do. You're gonna buy my beer at sixty-five a barrel. Your order is fifteen barrels, not ten. All credit, with interest."

"I buy my beer from Sal and Milo, not you," Spinelli sputtered.

"Don't you get it, old man?" Benny tapped the side of his head and pretended to think. "Sal and Milo aren't independent no more. They work for me now. If you want beer in this town, you buy it from me."

Spinelli quivered with indignation. "You want to put me out of business."

"Now you're catching on," Benny said. "Antonelli beer is my beer now. You either buy from me at sixty-five or you're cut off. Dry as a bone."

"You're a punk," Spinelli snapped. "A good-for-nothing punk."

"Why you--" Benny rushed at Spinelli.

Lombardo got there first. A fist like a sack of cement collided with Benny's jaw.

Stars circled his head. Benny managed to whip out the Colt Pocket Hammerless. "I've killed men for less than that, Sheik," he gasped.

Lombardo didn't move.

The Polish boys got out of the Cadillac.

Sal hustled Lombardo backward, away from Benny. "Nobody makes any money if there's shooting and the police show up."

One of the Polish boys racked his shotgun and laughed nervously. No one spoke. The night crackled with electricity.

"Sixty dollars a barrel," Spinelli said finally. "Ten barrels. Cash."

If trouble went down now, Benny wasn't absolutely sure the two Polacks wouldn't shoot him by accident. He lowered the Colt Pocket Hammerless. The deal was good enough for now.

Sal and Milo did most of the grunt work unloading and stashing the beer in Spinelli's cellar. Lombardo didn't offer to help but leaned against the wall by the door, sort of hunched to one side, face hidden by shadows slanting off the roofline.

Spinelli paid Sal. Sal handed the wad to Benny.

Lombardo had a pretty good sucker punch, Benny thought as he drove back to the pump house with his jaw throbbing and his sluggers jabbering at each other in Polish. Besides the Valentino face, the fella had all the makings of a crackerjack bartender and bouncer. Definitely worth a hundred a week.

It would be a shame if Sheik had to go for a ride, as Hymie used to say, before the Galliano Club belonged to Benny.

CHAPTER 41

Nasty little muzzle

Owen didn't like going into East Lido. The neighborhood was crammed with foreigners. It smelled like garlic and other revolting things that never graced a plate at Buckner's or the Bison Club.

Nick and his wife and kids lived in one of the double-decker houses that hugged the narrow streets. Two front doors, one for the Procopio family and another for the family that lived upstairs. Despite the cold temperature, laundry flapped across the top and bottom porches, the same as every other house on the block.

Yards were small and unkempt with the detritus of summer gardens. Frozen remnants of plants tied to wooden stakes with torn strips of cloth. Slimy brown vines poked through a light dusting of snow.

Nick answered the door. "What are you doing here?" he asked, whipping off the stained napkin tucked into the neck of his wool undershirt.

Owen kept his hand in his pocket. "Why do you think I'm here?"

"You got some dirt on Blick for me?"

"Blick? Forget him, he's untouchable. Where's that ledger?"

Nick shrugged. "It wasn't at Zambrano's house or his locker. It's gone. You ain't getting your money back, neither."

"You left Jimmy Zambrano's body at the Galliano Club," Owen said impatiently. "Obviously, whoever found him also found the ledger. Maybe it was the police, but wouldn't Chief Doyle have returned it to Benny by now? Common sense says someone who works at the Galliano Club found it. Maybe that owner you wanted to embarrass. Did you ask?"

Nick wiped his mouth with the napkin.

"You didn't," Owen accused.

"You think me and Spinelli go to tea parties together?" Nick balled up the napkin in one of his mammoth hands. "Maybe he's half in the bag all the time, but his keeper, Lombardo, would want to know why I'm asking. Forget it."

Owen swallowed hard. It was time for Ted's plan.

"Did you know that your cousin is wanted for murder in Chicago?" he asked quietly. "Killed a store clerk in cold blood in front of witnesses. I saw the Wanted poster."

Nick's eyes narrowed to suspicious slits.

"Unless I get that ledger back, I'm turning him in." Owen brought the revolver out of his pocket and pointed it at Nick's heart.

For a long, tense minute Nick stood like a statue focused on the nasty little muzzle. Owen was suddenly terrified that the bigger man would try to grab it. Ted hadn't mentioned that possibility.

"What about me?" Nick asked finally. "You plan on turning me in, too?"

"Think of that ledger as an insurance policy for both you and your cousin." Owen waggled the gun. "Before you even think of threatening me with the same fate as Jimmy Zambrano, you should know that certain members of the Bison Club have letters explaining everything. Zambrano, Rotolo, our plans, everything. And may I add that Chief of Police Doyle is a Bison. Anything happens to me, or my wife, and those letters get opened."

It wasn't true. No one knew, not even Ted, fellow Deke and master planner. Owen had carefully chosen what aspects of the partnership Ted could know. Certainly nothing about the contents of the ledger and why it was important that Benny Rotolo never see it.

"What would happen to your wife if you went to the electric chair?" Owen pressed, exhilarated by his newfound leverage. "Would Benny take care of her and the kids? I doubt it. He's probably off whoring right now."

Nick wiped his face with the napkin again. "The Galliano Club is closed on Sunday," he said. "I could bust in the back, make it look like a burglary, take a look around."

"I don't care how you do it, just get that ledger," Owen said. "Bring it to the mill on Monday. Wrap it up. Make it look like a parcel."

Nick went inside. Only when Owen heard the lock turn did he jam the revolver in his pocket and run to the car. If he'd learned anything at all from his partnership in the Lido Outfit, it was to never turn his back on either Benny Rotolo or Nick Procopio.

CHAPTER 42

Always, just for him

"The doctor is sending Aunt Evelyn to the spa in Saratoga," Tess said as they strolled along Hamilton Street after her dance lesson. "Mr. Howland is letting me go with her. We'll be gone almost two weeks."

"That's a long time," Luca said.

"Aunt Evelyn has taken a turn for the worse." Tess stayed close. Their steps synchronized. "The doctor said a course at the spa might help. 'Delay progression,' he said."

"I'm sorry." Luca didn't know what else to say.

"How are your ribs?" Tess asked.

"Good enough to take you to the Candyland Supper Club on Sunday before you go," he said. She hadn't questioned his story of falling down the stairs. Fortunately, the wound in his side healed quickly, although it still twinged if he lifted something heavy.

Tess's fingers tightened on his arm. "Oh, Luca. That would be lovely."

The Candyland Supper Club was the most elegant way to spend an evening in Lido, according to the advertisements in the *Lido Daily Clipper*. The price of admission included a buffet supper featuring Lobster Thermidor and Beef Wellington, along with sparkling soda. There was a full orchestra and upstate New York's biggest dance floor.

Luca bought a secondhand tuxedo from Silvestro, the tailor on Third Street. Vito let him borrow the Packard.

The car got a grudging look of admiration from Annie, that curmudgeon of a housekeeper, as she opened the door to let Luca in. She approved of his tuxedo, too, although not in so many words.

Tess came down the stairs wearing a sleeveless satin dress the color of emeralds and a matching beaded headband. The ensemble matched her eyes and showed off shapely ankles and white shoulders. Long loops of jet beads swung across her bosom, and she wore black gloves that reached to her elbow. The dress was cut low enough to see cleavage.

Luca's heart vowed to leap out of his chest and fall at her feet.

"Put your eyes back in your head, mister," Annie said tersely.

Candyland was a riot of skirted tables, velvet couches, glittering chandeliers, and imported hothouse palms. They sat at a table for two near the orchestra.

The buffet supper was elegant, although most of the food was unfamiliar.

But the meal was secondary to the thrill of dancing with Tess. She was just the right height to fill his arms during the slow dances, her forehead pressed against his cheek. The fast dances were fun but woke the pain in his side.

The best moment was when the orchestra's tenor sang "Always," the new hit by Irving Berlin.

I'll be loving you Always
With a love that's true Always

Tess put her cheek against his and sang along. Softly, as if every word was just for him.

The evening was staggeringly expensive but worth every penny, Luca reflected as they collected their outerwear from the coat check girl and walked outside. The night was clear and cold. Luca gave his chit to the valet who ran to get the Packard. It was only midnight, but Tess had to catch the early train. Luca didn't object; his ribs were telling him that the party was over.

"I had a lovely time." Tess rested her head on his shoulder as they waited for the valet to bring the Packard around. "Seventeen. Fifty-four. Twenty-four."

Luca immediately knew the solution. "Five."

"Yes, five." Tess smiled up at him. "That's how perfect tonight was."

Luc dipped his head, ready to kiss her. He didn't care who saw.

"Well, if it ain't the sucker-punching Sheik and his gal," a voice called out of the darkness. "Tessa, right?"

CHAPTER 43

Unexpected leverage

Of all the people Benny expected to see in front of the Candyland Supper Club on a frosty Sunday night, it sure wasn't Lombardo with some rich-looking tomato with a feather in her hair. A real high society type, but with spectacles.

He and Trixie walked up the steps. The look on Lombardo's face was priceless, a cross between a lovestruck moose and the real Valentino dead in his casket.

"Ain't you gonna introduce us?" Benny tipped his hat at Miss Green Feather. She had on opera gloves and a velvet cape with a wide collar. Probably smelled better than a thousand-dollar bill.

"Miss Tess Kennedy," Lombardo said, sort of strangled sounding. "This is Mr. Benny Rotolo. And his friend."

"Trixie Dawson," Benny supplied. Trixie was cooking with gas, in a barely-there gold lame gown and the mink jacket he'd lifted off Fisher. Her blonde hair was coiled close to her head, with pearly combs holding it in place.

"Pleased, I'm sure," Trixie said.

Miss Green Feather didn't say anything, just drew closer to Lombardo like she was too good to rub elbows with a working girl.

"Tessa." Benny wondered what ladder Lombardo had climbed to snag her. "Sheik been telling you about me?"

"No, he hasn't mentioned your association to me," said Miss Green Feather in a snotty way that got under Benny's skin.

"No?" Benny bared his teeth in a grin. "That's too bad. Him and me, we're gonna be in business together."

"Mr. Rotolo is one of the club's suppliers," Lombardo said. "That's all."

"Ask him to tell you the whole story. Like the offer I made him. It's a doozy." Benny winked at Miss Green Feather. "Or I can tell you myself. Why don't you come in with us? Make it a foursome."

"We were just leaving."

"That's too bad. Your gal's a real tomato, Sheik." Benny winked at Miss Green Feather again, trying to get a rise out of her. "He's pretty buttoned up for an Eye-talian though, ain't he? Bet he don't make you cream, does he? Any time you get bored with him, Benny Rotolo will show you a good time."

Miss Green Feather gasped at his vulgarity.

"That's enough, Rotolo." Lombardo steered Miss Green Feather down the steps as a big Packard swung into the drive.

The valet jumped out and opened the passenger door.

It was the same Packard as the one behind the Galliano Club the night that Benny and the Antonellis delivered beer. Lombardo hustled Miss Green Feather into the car, gave the valet a tip and sped off.

"Benny!" Trixie gave Benny a playful swat on the shoulder.

"What?" Benny grinned at her. "Hell, I was just pulling his crank. Lombardo needs softening up."

He felt really good as he steered Trixie into Candyland.

Miss Green Feather was an unexpected bit of leverage. Now all he had to do was figure out how to use it.

CHAPTER 44

For your own good

Luca drove to West Park Circle, occasionally glancing at Tess. She gazed out the side window, her face half hidden.

He coasted to the curb in front of the house, cut the engine and turned to her. "Say something, Tess."

"Rotolo was the name in that ledger, wasn't it?" she asked, still not looking at him.

"Yes."

"He's a gangster," she said flatly. "How are you mixed up with him?"

"I'm not mixed up with him."

"Then how did he know my name?"

"I don't know," Luca admitted.

Tess's lips quivered. "Are you a gangster, Luca?"

"No, of course not." Luca reached for her hand, but her arms were folded. "Look, Tess. I don't want to talk about Rotolo. He's my problem. Doesn't concern you."

"Doesn't concern me?" Tess flared. "I love you. Everything about you concerns me."

Luca was suddenly speechless. His brain required

an extra heartbeat to process her words. He swallowed hard. "I love you, too."

"Then tell me what's going on."

"Rotolo's a bad man. That's all you need to know."

"What aren't you telling me? How are you involved with him?"

"The Galliano Club buys beer from him," Luca admitted. "Bootleg beer. He forced out our usual supplier and is charging us a pile of money for beer. He wants to bankrupt Vito, my boss, and buy the club. He offered me big money to work for him. But he's a crook and I don't like him."

"Tell me what this has to do with the ledger," Tess said stonily. "His name was in it, or did you think I'd forget? Are you getting a slice of the divvy? Are you the fourth partner? Skimming that third off the top?"

"No. Nothing like that." Luca looked away, trying to think of a way out of the conversation that didn't involve mentioning Jimmy Zambrano and the ledger. The elegant park was deserted. The houses circling the park were dark, the exception being the lights waiting for Tess to come home.

"Then why did you ask me to look at it? Be honest. Are you and Mr. Fisher cheating Rotolo or are they cheating you?"

"The ledger's got nothing to do with the club," Luca

said.

"I deserve a better explanation than that."

"There is no other explanation. I found the ledger and wondered what it was."

"You said your boss found it."

Right then and there, Luca knew he was in deep trouble. "Sure, that's what I meant."

"How dare you," Tess exclaimed. "How dare you make me think we have something special and then lie to my face?"

"I'm not lying. I told you what's going on with Rotolo. He's a crook. I'm not going to work for him."

"But you've got his ledger. Are you blackmailing him?"

"You don't need to know anything more about the ledger, Tess. It's for your own good."

As soon as the words fell out of his mouth, Luca regretted every syllable.

"For my own good?" Tess spit out the echo, her face scarlet with fury. "What's good for me is a man who respects me enough to be open and honest."

Luca stared at her mutely, knowing the train wreck was coming and powerless to stop it. He couldn't say anything else about the ledger because if he did the rest of the story would spill out. How could he tell her about the horror of finding Jimmy's body spitted on that wire,

O'Malley's late visit, or the Antonellis' unexpected delivery? The splash in the river or Al Genovese's threat? What if she suspected him of murder? What if she hated him forever for deceiving Jimmy's family?

Tess bolted out of the Packard. Luca ran to get between her and the house, a spurt of pain slowing him down. "Please. Don't be mad."

"Good luck with all your secrets, Mr. Lombardo."

Luca didn't know what to do, what to say to make things right. "I don't want to fight with you, Tessa."

Her eyes swam with unshed tears. "Is that the best you can do?"

"I love you," Luca said desperately.

Tess ran into the house. The porch light flicked off.

Luca waited. His brain told him to go. His heart told him to stay.

Cold sleet began to fall.

A car rounded West Circle, headlights punching yellow accusations through the slurry. The break in the darkness sent the weight of all Luca's sins crashing down. He was a fool. The traitor's son who took with one hand and destroyed with the other.

Tess wasn't coming back outside.

Tessa.

He drove to the Galliano Club and parked the Packard in its usual spot behind the building. Through the streaky windshield and the furious rhythm of the wipers, a light glowed in Ruth's second floor window. She'd barely spoken to him in weeks. Perhaps they were no longer friends. Either way, Luca was hardly going to ask to cry on her shoulder at this time of the night. He went in the back door to the office, tossed the keys to the Packard on Vito's desk and dumped his hat and coat.

The blinds were drawn but moonlight trickled through the slats as he opened the safe. Luca filled a glass with enough Old Bushmills to slake even Vito's thirst and took a giant gulp.

The whiskey burned his gullet and exploded like a bomb. Luca slouched into the chair behind the desk, ready to have a blue dog day of his own. He ripped off his bow tie and the collar stud. The second glassful went down faster. He poured a third.

His thoughts descended into an abyss of self-pity. Until Orsini galloped into the olive grove with his soldiers, Luca did not know that his father was a military officer who had deserted. Were secrets the Lombardo family legacy? How many were woven into the very fabric of Luca's life?

His father's past was the first. Killing Orsini and allowing the man's death to be recorded as a suicide came next. Now it was hard to remember them all.

Hiding Jimmy's body. Lying to the police. Keeping the ledger. Rumrunning with Toby Gleason.

He'd piled one secret on top of another and tried to fool someone as smart as Tess Kennedy.

Luca gagged on the next swallow of Old Bushmills. Coughed and winced at the sting in his side.

A scratch answered him, coming from the darkness outside the office. Luca lurched to his feet and blundered into the hall, the floor wavering with every step.

The back doorknob rattled. The scratching resumed. Someone was trying to pick the lock.

Whiskey-fueled anger surged through his veins and Luca was instantly spoiling for a fight. He tottered down the hall toward the saloon, opened the hidden entrance to the cellar, slid down the stairs, and staggered past the barrels of Rotolo's beer to the alley door.

The sleet was still coming down. The Packard was covered. The gravel shone white, too. Across the alley, the maple trees had lost their last leaves, turning bare branches into gnarled fingers that clawed at a streaky night sky.

On the back porch twenty feet away, a man hunkered over the door lock.

"Hey," Luca barked.

The man whirled around. His lock-picking tool was a length of wire looped around one hand. It flashed the color of a copper penny in the sloppy moonlight.

"Nick Procopio," Luca slurred, pushing himself away from the open cellar door. "What the hell are you doing?"

"Coming to get what's mine," Procopio said.

Luca blinked, trying to push aside the fog in his brain. "What are you talking about?"

"You lifted an account book off Jimmy Zambrano," Procopio said. "He was right here."

"Jimmy? When?"

"I left him here," Procopio growled. "The ledger musta been in his pocket. You and Spinelli took it."

"You left Jimmy here?" Luca swiped a hand across his face to get rid of the wet. The ground kept tilting like a ride at Saint Rocco's summer carnival.

"Where's the account book?"

Luca swayed as truth penetrated the fog. "*Oddio*, Procopio. You strangled Jimmy." The point was worth repeating. "Strangled him. Because Vito kicked you out of the club. You wanted him to get in trouble. Get Vito convinted . . . I mean, convicted. Arrested. For murder. For killing Jimmy. But you killed Jimmy."

"Where's the book?" Procopio charged off the porch and approached through the sleet. "Got to have been in Jimmy's pocket because it didn't turn up in his house or his locker. Either you or Vito got it. You were the ones what got rid of his body, weren't you? Either you or the cops."

Luca registered the copper wire stretched between Procopio's hands. "Why did you do it? Jimmy was a good man."

"Wanted the damn book back."

"The ledger is your divvy sheet," Luca said. The wire moved in and out of focus as the sleet came down. "You and Rotolo and his pack of Polish gangsters. Pushed Sal and Milo Antonelli out of the beer business. Fisher keeps your books."

Procopio came closer. "Gimme the ledger and we're square."

Laughter bubbled up inside Luca, Old Bushmills fizzing the situation into outright hilarity. *Rotolo's own partner was cheating him!*

Tess was so smart; she saw the pattern but they'd both missed the truth. Nick was looking for the ledger, but Fisher's handwriting was all over it.

"Fisher is skimming off the top," Luca chortled. "A third off the top."

Procopio came at him fast. Luca made a lurching start for the maples only to be pulled up short.

The copper wire snugged against Luca's neck, a

snare that caught not only bare skin but the stiff collar of his tuxedo shirt. He pushed two fingers inside before the snare was yanked tight and felt the wire slice to the bone. Blood flowed down his hand.

"You fucking shit," Procopio snarled in his ear. "Bet you dumped Jimmy in the river. In the fucking river."

Luca didn't have enough air to reply. On the verge of choking, he twisted like a madman, desperately trying to break Procopio's grip. They stumbled across the gravel, locked together in a gasping fight to the death. Sleet turned Luca's elegant wool tuxedo into a suit of sodden armor.

Grunting with effort, Procopio cinched the wire tighter. Luca's vision darkened.

The two men slammed against the Packard and ricocheted off the back wall of the building. Luca kicked out wildly. His foot caught the open cellar door. It slammed shut.

An angry billow of cold air rattled the window on the second floor.

CHAPTER 45

The same scene that haunted her dreams

O'Malley didn't bring Ruth anything that Sunday, as if he knew the charade was over. And it was. Ruth met him at the door in her shabbiest flannel nightgown. There would be no more pretending that he was a gentleman caller, no more attempts to court her.

Occasionally looking at the clock, she sat in sullen silence as he talked. Eventually he got the message and pulled her into the bedroom.

When O'Malley finished pawing and panting, he rolled off her and onto his back, still in his long-sleeved undershirt and marled socks. His chest rose and fell as he got his breath back. Ruth pulled her nightgown over her hips.

"Now that wasn't too bad, Ruthie June," O'Malley said. He shifted to face her. "We really--"

"I'll heat up your supper," Ruth interrupted. "A piece of roast pork--"

A door slammed directly below the bedroom window. Scuffling footsteps grated on the gravel. Sounds of struggle sent fear rippling down Ruth's spine.

O'Malley sat up. "What's in God's name?"

Ruth leaped off the bed, twitched the curtain aside, and screamed. It was the same scene that haunted her dreams. Sleet rendered the violence in sharp relief. The fight was closer, too.

"Jesus, Mary, and Joseph," O'Malley shouted. "Find my pants, woman!"

In the blink of an eye, he had pants, boots, nightstick and was running for the door. Ruth threw on her flannel dressing gown and rushed after him. She caught up to O'Malley as he pounded down the stairs and swerved around the side of the building.

O'Malley plunged into the messy strip of wet leaves separating the Galliano Club and Panetta's Hardware like a champion runner. Ruth kept up, barely noticing the freezing sting of dirt and sticks and rotting foliage under her bare feet.

The sounds grew louder as they neared the alley. Grunts and gagging. The rattle of gravel being brutally disturbed.

O'Malley disappeared around the corner. Ruth heard shouts of "Police! Police!"

She emerged onto the gravel. Through the sleet, she saw a burly man strangling Luca with loops of copper wire. Luca's efforts to get free were making them both jerk and flop like dying fish on a line.

"Police," O'Malley shouted again as he raced into the fray.

He swept the nightstick into the skull of the man trying to strangle Luca. The stout wood connected with a night-shattering crack.

Once.

Twice.

Three times.

CHAPTER 46

A dying man's confession

Locked against Procopio, Luca felt the other man stiffen. Slick with blood, the wire that was slicing into Luca's hand and throat suddenly slackened.

Another crack propelled Procopio forward. Still roped to him by the wire, Luca toppled into the gravel, buried beneath Procopio's weight. He fought for breath and then the burden moved away. The wire snare choking his life away loosened. As Luca sucked in air, hands helped him sit up.

"Luca! Can you speak? Oh my God, there's blood everywhere!"

It was Ruth, he realized dizzily. She knelt by him. Tears streamed down her face.

"You gonna live, Lombardo?" A man squatted on his haunches next to Ruth.

Luca recognized Officer O'Malley, albeit minus helmet, tunic, or badge.

"He nearly garroted you," O'Malley said. "Do you know this feller?"

"Nick Procopio." Luca's throat was raw. The words

came out in a sandpapery whisper. "He works at Lido Premium."

O'Malley stood up and kicked Procopio onto his back. The coil of copper wire was clutched in one blood-stained glove.

Procopio's eyelids fluttered. "River," he breathed. The word was barely audible. "In the river."

O'Malley grabbed the front of Procopio's jacket and yanked him to a sitting position. "You got something to say?" the policeman snarled.

Procopio's head lolled back. Blood dribbled from the corner of his mouth. O'Malley let go. Procopio's skull hit the ground with the dull thud of a baseball bat smacking home plate.

"He's done for," O'Malley announced.

"He's dead?" Ruth put her ear on Procopio's chest. More blood leaked from his ear and dissolved into the gravel.

"Leave him alone, Ruthie June." O'Malley pulled Ruth away from the dead man before transferring his attention back to Luca. "What happened, Lombardo?"

Once again Luca registered that the policeman was only half dressed. Ruth was barefoot and wearing her nightclothes. O'Malley kept his hand on her arm as if he owned her.

"Can you talk, Luca?" Ruth asked.

A deep breath helped but his side was on fire and breathing only made it worse. He began to tremble from shock and was powerless to stop.

"He killed Jimmy Zambrano," Luca said as best he could.

O'Malley gave a start. "Killed Zambrano? The missing foreman?"

"He admitted it. He killed Jimmy. Strangled him just like he was trying to do to me."

"Jesus, Mary, and Joseph," O'Malley exclaimed. "Didn't he say 'river'?"

"Yes," Ruth said. "He said, 'In the river.'"

"You heard a dying man's confession, Ruthie June," O'Malley yelped. "This feller killed Zambrano and dumped the body in the river!"

"Oh my God," Ruth gasped.

"Yes," Luca said as his entire body shook. "That must be what he meant."

CHAPTER 47

On the riverbank

Ruth stood on the riverbank near the old city dock with the rest of the spectators, unable to shake the uneasy feeling that the entire city was staring at her. Calling her Ruthie June.

A foolish notion, of course. No one was shaking a finger at her. All eyes were riveted on the divers. She was just one more gawker, hoping to see a dead man pulled out of the river. Vito stood next to her, coattails flapping, the stub of a cigar jammed into the corner of his mouth.

The two divers were transformed into alien beasts by their padded leather suits. Air hoses sprouted from giant onion-shaped brass helmets and tethered the divers to a gleaming pump apparatus on a boat waiting offshore.

O'Malley was closer to the action, waiting with the other blue-coated Lido policemen inside the cordon that kept the public at a distance. He was Lido's hero for saving Luca, extracting a confession out of a killer, and solving the vexing disappearance of Lido Premium's foreman.

Ruth wondered if O'Malley expected her to be grateful that she wasn't mentioned in any of the reports. Of course, mentioning her would only incriminate himself.

If she was grateful to anyone, it was to Luca. He didn't have to protect her, but he did. The *Lido Daily Clipper* reported that Luca was in the Galliano Club's office after an evening at the Candyland Supper Club, which explained his tuxedo. He was there to leave the keys to his employer's Packard after attending an evening event.

Nick Procopio attempted to break in. Luca confronted him and Procopio claimed to be seeking revenge for having been ousted from the club several months ago. In the course of the interaction, Procopio admitted to strangling Jimmy Zambrano and leaving his body in the river. Procopio then became violent and attempted to kill Luca in the same fashion.

While making his rounds on Hamilton Street businesses, O'Malley heard the scuffle and intervened, saving Luca from certain strangulation. Both Luca and the policeman heard Procopio's last words admitting to the murder of Jimmy Zambrano.

Both Luca and O'Malley claimed there were no other witnesses.

Three days later, the story still rode the headlines. The Bison Club planned a dinner to honor O'Malley. The City Council voted to give him the keys to the city. He'd been invited to Albany to address a police conference. He was close to the dock, with the other policemen on hand for the event.

Luca was there, too, his good looks accentuated by white bandages around his throat and hand. The *Lido Daily Clipper* had published his picture several times. The captions were all versions of *The handsome and stoic survivor*. Photographers swarmed Luca again today until preparations for the gruesome search began in earnest. He was on the edge of the crowd with a man Ruth didn't recognize.

The divers waded clumsily into the river. The water slowly swallowed them up. Ruth could see the helpers on the boat gesture, but the constant burble of excitement from the crowd, as well as the legions of newspapermen running along the riverbank prevented her from understanding what was happening.

Many of the reporters were from as far away as New York City, following the scent of a murder mystery like a pack of baying bloodhounds. Even a Boston newspaper sent a couple of hacks to capture the stunning sequel to the story of Lido Premium and the Boston shipyard. So far, Ruth had avoided the reporters who seemed to have nothing better to do than cruise up and down Hamilton Street all day.

The crowd inched along the riverbank, following the slow progress of the boat and the hoses that disappeared into the water. Ruth found herself nearly at Luca's elbow and caught a snatch of conversation. His friend was unmistakably Irish.

A shrill whistle cut the air. The boat puttered back to the dock, the hoses still snaking into the water. At length, brass helmets broke the surface. The divers plodded up the bank, aided by a number of helpers who waded into the water. They carried an unwieldy bundle to the pier. It was shrouded in fabric tied at both ends and stained dark by silt.

Once upon a time, the fabric might have been Ruth's second-best linen sheet.

CHAPTER 48

Gift from the river

Luca felt guilty for many things, but not for letting another man take the blame for putting Jimmy in the river.

A policeman carefully cut the rope and pulled away the fabric. Jimmy Zambrano looked up to heaven, hands crossed over his chest, his skin bleached white by the water. Coils of copper wire, testament to Nick Procopio's guilt, flashed in the sunlight.

Sobs and cries were wrenched out of the onlookers. Detective Dooley practically carried Carmella Zambrano forward to identify her husband. Sonny propped her up on the other side, his face expressionless.

Luca wanted to turn away but forced himself to stay where he was.

"Jesus wept," Toby murmured. "Dooley's a saint. I'm glad my Mary Kate isn't here to see this."

Carmella bent over her husband's body and reached down with a trembling hand to touch his face. Her lips moved.

The wind frothed the river and rustled the last leaves of fall. Clouds scudded overhead. Luca's side throbbed. The cuts around his neck itched under the bandage. The crowd quieted to a few soft sobs. Even the troopers paused their instructions to the divers and the men overseeing the gear aboard the boat. Carmella's wordless goodbye to her husband was heart-wrenchingly poignant.

Toby blew his nose on a clean handkerchief. Luca thought about Tess. What if he died? Would she be as devastated as Carmella Zambrano?

Al Genovese broke the spell, muscling himself next to Luca. "Figured I'd see you here."

"Hello, Al." Luca took grim satisfaction from the disappointment plastered across the other man's face. Anyone with a lick of self-respect would apologize, admit he'd been wrong about trying to blackmail Luca into marrying Annunziata.

"Saw your picture in the newspaper," Al went on. "Annunziata cut it out and kept it."

"You send her to school yet?"

Al curled his lip, shoved past and walked away.

"Friend of yours?" Toby asked, pocketing the handkerchief.

"Genovese is a club member. Owns a farm near my cousin. Wanted me to marry his sister and got sore when I said no."

Toby raised his eyebrows. "What of Miss Tessa?"

Luca felt the hurt all over again. "You were right about her."

"How's that?"

"She's in Saratoga. I don't know what will happen when she gets back."

"Ah, now that's a sad thing to hear." Toby shoved his hands in his pockets as the crowd shifted restlessly, waiting for something else to happen.

The newspaper in Saratoga carried an account of Procopio's attack and subsequent death, prompting Tess to write. She hoped Luca was well and promised that they could talk when she returned, but only if Luca was ready to be honest with her.

He had yet to reply.

Dooley gently helped Carmella and Sonny away from Jimmy's body. An ambulance backed to the dock and the body was swiftly loaded in. Carmella and Sonny were escorted to a car and left.

Luca saw Benny Rotolo on the other side of the crowd, just another onlooker in overcoat and black fedora, save for the poison in his eyes.

"That's done, don't you think?" Toby asked.

The drama seemed to be over. The mystery of the missing foreman was finally solved. It was oddly disappointing to think that Bolsheviks weren't to blame. When Luca looked again, Rotolo was gone.

The divers clumped back into the river. The boat whistle sounded again. The crowd gave a collective gasp of surprise and alarm. Those who had strayed toward the cars parked on the frosty grass rushed for the rope barrier again.

Engine throbbing, the boat full of equipment chugged ahead. The air hoses inflated into thick snakes and trailed over the stern. The boat retraced its route up the river and out of sight.

Rumors circulated like wildfire. For the next ten minutes, the crowd buzzed with wild speculation. Luca and Toby stayed where they were.

The boat and the divers returned. A second bundle was laid on the dock. Like the first gift from the river, it was shrouded in sodden linen. This one was weighted with a sack of rocks attached to one end.

As the fabric was stripped away, the body of a young woman flopped out, all arms and legs and chin-length platinum hair. She wore no clothing save for a camisole plastered to her torso and made transparent by the water. A scrap of dark fabric was knotted around her throat, calling attention to a ring of dark bruises.

Her naked limbs were long and slender and the color of wax.

Find out what happens next int

BLACKMAIL AT THE GALLIANO CLUB

Acknowledgments

Sincere thanks go to Maria Rich of the Rome Arts Hall of Fame, who planted the seed for the Galliano Club series. I'm grateful for the assistance of Arthur L. Simmons III at the Rome Historical Society and Patrick Reynolds, Director of Public Programs at the Oneida County Historical Society. Thank you to Linda Iannone for a private tour of nearby Utica's incomparable Stanley Theatre. Steve Hamilton and Tom Wynne answered all my questions at the West End Brewery in Utica, famous for being first to ship beer when Prohibition ended.

Last, but not least, my thanks go to James R. Guy, president of the real Galliano Club in Rome. In September 2020, he kindly gave permission to use the Galliano Club name. The 1920 building still stands, smaller than the fictional club, but with the same twin doors and dance studio on the second floor where I learned to tap dance.

Carmen Amato
October 2022

422

About the author

Carmen Amato turns her 30 years with the Central Intelligence Agency into fiction loaded with danger and deception.

She is the award-winning author of the Detective Emilia Cruz police series set in Acapulco, the Galliano Club historical thriller series, two standalone thrillers and the Mystery Ahead book journal for mystery lovers.

Find out more at carmenamato.net.

www.ingramcontent.com/pod-product-compliance
Lightning Source LLC
Chambersburg PA
CBHW072020020726
47501CB00006B/1880